Contents

Friday night is always chicken and french fries night for Mom, Lela, and me. Wee Ling makes the best takeout. You should taste it!

Before I leave the house, Mom says, "Mark, be careful, and don't be gone too long." She always says that.

"A roasted chicken and fries," calls out Wee Ling.

That's me. I dash to the counter, pick up the food, and tuck it under my arm. Outside, it's getting dark. Usually, walking on my own in the evening doesn't bother me. I've done it lots of times. But tonight it seems really spooky.

There is a mist that makes the lights in the houses look like mean yellow eyes, and it feels like they're all watching me.

I try to keep the creepy feelings from taking over my thoughts by thinking about other things.

Still, at least I didn't have to bring my little sister with me tonight. When I take her, I have to walk really slowly. But without her, all I can hear is the echo of my footsteps. The street is strangely quiet. I clutch the bag of chicken and french fries.

Then suddenly a shiver runs down my back. Out of the blue, or more like out of the mist, I have the strongest feeling that I'm being followed. Don't ask me why. I just do.

I sneak a quick look over my shoulder (not that I can see much).

I walk quickly around the corner and onto Fox Street. Who'd want to follow me? And what for? I don't really have any important secrets, except for maybe that one about Mr. Pedosky.

Mr. Pedosky lives next door to us. He's very old, and he has a glass eye. Mom told me he lost his right eye in the war. She told me not to stare at it. But now that I know about it, I notice that the glass eye doesn't move. Anyway, I guess Mr. Pedosky is pretty mysterious and sort of scary.

I try to stop my own scary thoughts as I run across the street. The person behind me is getting closer. It's not that I'm scared. Well... not *really*. It's just creepy not knowing who it is. Then a thought hits me. It's probably some kids from the Snoopers Club.

They are always playing tricks on everyone and trying to stir things up. At that moment – from out of the mist – someone jumps in front of me. "Got you!" he hisses.

I nearly collapse with fright until I realize that the person who was following me is Scott, my best friend.

"What did you do that for?" I yell. "Now look what you've made me do." The bag of chicken and french fries is on the ground. As I bend down to pick it up, I hear a small sound a few paces behind me. Another enemy? Right! Whoever it is can get ready to have a showdown.

"Sorry..." Scott stammers.

"Shhh!" I say, pulling him down beside me.

"What is it?" he whispers. "What did you grab me for?"

"One of the Snoopers," I say, pointing in the direction of the sound. "They've been following me. It's time for a showdown. You in?"

Scott nods.

"OK, now," I say in a soft voice.

We pounce. The air is full of tension as Scott and I try to trap the enemy. But it's not a Snooper. It's a mangy cat!

"I thought you said it was one of the Snoopers," says Scott in disgust.

"Ouch!" I exclaim, trying to untangle myself from the wild ball of fuzz clinging to me. "Get off..."

The cat is not very big, but its claws are like needles. "Scram!" I hiss once I'm free.

"Whose cat is it?" asks Scott.

"I don't know," I say, running back to get the takeout.

"It's following you."

"What!" I exclaim. "Not again. What's its problem?"

"Maybe it's looking for a home," says Scott.

I shrug. "I can't take it. Mom wouldn't ever agree to it. Cats are at the top of her 'most unfavorite animals' list."

Then Scott says something smart. "I bet it's after a piece of chicken."

I tuck the bag under my arm. "Well, it's not getting any."

Just then, Scott's mother calls out. She has a voice like a loudspeaker. "Scott! Scott!"

"Coming!" He turns to me. "I have to go," he says in a whisper.

I grin. Poor Scott. The last time Mrs. Rapson was at our school, her loud voice was all over the place.

"See you," he says.

"Don't forget our club meeting tomorrow," I remind him.

Scott nods and waves, then he disappears into his house before his mother can start yelling again.

Our club is planning to counterattack the Snoopers on our field day next week. Last year, the Snoopers started a fruit-juice fight, and guess who got the blame?

When I finally make it through the kitchen door, Mom is angry.

"What took you so long?"

"I saw Scott," I say.

"You see him a hundred times a day." She shakes her head. "I don't know what you two talk about."

"I'm sorry, Mom," I mumble, desperately hoping she doesn't notice the dirty marks on the take-out bag.

The next second, my little sister is squealing and pointing to the scraggy ball of fur that has sneaked into the kitchen behind me.

Hey, Fuzz! Give us a break!

The cat takes no notice of my frantic telepathic thoughts. It is now sneaking over to Mom. It's about to rub itself up against her legs. I can't watch. Don't do it, Fuzz! Get a clue!

But it's like the cat has some sort of death wish.

For a split second, my mind blanks out and I feel frozen to one spot. Then I dive into action. I rush to grab the cat. It gets so scared, it flies up Mom's back. She lets out an ear-splitting screech. The chicken and french fries go sky-high. Lela claps her hands and laughs out loud.

In the middle of all this, our neighbor Mr. Pedosky appears. Even in normal times, I think he looks like a vampire. He has long front teeth, and he's always shouting stuff about us kids "curdling his blood."

And now, standing in the dark doorway, Mr. Pedosky looks like he just stepped out of an old movie. He has a dark coat and is wearing a black patch.

I let go of the cat. It disappears behind the trash can. Mom is still yelling.

Mr. Pedosky nervously says, "This is not a good time. No?"

"What? Is something wrong?" asks Mom. Her voice is a little shaky.

"Um. No. Yes. Ah, maybe..." Mr. Pedosky's voice trails off.

"Mark!" says Mom, interrupting Mr. Pedosky's confusion. "Get that cat out of here! And when you've done that, pick up the takeout."

Anyone would think everything was my fault – like I brought the cat home on purpose.

"I'll come back," says Mr. Pedosky.

"No, no. Come in," says Mom, using her quiet voice – the voice that I have now learned from experience is the one she uses when she's really fuming inside. (One day, I think, she'll go up in flames.)

Mr. Pedosky is still hanging around the doorway. That's the big difference between him and a real vampire – a real one would have sucked out half our blood by now.

I move toward the cat, tip-toe, tip-toe, slowly, slowly. Then WHOOSH! Before it can draw a single claw, I snatch it up and into my arms and rush for the door.

The two of us fly past old Mr. Pedosky faster than a zap of lightning, faster than a turbo football, faster than my friends leaving the school at the end of the day.

When I reach the far end of the yard, I release the fuzzy cat. Then I shoot back inside before it can get any more ideas about following me.

Chapter Four

Five minutes later, everything is calm. We're at the table, eating our chicken and fries. Yuck city. Hard fries and soggy chicken. And cold! Mom cleaned the food with a wash cloth before we were allowed to touch it. Mr. Pedosky is telling us a sad story about his glass eye. He doesn't seem worried that my ears are flapping, taking in all the gruesome details.

"I am putting my eye on the counter." He takes a mouthful of the strong coffee Mom made him. "I do some other things. Then I am wanting to put it back... but it is gone." He pauses and looks at me fiercely.

"My eye is not there. It is not anywhere. It has just vanished."

"Well, it couldn't have gone far," says Mom. "It must be somewhere." She leans over and removes a french fry that Lela's busy mashing into her hair.

"I look all over. But it's hard..."

"Yes. Of course," says Mom hurriedly, in case Mr. Pedosky decides to give us a detailed description of life with one eye.

"I am thinking..." continues Mr. Pedosky, "that it is running away somewhere."

I giggle. Pictures of a glass eye with little legs running away fill my head. Then I quickly change the laugh into a cough when I see Mom frowning at me. But the pictures won't go away. Maybe Mr. Pedosky's eye has gone to visit other glass eyes.

And they'd all be cross-eyed, staring at one another. I splutter, and an explosion of french fries and giggles comes out before I can stop it.

Mom glares at me. "Mark will be happy to help you look for it."

Oh, yeah! Mark, the great "glass eye hunter." Why does my mother volunteer me for things that I don't want to do?

"Won't you?" says Mom, smiling.

I would rather eat a big bowl of dirt. "I guess," I mumble.

It's not that I don't like Mr. Pedosky or anything. But my favorite TV show is on in five minutes. It's up to a really exciting part. Now I'll probably never find out where the jewels are hidden.

"Mark!" says Mom, interrupting my thoughts. "You can go now."

I open my mouth to ask if later would be OK, but Mom's face tells me she's "brewing a storm." So, I go off with Mr. Pedosky, into the night.

We squeeze through the hole in the hedge that Mom uses when she visits Mr. Pedosky – she says it takes too long to go around the block. Mr. Pedosky's back door is wide open.

"Ah, strange," he mutters.

I stop. "What? What's strange?" I ask. My voice crackles.

"The door," he says. "I did not leave it open this much."

Oh great! Now there's probably an intruder in on the act as well. "I'll go first and see," I whisper, hoping that Mr. Pedosky will stop me – hoping he'll pull me back.

Instead, he says, "That is good."

Knees knocking, I move toward the house, slower than a bike with no wheels. I creep inside the house. The kitchen is in darkness. I hear a scuffling sound. What is it? I wait. No more sounds. Go, hero! Get the light! I put my hand around the doorknob... SPIT. HISS.

I flick on the light switch. Yep. I knew it. That Fuzz doesn't know when to give up. We give each other the fish-eye stare for about half a second, then I lunge. But before I can grab the pest, it goes behind the oven.

Mr. Pedosky comes in. "I am hearing..."

"It's OK," I say. "It's the cat..."

Mr. Pedosky interrupts. "I am thinking it is hungry. Poor kitty." He goes over to the fridge and gets out a carton of milk.

I shrug. Well, if he wants to make a fuss over it, that's fine with me, but I want to get back to my TV show. If this doesn't take too long, I can still see some of it. "Where was your eye before it got lost?" I ask.

"Over there," says Mr. Pedosky, pointing toward the kitchen counter.

I search high and low, but there's no sign of the glass eye. I don't like to say it, but I think it rolled into the sink and down the drain.

Old Mr. Pedosky seems more interested in pouring milk into a saucer and putting it on the floor than in discussing the situation. "Here, kitty," he says, kneeling on the floor and peering into the gloom behind the stove.

"I can't find it," I say.

But Mr. Pedosky isn't listening. Fuzz is all he cares about. A pink nose, two bright eyes, and bunches of whiskers are sticking out from behind the oven.

Talk about looking halfway decent. What a con artist that cat is. It's got Mr. Pedosky completely fooled.

"A long time ago, I had a cat," says Mr. Pedosky.

"Mom hates them," I say.

At the mention of my mom, Fuzz disappears behind the oven again. I go back to the matter of the glass eye. "Maybe I can come back tomorrow and do another search then."

Mr. Pedosky nods. "That is all right." I'm halfway to the door, thinking about my TV show when I hear a RRRRRRrrrrrr. Something rolls out from behind the oven. A black paw follows. SWAT. SWAT. The thing rolls across the floor, followed by the black-and-white Fuzz. What the...?

SWAT. SWAT.

The thing rolls in my direction and stops. I look down. Help! An eye stares back at me.

"A-ha!" says Mr. Pedosky, smiling, his large front teeth in full view.

Chapter
Seven

As I bend down to pick up the lost
eye, I'm beaten by a paw. Again, Mr.
Pedosky's glass eye rolls across the
floor. Then the cat, almost reaching it,
suddenly smells the milk. Game
forgotten, it makes a beeline for the
saucer. While it's busy guzzling, I
crawl under the kitchen table and pick
up the small ball of glass. Totally,
totally weird.

I bet there aren't many people who
can say they've held an eye in their
hand. I give it to Mr. Pedosky, but he
hardly notices. He's too busy making
a fuss of Fuzz. And Fuzz is making
the most of it! Sly cat!

ISBN 13: 978-0984332557
ISBN 10: 0984332553
Cover concept by Joy Deja King & www.MarionDesigns.com
Cover layout and graphic design by www.MarionDesigns.com
Cover Model: Shanel Nelson
Typesetting: Keith Saunders
Editor: Joy Deja King
Copy Editor: Linda Williams and Suzy McGlown

Library of Congress Cataloging-in-Publication Data;
A King Production
Mafia Princess Part 2/by Joy Deja King & Michelle Monay
For complete Library of Congress Copyright info visit;
www.joydejaking.com

A King Production
P.O. Box 912, Collierville, TN 38027

A King Production and the above portrayal log are trademarks of A King Production LLC

Dedication

This Book is Dedicated To My:
Family, Readers and Supporters.
I LOVE you guys so much. Please believe that!!
—Joy Deja King

A KING PRODUCTION
MAFIA
Princess
Married To The Mob
PART 2
A NOVEL
JOY DEJA KING
AND
Michelle Monay

Prologue

Present Day

The turbulence from the severe thunderstorm caused the private jet to dip wildly as Semaj and Vega flew into New York City on the Learjet 60. Semaj gazed out of the small window. The scattered sounds roared thunderously as the lightning lit up the night sky. Her adrenaline pumped with anxiousness, but it wasn't because of the striking rain clouds or the shaky aircraft. The average person would've been shaken, but the severe downpour was the last thing on Semaj's mind. There were three oversized crates full of all white bricks aboard, and she knew the shit was straight up federal. No matter how many times she'd jet set pure coke, she never got used to transporting cocaine across the U.S. border from the Dominican Republic.

"Fucking wit' you and yo' peoples, I done flooded East and West Baltimore with keys," Vega said as he laid his head atop her lap with a U-shaped plush pillow tucked underneath his neck. "Went from copping twenty kilos to flying out to foreign places to pick up five hundred bricks plus, e'ry trip now, ma."

"Yeah, and now that I introduced you to my Uncle Ortiz, shit gon' be even better for you, bay," Semaj said, rubbing his Caesared-cut hair as she smiled slightly at him. It seemed as if she was staring down at a virtually perfect man. Most of Vega's face was flawless, but there was a bad scar that ran from his wrist to the right side of his mouth. His right arm, shoulder and neck were burnt

from the explosion, but the thought of Paris's death caused her smile to broaden. *Snake ass bitch*, she thought as she noticed them approaching the small private airport.

The captain made an announcement that the private passenger plane was about to descend and to prepare for their arrival at the landing strip. Once the aircraft was on the ground safely, the Milano family's head henchman, Arturo exited the awaiting limousine, large umbrella in hand as he made his way to service them.

The piercing sound of the opening plane door urged Semaj and Vega from their seats, and they walked towards the exit to get off of their private flight.

"Hello. I hope you had a pleasant flight," he smiled at Semaj. Do you need me to take your suitcase?" Arturo asked as he stood at the bottom of the boarding steps.

"Nah, I'm good. You can grab them crates once you get me to the car and unload them into that black Lincoln that's coming through," Semaj instructed as she cautiously looked around before proceeding off the jet.

Rain poured heavily from the darkened skies and the illumination from the Town Car's headlights appeared close. "Damn, it's storming cats and dogs out this bitch!" Semaj pulled the knitted hoodie over her head and wheeled her designer luggage across the wet pavement as she walked underneath the umbrella the bodyguard held for her. "Fuck is this nigga pulling so damn close for?" she frowned in annoyance.

The Lincoln Town Car blocked the backdoor of the limo, but before another thought could register in her mind, the dark tinted window rolled down. Semaj's eyes grew wide as she watched a dreadlocked Jamaican behind apparent night vision goggles emerge with a small handgun emitting an infrared beam. Her heart thumped in fear and she closed her eyes as she waited for the bullet that would end her life.

"Boom! Boom! Boom!"

Bullets whizzed past her, and when she turned around she saw Arturo with a hole blown clear through his forehead and a chrome .40-caliber pistol dangling from his hand as he crumpled to the ground. The side window on the small plane was shattered and the captain lay slumped over the control panel. Her head spun wildly and the hailstones hit her in the face as she turned quickly to check the status of her husband. When she saw Vega sprawled awkwardly on the pavement she screamed, "Oh my God!" Her hand shot over her mouth as she repeated this over and over again in a panic.

Three men dressed in dark-colored clothing hopped from the backseat of the vehicle and ascended the jet's boarding steps. "Don't move, bitch!" the Jamaican driver barked as he held his gun out aimed directly at Semaj, daring her to move.

Before she even realized it, the men had grabbed the crates, jumped back into the Town Car and screeched off recklessly. They were gone, and Semaj was without a half ton of Gio's potent bricks.

Hit with lead, a round splotch painted Vega's white button-up shirt crimson. He gripped the blood spot with both of his hands simultaneously as his face grimaced in horror. The hot metal spread through his flesh like a California brushfire, burning up his insides. His eyes closed in agony as the cold rain fell on his injuries, doing nothing to chill the open wound.

Everything happened so fast and unsuspectingly that it wasn't until Semaj saw Vega's blood wash up onto her cream loafers that she snapped out of her shocked trance. She looked around for assistance and immediately reality settled in; she was all alone. "Vega!" she screamed as she fell to the ground beside him. "Please get up, baby!" she cried as she unzipped her purse to retrieve her phone. "I'm calling for help! Just hold on!" Her shaky hands were barely able to dial 911, but she managed, and cradled the cell phone to her wet ear.

"Nine-one-one. What is your emergency?" the operator answered.

"Please, somebody help me! My husband—he's been shot!"

Semaj mumbled hopelessly and scooped up the umbrella in an attempt to shield Vega's body from the torrent, as she compressed the wound with the clothes that she'd grabbed from her suitcase in order to stop the bleeding. "I need help! Hurry! Please, hurry!" After she told the operator her location, Semaj dropped the phone and concentrated on Vega.

The heat flaming inside of his body was unbearable. The ache was excruciating. He was unable to speak. All he could do was gasp for air and groan as he grasped the bloody garments while attempting to stare Semaj in the eyes with desperation, but the rain was obstructing his vision. He could see nothing. He reclosed his eyes as rain sprayed his face, and the sluggish thump of his pulse caused him to shudder violently. He was dizzy. He was losing way too much blood. He gulped as he tried to suck in oxygen, but the water got in his lungs and he began to choke on his own blood as it overflowed from the side of his mouth.

Semaj's eyes burned as the rain mixed with tears fell from her face and onto Vega's cheeks. The crying sky wasn't letting up, as if Mother Nature was sobbing with her. Her throbbing head spun out of control and she felt like she was floating through air. Her chest ached, and she tried to inhale, but each time she tried to suck in air a twinge erupted through her heart. She was devastated. "Please, I need you, Vega! I can't lose you too!" She closed her eyes and shook her head from side to side as if she were in disbelief.

"Semaj!" he whispered, weakly. He heard her voice in his ear and it had given him enough strength to speak. She didn't know it, but she was the one keeping him from slipping into unconsciousness. Her sweet tone was in the distance, so far away, but her soft, pleading mutters caused his eyelids to flutter wildly. Her melody was a temporary distraction from the agony. She was his dose of energy and there was no way he was going to let a gunshot wound tear them apart. They had things to handle—he had scores to settle, and until then he would remain in the flesh.

"You're going to be okay. Just hold on. Hold on, Vega!" she

pleaded. Semaj heard the strident sirens nearing and the flashing red, white and yellow lights lit up the darkened black night skies as if it was a *son et lumière*.

Semaj stared at her bloodstained hands as she nervously paced back and forth in the hospital's emergency waiting area. Her clothes were drenched in blood and her hair was matted down on her face. She walked to the oversized window and waited for her grandfather to arrive as she watched the sky fading from black to a dull gray. Dawn had set in on the horizon, but due to the constant showers, the gloom barely allowed illumination to the city streets. The dreariness matched Semaj's somber mood; it seemed to fit the occasion. For the life of her, she could not wrap her mind around what had happened. Vega was undergoing surgery and hundreds of bricks were missing. She was clueless to the fact of who would want to rob them—who were bold enough to rob them—and the ache she felt in her soul hurt horribly.

When Semaj saw five black bulletproof Hummers pull up to the hospital's door, one behind the other, a wave of relief washed over her. Out stepped the Milano Hitters from the lead truck, clad in their usual trench coat attire. Their long, jet-black hair flowed as if the four of them were about to walk down the catwalk in Milan instead of guarding the hospital's front entranceway for the Milano mob.

Shortly after, Gio climbed from the backseat of the last vehicle and entered the building with an entourage of sixteen armed Dominican men behind him. Members of the Milano organization scattered around the area, preventing anyone from entering or exiting the premises. Four of Gio's most efficient henchmen followed behind him over to where Semaj stood with a look of devastation etched to her face.

"Excuse me, sir," one of the front desk medical receptionists

said as she stood up from her post. "You all just can't have people blocking all entryways. It is a fire hazard."

Gio disregarded her protest and never acknowledged her as he kept his stride. "Pay her!" he ordered. His lead worker slipped her a stack of money and didn't lose his step alongside the boss. "*Arretao', perra!*" Gio ranted, cursing the bravery of the nurse in Spanish. "See what it will take to have a medical care flight to transport Vega to the private hospital. Whatever it takes, make sure it gets done quickly and quietly," he whispered as he spotted his soaking wet granddaughter.

"G-Poppa!" Semaj ran to her grandfather and hugged him tightly. "I'm so sorry, Poppa! I didn't know! I don't know who—"

Gio placed his index finger on his lips, indicating to her to calm down. He hated for attention to be brought to him. He was discreet and preferred to talk in private. "Let's take a step outside, Semaj," he suggested in a thick Dominican accent. He removed his suede blazer jacket and wrapped it around her shoulders, then gently grabbed her hand as he led her to the forecourt of the hospital. An elderly man sat in a wheelchair out front, a winter scarf covering half his face as a lit cigarette dangled limply in his trembling hand.

Gio pulled Semaj's arm and headed to the crosswalk out of earshot of the old man. "Now, tell me what happened," he said as he looked around to see which of his people were paying attention and the ones who were cautiously on the lookout. He noticed Emilia on the phone, apparently in a deep, serious conversation. Her facial expression was emotionless and her gaze was distant, as if she was staring at something in particular.

"When we got off the plane, the Lincoln Town Car that usually picks up the work to deliver them to Uncle Bonjo's pick-up spot pulled down. I knew something was wrong because of how the driver blocked my path," Semaj admitted. "Instead of José being behind the wheel, it was a Jamaican. He had a gun hanging outside of the window, and before I could blink, he fired off shots

killing our pilot and Arturo." Her head dropped in sadness as she continued to explain. "By the time I noticed Vega had been shot, three dudes popped out of the backseat and grabbed all of the crates and got ghost."

"Uncle Gio!" Emilia called as she approached them. "I was just on the phone with some of our higher-powered sources who said they found the Town Car a few blocks away from the private airport, along with José's corpse in the trunk, stabbed several times in the neck and a single gunshot to the head." She looked over her shoulder and noticed the same Dodge Caravan creeping down the block that she saw when the call first came through. "Fuck this lil' ass van keeps coming past here for?" she asked with suspicion in her voice.

The three pairs of eyes glared, eyeing the darkly tinted van that stopped in the middle of the street. Gio felt something was odd, and he stared at the vehicle closely. Although all of his soldiers were strapped up, he still reached in his waistband as he simultaneously stepped off the curb and pulled out his Desert Eagle semi-automatic pistol. He let it rest in his hand by his side. He threw one of his hands up threateningly as if he was inviting the occupant behind the wheel to step to him.

The van immediately sped off, leaving Gio standing there with his hand in the air. He felt he was too old for this shit, but then again, he was never too old to murder a man. "Stupid motherfuckers!" He smoothly replaced the powerful gun into his leather holster. He waved his hand in dismissal, pulled out a Cuban cigar and lit it as he returned to the girls.

Emilia leaned close to Semaj's ear and whispered, "Some bullshit is happening."

"No doubt," Semaj agreed. "Fuckin' niggas getting real fuckin' bold, nowadays. Fuck is behind all this bullshit?"

"The only mu'fuckas I can think that even got the balls to pull some shit like this is them bitch ass Jamaicans. Ox's people," Emilia replied matter-of-factly.

7

Gio immediately thought of the beef he had with the Rasta boys and regretted not killing them all off and everyone associated with them. He knew that Ox was pissed behind the massacre of his people, but who would've thought he'd have his private jet robbed upon landing? "Emilia, I need you to put your ears to the streets. See who's talking and who knows what. If you have to fill pockets to get information, then you do that. It's time to cut the bullshit out," Gio said, never raising his voice. "Get people on the phone now and see what you can find out."

Semaj noticed something wasn't right. As she looked around, everybody seemed to perfectly placed. There were two overly-dressed men perched at the bus stop bench with their heads buried in the newspaper, and also three white windowless minivans exiting the parking garage booth. By the time she realized what was going down, it was too late. The daring Jamaican posing as an elderly man removed a Tec-9 from the side of the wheelchair and pointed in their direction. "It's a hit!" Semaj screamed as she tried to warn everyone.

Emilia was always ready, on-point, and swift with her shit. She ripped her trench coat open and pulled out the AR-15 automatic assault rifle and fired first as everything seemed to happen in slow motion. With precision, she let off shot after shot that filled the foolish imposter up with lead. The force of the barrage of military bullets threw him back and slammed him into the handicap seat before he could ever pull the trigger.

All of the sudden, the two Jamaican men hopped onto the bench like frogs, both their feet planted firmly with machine guns in their hands, and began letting off shots at the Milano family. The three vans stopped at the hospital's front entrance, and in the blink of an eye the backdoors on the vans seemed to open at the same time. Four men jumped out of each van, all of them carrying army weapons. The bullets from the automatic assault rifles filled the morning's atmosphere:

"*Rat, tat, tat, tat, tat, tat, tat, tat!*"

Tiny flashes of fire danced around in the air intending to take down the Milano's family—and in particular, the "Princess". Pedestrians screamed and ran for cover in an attempt to escape the warzone while dodging bullets. It was complete pandemonium as shots rang out, hitting innocent bystanders and outgoing cars all in a special attempt to lay down Semaj (Milano) Richardson forever.

Gio had grabbed a nine-millimeter from the side of his Ferragamo boot while firing at the Jamaicans who were closing in on him. Semaj caught the gun in midair that her grandfather threw to her. She spun around, adrenaline pumping, heart pounding heavily in her chest as they shot it out with the shottas from Kingston, Jamaica. Her eyes darted wildly around the temporary parking area as she aimed her gun and released one shot after another.

"Pow! Pow! Pow!"

They returned fire.

"Boom! Boom! Boom!"

Bullets crashed the windows of the car Semaj was ducked behind, sending glass flying everywhere. She reached over the car's hood and shot back, holding her own as they went against Ox's hoodlums. Hospital employees, patients and visitors scattered in a frenzy trying not to be the ones caught by stray bullets.

"Click-Click!"

The audible indication that she was out of ammunition caused Semaj to scramble to run behind the Corinthian-style column as she realized her clip had quickly emptied, but the gun battle continued in full force. *Fuck!* she thought defenselessly. Crouched low, she ran while bullets flew around her head as she inched as quickly as possible to shield herself behind a concrete wall.

Meanwhile, Emilia had traded shots with the Jamaicans and managed to keep them off long enough for her sisters to come and assist. She yelled, "Buquí! Y'all wanna get ratchet?" and continued to let her weapon spew. "Learn how to shoot first, mu'fuckas!"

The Milano Hitters had a marksman's aim, and due to the reckless shots that the Jamaicans sent gave Emilia and her sisters a

slight advantage.

"Kill all these muthafuckas!" Sosa shouted mercilessly as she stood next to her younger sibling, Marcela. Both with a "street sweepers" in their hands, bullets flew loosely, killing everyone in plain sight.

These mu'fuckas must ain't checked our background, Emilia thought, her facial expression in a furious scowl.

Fearlessly, the Milano Hitters blasted off on the incompetent hired guns that had been sent by the infamous Ox. It was obvious that he was out for blood and her family was the target, but Emilia knew her trigger-happy knack was flawless, and Ox's hooligans couldn't match her body count alone; not to mention their numbers tallied together. *Make sure to send these bumbaclot pussies back in a fuckin' body bag!*

The four female siblings were magnificent when it came to gunplay. As Emilio's daughters, the girls had been taught by the very best, and popped off nothing but deadly headshots as the hot lead penetrated skulls, causing brain matter and mucus to spill gorily from nearly half of the dreadlocked heads.

"Arghhhh!" LuLu, the baby sister shouted piercingly as she handled her weapon skillfully and relentlessly like a madwoman. Enraged, LuLu blazed off and the Jamaican bodies fell like dominoes.

Although by now the rest of the Dominican crew had come to their defense, the Milano Hitters had their murder game looking like artwork as they painted the city streets red. In the beginning, they were outnumbered in bodies, but with a sharpshooter's ability, the female gunners were more than their equal, and had drastically slashed the Jamaican men's number down by more than half.

"This ain't what y'all want!" She was so ill with an AK that you would have thought she had invented it, and one would have never known that she reloaded her weapon. LuLu fired a trail of shots while boldly moving toward the Jamaicans, who were now backpedaling and trying to make it to their waiting transportation.

The rapid spray of endless bullets was more than the men left standing could handle, and they backed down.

"We kills cha e'notha time!" a thickly accented dread roared.

Semaj heard one of the Jamaican gunmen's threat as her ears rang deafeningly from the loudness of gunfire piercing their surrounding like it was the Fourth of July. Her damp hair hit her in the face as she spun her head quickly and peeked around the granite-stoned pillar. Her mouth fell open in horror as she saw an onslaught of bullets fill LuLu's chest, leaving her body violently jerking from left to right as her gun continued to rain bullets while hitting the ground. The three remaining Jamaicans hurriedly hopped into their vans and peeled off, leaving a cloud of smoke behind from the burning tires.

Semaj saw her cousin's body drop to the ground, and the bullets left LuLu lying motionless in the middle of the hospital's front entrance.

The entire scene was of complete carnage with dead bodies littered all across the pavement. It was something like no other. The innocent were dead at the hands of "street violence" that had showed up unexpectedly to the location. More than a thousand shell casings were scattered over the street, and the Dominican Mafia and the Jamaican gang were the cause of the gunfire melee.

"LuLu!" Semaj screamed at the top of her lungs. Her eyes began to water and she shook uncontrollably as she ran full speed to her cousin's side.

Emilia was on bended knee, rocking her sister's bullet-riddled body back and forth as she held her with silent tears flowing from her eyes. Her worst fear had surfaced, and her head fell low as she stared into LuLu's weakening gaze. Blood was spilling from her neck and her body had been struck still. "Please, Lu... you gotta... gotta get up, ma! C'mon!" Emilia yelled, and looked back at Semaj for help. "We gotta get her into this hospital. Help me please!" she pleaded in desperation and panic as she tried lifting the deadweight.

11

Gio looked around at the bloodbath that he and his family had contributed to. People lay dead everywhere; it resembled a battlefield after combat. He heard sirens in the distance and knew the sounds were coming from a procession of patrol cars and ambulances to assist with the aftermath of the early morning slaughter.

Two of the Hummer trucks pulled up directly in front of them and the doors immediately flung open.

"We've got to get the fuck from here," Gio stated as he grabbed Semaj by the arm and they slid into the truck. "*Obtener el mi la familia!*" He ordered his henchmen in Spanish to get LuLu into the other Hummer. "Come on, Emilia, let's go before the police show up. And, I need you to get someone on the line that can pull the hospital's surveillance tapes before authorities arrive on scene."

Emilia conceded and released her sister from her embrace after she kissed her forehead and then hopped into the Hummer beside Semaj as a frown of pain crossed her face while speed-dialing numbers.

The Jamaicans had shown the ultimate sign that they were declaring a war, and they were stopping at nothing. Two ruthless incidents within hours from each other weren't coincidental, and at that very moment Semaj realized that she was *literally* married to the mob. She closed her eyes and cried silently as she thought about all the things that had been done to bring her to this point.

Chapter 1

Six Months Ago

It was a cloudless, balmy Sunday afternoon and the temperate conditions were just right for the ceremonial christening for baby Niran, Semaj and Vega's sole child. Semaj's grandfather invited the family and their greatest criminal-minded organization's chiefs from all regions of the country to come celebrate the naming of his first great grandson at St. Patrick's Cathedral.

Semaj and Vega stood at the altar of the Catholic Church, her baby boy in her delicate arms as she held him over the baptismal font. Tears of joy slipped down her cheeks as she looked down at her son. She watched in silence as the priest anointed Niran on the crown of his head with sacred chrism. Elation filled her, and it seemed as if her very own sins had been washed away with the holy oil pouring down her little man's head. She had committed the unforgivable to most, but for some reason she felt that her son was her forgiveness for every sin and penalty living in her. Now, her days of destruction were in her rearview mirror, and when her grandfather stepped up, she was certain that she had been purged of all the evil she'd once known. Gio was her protector, and there was nothing for her to worry about.

Semaj had no idea that she would soon step into a world that transcended the 'hood life; a way of life that would forever change her.

The sanctuary was packed, and the purity of the occasion lent an ambiance of sheer happiness for the newest edition of the Milano family. Semaj was aware that she was amongst a congregation of the righteous and saved, but also knew that real gangsters and true soldiers surrounded her.

She glanced over at her grandfather, who was positioned at her right side. He winked at her and flashed a supportive smile. Although he was always a serious man, he delighted in surprising many with his affection for his only weakness—his granddaughter. Semaj returned the gesture graciously, and it still amazed her how one man could always make her blush. It was a natural instinct, because even though Gio missed so many years of her life, she was his pride and joy, and he treated Semaj like a princess and doted on her. She loved him dearly, and although she never knew of a man's adoration and protection stronger than her deceased father's, Gio's security was equal.

She stared into her Uncle Paulie's eyes, and everything about him reminded her that he was her mother's twin brother. From his unblemished skin tone, striking features and confidence in his bossed-up swagger and conversation, Semaj knew that from the small remembrance to her mother, that he too was one that would get the job done.

Gio hadn't touched drugs in what seemed like forever, but the Milano family's lucrative drug cartel was one of the few good ones left standing stateside, and it was obvious that Paulie was his father's successor.

She shifted her gaze and looked at Gio's only nephew, who he considered his own son and called him as such. Semaj loved how her uncle was respected in the streets and was feared by most. Unlike Paulie and many others, Bonjo was a real street nigga, and while the family business was a wholesale market, Bonjo set up shop on corners and in dope houses. He kept it all the way 'hood, and sold it whichever way one preferred. He had buyers and workers, and the Mafioso members knew he'd gotten his "grinding to get it

all" mentality from his African American heritage. He was ratchet, business and street savvy, but most of all, Semaj admired the bond he had with his wife. Something told her that his wife, Jah-Jah was the Bonnie to his Clyde.

Semaj looked out at the front pew reserved for immediate family only. Her cousins were full-blooded Dominicans, and to the average person the four girls were undeniable beauties and supporting their family, but inside their fashionable belted, short-sleeved Donna Karan trench coats was the only supportability that mattered to them—long guns and plenty ammunition. Their natural almond skin glowed, and their different colored catlike eyes made some men make fatal mistakes. Although they were whole sisters, they each carried a distinct feature about themselves.

But the one thing all of them had in common was their murderous ability. It was in their blood to be killers. Throughout the eighties and nineties their father, Emilio Milano ran one of the most notorious gangs of contract killers and career robbers that the streets had ever seen. His daughters had been murderers for hire in the making. After their father received two consecutive life sentences, with small feet, they had filled the big shoes of the legendary mobster and were leaving huge footprints on the game. Although they were gorgeous women, they were also stone-cold killers, and it was a known fact that between the four of them, their body count was in the triple digits. They were "mob bitches" by all means.

Semaj lifted her baby from the font and handed him to Paulie, who accepted the role as godfather. He had her son dressed to the nines in a pure white, luxurious silk Dupioni christening suit.

The celebrant grabbed the Paschal candle and said, "Receive the light of Christ."

Vega flickered on the Caran d'Ache lighter and lit the candle, and an orange flaming glow emitted. The expensive 14-kt gold lighter was given to him by Gio. Every man in the Family had one. It was a token of family loyalty.

The high priest then added, "Parents and godparents, this light is entrusted to you to be kept burning brightly. This child of yours has been enlightened by Christ. He is to walk always as a child of the light. May he keep the flame of faith alive in his heart. When the Lord comes, may he go out to meet him with all the saints in the heavenly kingdom."

The words touched Semaj's heart, and as the Lord's Prayer began, her mind drifted back to the day that her world had been blessed by her family's presence and the day she knew that Niran would never have to commit the sins of the Family or take risks as she once had before she knew she was a Milano heir—they were all living so that the next generation would be able to live in a lawful world and enjoy their inheritance without fear.

Three Months Earlier

"Everyone, I want you to meet my granddaughter, Semaj and her significant other, Vega. Semaj, I don't know if you remember, but this is your mother's twin, Paulie Milano. Then this goodfella here," Gio chuckled, "Is my sister's son, Bonjo, and this beautiful lady right here is his wife, Jah-Jah. Then, these lovely young women are my nieces, Emilia, Sosa, Marcela and LuLu. We call them the 'Milano Hitters'. These are my 'problem solvers'. If you have any problems, let them know and they'd make the issue disappear. These are the immediate family members up here in the States. Everybody here is trustworthy and loyal and everyone else is questionable. And remember, anyone that is a doubt we don't trust."

Everyone greeted Semaj endearingly and welcomed Vega into the Family because of her.

"Paulie, she looks just like you and Kasey. It's uncanny, fam," Bonjo said, remembering Semaj's late mother.

From his street clothes, Semaj could tell that he was a straight

'hood nigga, and through his gaze she could read savage, but yet calculating and took an instant liking to him. Beyond the expensive Chanel threads, Semaj knew that his wifey was cold and cunning. From one thorough bitch to another, Semaj had peeped her whole swag. For the Milano Hitters, she knew what was understood didn't need to be explained.

"Let's eat," Gio said as he took his seat at the head of the rectangular dining table. Semaj sat directly across from him at the other end.

For the first time since she was a little girl, Semaj felt whole because she had a complete family... a family that she could count on, and she fell in love with the concept. Their interactions were so natural that they appeared as an old traditional family. They popped bottles of vintage wine and ate good as they all got to know her, and before they realized it, hours had gone by.

The amazing joy Semaj felt right now in the present made her begin to reflect on her past. She excused herself from the table, as she needed a moment alone to work through the feelings that had suddenly overcome her. She headed out of the twelve-foot French doors and walked out onto the balcony. "This is beautiful," She said as she looked out into the perfect night. The rain had stopped and a full moon had bloomed. In silence, she stood and stared into the glittering stars. The sky was lit up and the cold wintry draft caused her to wrap her arms around herself.

She closed her eyes, and her tears began to fall. Her mind had granted her memories of her past, but there was one that stuck out; Quasim. As hard as she tried blocking him out, she couldn't. His presence was always felt and she had never let go... not completely. She rocked hard with Vega no doubt, but although she hated to admit it, Quasim had been her rock. He taught her how to survive in a different light, but as each day passed, she noticed the light dimming even more. Dreams of yesterday seemed to be dreams that weren't even in the cards for today. Too much had happened, and Semaj felt like her tomorrow was just as bleak.

Quasim was a constant reminder of her past life. What she was, who she was becoming, what she could have been, and in a blink of an eye it had all been taken away from her. *He* had been taken away from her. Not knowing if he would've forgiven her haunted her every day. She relived the last moments she had with him, which was brutal, but that didn't matter to her. All that mattered was their last phone call. It ended with him giving her hope. *He was a real nigga*, she thought guiltily, still hating herself for deceiving him. *I just wish I could have at least told him one last time that I was sorry.*

Semaj was lost in her thoughts as her grandfather stood behind her and kneaded her tensed shoulders. This was a ritual that he'd always done when his daughter was younger, and every Friday he had decided that this would be one of the ways he bonded with his granddaughter. He had to make up for lost times. "What are you crying for, Semaj?" he asked as he began to rub her hair.

She reopened her eyes, and it was unfathomable how he heard her silent cry, "I'm just thinking about a lot of things. Nothing really."

What she didn't know was that Gio already knew her reason. "Semaj, you remind me so much of your mother. But know that just like I could read everything about her, I know how to read you like an open book, too." He turned her around to face him. "I know you miss, Quasim. He was a man of great honor, but I must tell you that I'm glad I was not the one that had to kill him."

"But how did you know?" she gasped as her brow rose in astonishment.

Gio laughed lightly, because it was always the same response he received from her mother. "I know everything that goes on with my favorite girl," he winked matter-of-factly. "I was going to wait, but since we have some alone time, there is something I need to speak to you about."

"What is it?" she asked.

"I know Vega is your boyfriend, but it is a part of our family's

tradition that when our women bear a child, the mother and father must be wed in holy matrimony. So, I need for you to get your head together. You and Quasim wouldn't have ever made it. Fate forced y'all apart before the two of you met, Maj. I recognized that the both of you loved each other the night of your birthday at my yacht, because he was about to give up the game for you; something he said he'd never do. But sometimes things are left better as is," he said, and kissed her on the cheek and walked back inside.

He turned around at the door and smoothly put his hands in his gray Burberry London slacks. "You all will get married, and two weeks later, Niran will be baptized," he said with dominance in his voice, but in actuality, Semaj knew that this was the softer side of her grandfather. He saluted her and left her to her own thoughts.

She gripped onto the railing of the balcony and released some of the anxiety that she was feeling with a long sigh. Her eyes got lost in the shooting star as she tried to shake her past from her thoughts. "Married! I'ma be a wife," she confessed to herself.

Semaj knew that she didn't have time to dwell on the past. She had to focus on her family, her life, and find out what her future held, but she would soon discover that it held more than most men could handle—a life that her mother got introduced to at a very young age. Gio had been the one to inform her on her mother's involvements with the family's drug business.

When it came to Semaj, Gio held nothing back. He ran her entire family history from jump, wanting to give her the game, the ins and outs of the illegal business so that she could stay on alert just in case something happened. She knew her grandfather was a drug lord. It was no secret, but she knew not to discuss the Family to outsiders. It was an unspoken silence, and she was well aware about keeping her mouth shut. It was called "Family Secrets" next to Omerta; a code of silence.

But soon, Semaj would learn that she wasn't only born into the mob, but built for the Mafia.

*****

Semaj and her family walked out of the building with an entourage of six men in black suits following them. It was unusually warm and gorgeous outside for it to be mid-winter, and on the perfect, sunny day her son had been christened. But little did Semaj know that it wouldn't stay perfect for long, and the block was about to get hot.

As they walked down the forty-four courtyard-styled church's steps, laughing and making their ceremonious farewells, Paulie took a sleeping Niran from Semaj's embrace. He squirmed around as Paulie cradled him against his blanketed chest. "Poppa gon' have you out here all day, Maj, introducing you to the family. This baby boy is drained and worn out from today's occasion. I'll be waiting in the car for you all to finish up. Take your time. I have some important calls to make in private."

An eerie feeling came over Semaj as she watched as her uncle descended the staircase with her baby in his arms. The further he got down the flight of steps, the more she felt as if he was leaving from her life permanently. Her heartstrings seemed to be pulling towards her son, and as she fixed her mouth to summon him back in her care, Gio directed her in the opposite direction.

"I have someone that's been dying to see you again." He put his hand on the small of her back and led her to the limo waiting curbside as she watched the congestion of cars pass by and Paulie look both ways before crossing the busy street.

Paulie slid into the backseat of the bulletproof limousine after the chauffeur opened the door and stood waiting for the rest of the family.

"Your great-great grandfather, Marriano Milano, the man that started it all!" Gio boasted with a wide smile. "He's one-hundred-and-one years old, but has a memory bank as clear as a bell."

Without averting her attention from the limousine, Semaj extended her hand and replied, "It is really nice to see…"

"BOOM!"

Metal and glass fragments flew everywhere, showering the city streets as the limousine exploded right before Semaj's eyes and damaged all the cars in its vicinity. The ground shook violently beneath her feet as if an earthquake had hit Manhattan, sending her flying backwards onto the pavement, along with knocking many others from their feet. Her ears went deaf to everything around her as the loud explosion and blaring sound of her head throbbing rang loudly in her ears.

The sight of amber flames engulfing the car and creating a black smoky cloud in the air forced Semaj to scramble to her feet. "Nooo!" she screamed as she ran toward the burning limousine across the street. She sprang over all the destruction as she watched the fire swallow up the car. She saw the blaze swirling, causing the large trees and bushes near to catch fire. A fear incited her that she had never known as she was approaching the wreckage.

Debris from the car scattered all across the street while the remains was quickly burning. She knew it was only a matter of time that the fire would spread to the gas tank, but that didn't stop her. She was out of her mind and at this point delusional. Her baby was inside that car, and she needed to get him out so that he could go home with her.

Her entire body went numb, as she maneuvered through the dispersing crowd, and realization settled in as she bent over in disbelief. The agonizing thought of her son charring caused her maternal instincts to kick in, and she opened the blistering door despite the excruciating pain the hot metal produced. When the door flung open she saw Paulie lying on the limo floor hunched over her son's body. Instantaneously, she felt strong hands tugging at her, but she ferociously fought them off. "No! Please! My baby!" she screamed, squirmed and swatted the rough, rigid hands as she turned to see that her grandfather was dragging her away from what had already been destroyed as fire trucks and paramedics surrounded the scene and jumped out in their required gear and

equipment in an attempt to snuff out the fire.

But it was too late. Baby Niran and Paulie had died in the detonation of the car.

"Please! I have to get my son!"

The explosion was very intense, and it was obvious that they were gone. Her son was gone. What was supposed to be a joyful affair turned into a horrid tragedy, and it broke Semaj down to her knees.

As Gio looked his granddaughter directly in her eyes, he saw the unbearable pain embedded deeply within her puffy, bloodshot, devastated gaze. A rare emotion of pain passed over him, and at that moment he knew a war had just begun, and he would stop at nothing to see the persons responsible for the bomb plot buried six-feet deep; Dead or Alive.

Welcome To The Mob....

Chapter 2

Gio's head rested against the plush seat as he watched the tiny ice pellets fall from the murky skies as the driver pulled into the gated community. It had been over fifteen years since Gio lived in New York, but the chaos surrounding him and his family forced him into a long-term stay back on the East Coast. He was enraged by the unforeseen ambush that had been committed against his family. And as he rode in the backseat of the Rolls-Royce Ghost, retaliation consumed him. His anger reached such a boiling point that it now had a mind of its own, and anyone he assumed guilty would die.

As the driver pulled up, Gio observed the picture perfect mansion that would to most appear to be the ideal family home, but there was nothing ideal about the Mafia.

Gio was the mastermind of the international drug operation and made sure things ran smoothly. Although they were a part of the underworld, he made sure to keep his family almost undetectable. So, the Family Business existed, even to the authorities, like some sort of UFO. There were even mentions about the Family, but there wasn't any solid proof of their existence like various other Families. Gio's main priority was to keep them under the federal government's radar, and that was his sole reason for aligning himself with great political figures.

The Milano's had numerous legitimate businesses, all the while holding reign over the drug trade, further cementing

the Family's power. They owned a chain of private hospitals, mortuaries, funeral homes, and cemeteries, all of which proved cleaver—for both drug smuggling and also safe hiding places. He had an international aircraft travel business for the deceased as a front to transport drugs, where bodies were stitched with narcotics. He knew his investments would be perfect because it would also help them conceal the evidence of the murders they might partake in.

As Arturo opened up the backdoor, Gio stepped out in a floor-length wool trench, and out of habit he looked both ways. He took a deep breath as he prepared himself for what he was about to encounter, knowing his pain didn't compare to that of Semaj's heartache.

There were many henchmen stationed around the house, but Gio was so bothered that he didn't acknowledge any of them as he passed by and proceeded into the Milano family home.

"Uncle Gio," Emilia mouthed as she pointed at the phone cradled to her ear, indicating that she was collecting information on the other end. She was the most resourceful of the sisters and always had her ears to the streets. Emilia was the brains, and she was the oldest. She seemed to be the one with useful tactics, and it never took her more than a week to gather the specifics. Don't ask how, because even Gio didn't know, but she had major connections. The perfect leader of the professional murderesses, Emilia was cold-blooded but brilliant.

He greeted her with a head nod and was well aware that she was already on top of things.

LuLu noticed him and immediately walked over. "Don't worry about nothing, Uncle Gio. The people that murdered our family will suffer a painful death. We won't stop until we take what they took of ours three times over."

Gio knew that she was serious. Although the youngest of the Family, at nineteen LuLu was the nuttiest and was a natural born killer. She was the one to shoot first and never asked questions later.

There was nothing hesitant about her when it came to her murder game. She put it down like no other.

"I know, Lu." He wanted to pull his niece in for a hug but he knew that wasn't her style. There wasn't a sensitive bone in her body, and Gio respected it. LuLu reminded him the most of his brother. For lack of better words, LuLu was a "goon" and she kept it gangster. "Where are the rest of the ladies?"

"I'm right here, Uncle. Marcela is upstairs with Semaj," Sosa said as she emerged from the kitchen. She was what you called the different one. She could have easily passed for a 'hood chick. Her butter-pecan complexion was the darkest, and with shoulder-length caramel-layered hair and hazel eyes, her natural beauty had been the perfect bait for their victims. Feisty as they come, Sosa had a fetish for designer threads and powerful Glocks. Needless to say, she was a fashion junkie and an addict for murder. The ghetto one out of the bunch, Sosa was a loudmouth, but there was no denying that she was a real bitch.

Gio ascended the steps two at a time and sighed as he walked past Semaj's bedroom where two armed bodyguards stood. He headed down the hallway to the guestroom Vega was in and knocked on the door.

"Come on in," Vega called out as he stood staring out of the window solemnly, watching as the snowflakes fell from the skies. He turned around and saw Gio standing in the doorway. He grabbed his suit jacket and eased into it comfortably. He was dapper in a black-on-black custom fitted suit, but the dull pain inside made him feel like shit. He was supposed to be his family's protector, and right underneath his nose their most innocent member had been killed, and now he and Semaj were forced to bury their infant son. What had been a great dream had quickly turned into their worst nightmare. Niran had been what had solidified their love, and Vega just hoped with him gone their love would survive.

While grieving the loss of their child, at the same time Vega had to be strong for Semaj so she wouldn't fall completely apart.

25

He watched as she forced herself to sleep at night, and even though he tried to console her, emotionally she seemed to be trapped in her own world and unwilling to let anyone in, including him. But Vega understood that she was more than likely trying to fight off the same haunting images of their son that consumed his every thought.

At the same time, he knew that if he didn't step up and remain strong, that this devastating tragedy would destroy them both. Vega refused to let that happen, so instead of wallowing in his grief, he had his own crew searching for a leak. There was no doubt in his mind that Gio had all of his people on it, but sometimes the most useful and important information comes from street sources that Gio might not have access to.

"It's time," Gio said, walking inside the room. "But first, there is something that needs to be addressed, my son."

"What's up, Poppa?"

"Call me Gio," he corrected, not even giving him the respect of facing him. He walked over to the bay window and pulled out a cigar. With his back turned to him, Gio wrapped his chubby finger around the cigar and toked on it as he stared out the window.

This nigga can call me son, but I can't call him Poppa, Vega thought. He knew Gio wasn't too fond of him and only dealt with him because of Semaj, but Vega didn't care, because the feelings were mutual. *It's only a matter of time before my plans come into play,* he thought treacherously. *Fuck this nigga wanna talk to me fo' anyway?*

It seemed as if hours had passed before Gio finally turned to Vega, but when he did he stared him in the eyes coldly. "I'm aware that you have people seeking out who was behind the hit. But that is an area you need not tend to. Your main concern should be helping Semaj get through these difficult times. Trust me; you don't have enough power to back you up. This life is deeper than the 'hood shit that you're used to, my friend. Handle your people in Baltimore and ensure your wife's safety, and your job is done.

Anything outside of that will result in your death." Without waiting on his response, Gio brushed passed him hard.

It took all of Vega's willpower not to go for his pistol and shoot Gio in his back. He felt totally disrespected, but he knew that he might as well turn the gun on himself if he did that. *My son was killed and this mu'fucka thinks I'm just 'pose to sit and watch like a sitting duck or some shit? Got me all the way fucked up. I'ma show this slick-haired fuck just the type of niggas a 'hood nigga recruits,* he thought as he shot daggers as Gio exited the room.

When Gio approached Semaj's bedroom, he stopped as he looked at her through the full-length mirror she stood in front of.

She was dressed in an all black Prada pencil skirt set that he specifically picked out for her to wear. It was tailored to fit her five-foot-seven frame perfectly. Her long, coal black hair was pulled back into a sophisticated donut. As she slipped her left hand into the black satin glove, she repeated the same gesture, but this time she slowly slid her blistered hand inside, careful not to scrape her scalded palm. The beyond scorching door handle she latched onto had caused it to bubble up badly, but the injury was very minor compared to the battle wound of losing her only child.

Semaj spared herself of any makeup because her crying would eventually ruin it. Her beauty was natural anyway, but even so, an ugly pain within was written all over her face. Although there weren't any tears, her eyes were bloodshot red and swollen, and it was obvious that she had been crying nonstop.

Marcela had helped Semaj prepare for the dreadful task that awaited them. As a matter of fact, she hadn't left her side since Niran's untimely demise. To have to bury the youngest member of their family was daunting, but Marcela knew that the united strength of the family would pull them through it.

Marcela was quiet and laidback. A woman of very few words, she didn't speak unless she had something important to say. Although close with all of the girls, she and Semaj shared a tight bond. They were the same age and Marcela was an all out

sweetheart. But don't get it twisted, because she had a heart as chilly as an Antarctica winter, and when she came through, she came *through*, and it was one bloody murder one after another.

"Marcela, I appreciate you being by Semaj's side while I was away. I heard you've been her rock, and for that I thank you."

"We're family. You know I'ma always make sure the Family is straight," she replied. Marcela walked over to Semaj and whispered in her ear, "I'll be waiting for you downstairs." She stood on her tiptoes and kissed her uncle's cheek before she exited.

When the two of them were alone, Gio walked towards his granddaughter. For the past six days, Semaj hadn't eaten or spoken a word, but somehow her granddad's presence made her feel comfortable and eased her weary soul a bit. She was grateful that he was there so she could finally express herself. "Poppa, I'm feeling as the time nears that I can't do this...I don't want to do this. It's as if when the bomb went off and took my son, I died too," she said, and as her legs had given out underneath her, she fell onto the ottoman and buried her head in her gloved hands.

Gio rushed to her side, and as he sat beside her he intertwined their hand. Wrapping his arm around her neck he pulled her closer to his chest as her tears poured from her soul. He knew that she would take her son's death hard. He too felt the pain of losing a child. Actually, he had lost all of his seeds. He had no living children. Semaj was the closest thing that he had to an offspring, and now he definitely had to do everything in his power to protect her. His eyes filled with tears and threatened to fall, but he willed the tears away as fast as they had come.

"I know this is very difficult for you, Semaj. It is difficult for all of us. But you have many people that love you. Many people that are doing everything that they can to bring us some answers. Saying good-bye will be hard for us to digest, but I promise you that we will get through this as a family."

"But why me? It seems like everything I love gets taken away from me. First, my mom, then my auntie, then my dad, and now

my son. Uncle Paulie too. How much more does God think I can take? He was only a baby, and it's like his life on Earth didn't exist to begin with!" she cried. She felt as if she was dying a slow painful death with no timeline on when the suffering would end.

"Know it will take time for you to heal, but your son, my great grandson is gone, but his memory will live on," Gio said soothingly. He stood up with her still held in his arms and kissed her on the top of her head. "Dry your tears, because we don't play fair. We don't believe in an eye for an eye. Take one of ours, we need three, four, five of yours. That's just how we play, and we play for keeps. We will avenge the murders. You understand that their death will not go unpunished, Maj?" he asked.

Semaj nodded her head unsurely as they walked down the long hallway and descended the steps. Their relatives were already waiting in the foyer for them, and together they all walked out of the house, unprepared to say their final farewells to Paulie and baby Niran.

Paris stood on the third floor balcony and hid behind one of the cathedral's many confession booths as she looked out of the window and noticed Semaj and her family had arrived. Five black Rolls-Royces pulled up curbside, and each car came to a slow stop in front of the church doors. Paris had to admit that Semaj and her people had security "virgin-tight", and there was no way a person would be able to bring drama to the church without getting murked. The road was barricaded within a mile radius, and nobody was able to attend the private funeral unless one was a part of the family. A slight smirk crossed her face at their effort of protection.

A silk scarf and a large hat concealed her identity, and the member nametag confirmed her position. Paris had snuck in before anyone had arrived earlier that morning and posed as one of the sister's of the ministry. She knew being there was very risky,

but she just had to witness Semaj fucked up, and was crazy enough to attend. She was glad that Semaj hadn't died in the explosion, because seeing how she affected her life firsthand was hilarious to Paris.

As she watched henchmen of Dominican descent walk up and surround the vehicles, Paris's nose turned up. She was sickened with disgust as Vega stepped out the back of the car and held his hand out for Semaj. *Sucka ass nigga. What kinda nigga marries a bitch that set your people up? Fuck type shit is that?* Paris shook her head, and as she zeroed in on the pair, vomit tickled the back of her throat. She despised them, and the sight made her want to throw up on the track.

Draped in a maxi-length mink coat and a pillbox hat, Semaj's devastation was hidden well behind large Gucci sunglasses. She looked like old money. *This bitch's really trying to be on some real Mafia Princess shit. Ha! Fuck she think her grandfather is? John Gotti or some shit? Fuck outta here!* Paris thought.

Vega placed his hand on the small of her back as Semaj attentively looked around. As if Paris's intense energy had whispered in her ear, Semaj looked up at the building. Unfortunately, the window was opaque and she saw nothing. She turned her head to each end of the block. The vicinity was sewn up with bodyguards. Seeing her surroundings, she knew that she was good. Her husband led her through the crowd of unfamiliar faces, and her family followed closely behind.

Once Semaj entered the sanctuary, her insides felt like they were about to explode. She began to hyperventilate and felt claustrophobic in the tiny space. Seeing the huge picture of her newborn baby displayed at the front of the church caused her limbs to shake uncontrollably and her breathing became shallow.

A tiny, silver-plated casket sat next to her uncle's coffin at the head of the aisle, and both sat among hundreds of gardenias. Each casket was closed, and the sight caused Semaj to stop walking. *Why me? Why my baby? This is too much! I'm not ready to say goodbye to my*

son. He was supposed to bury me, not the other way around. It was as if her heart went up into flames and died right along with her baby, and she felt as if she no longer had a purpose to live.

Just as she was about to turn around, Semaj felt a hand on her shoulder. "Maj, you gotta do this for your little man," Marcela whispered in her ear. "I'm not going to say that everything is going to be a'ight, because I know it will take time for you to be even half way right. But you have to get through this for your son. Niran knows his mom loves him, and that you'll meet back up with him one day. He was just too perfect and good for this world. God removed him from your life so that he wouldn't be caught up in the middle of what's about to go down," Marcela said.

Semaj stared down at the carpet as her feet shuffled nervously from side to side, and she allowed her tears to flow freely. It was almost as if her cousin's words fell on deaf ears and the twinge in her heart was unwavering. She had never experienced a loss so great, and she felt lost without her son's pleasant smile to cheer her up. She forced herself to get a whiff of his scent and tried her hardest to think about each day that she had with him. Thoughts of happy times with him gave her the strength, and she lifted her head up. She nodded weakly and allowed Vega to continue to escort her to her seat.

Before Semaj sat down she scanned the crowd to see all of the Milano family members. When she glanced up at the balcony, her eyes bugged wide in astonishment and she almost lost her balance, but quickly grabbed the wooden bench for support. A lump formed in her throat, and her neck whipped toward the third floor for a double take. No one stood there. *What the fuck*, she thought, and could have sworn that she saw Paris. *Semaj, you is really buggin' the fuck out*, she told herself as she took her place on the front pew.

Focusing in on the priest, Semaj tried to focus in on the eulogy service as the catholic minister that baptized her baby a week prior delivered a sermon on a new day, and sent her son Home.

When the service was over, Semaj stood to leave. She was

amongst a community of Dominicans, and everyone came up to her expressing their condolences. Besides Gio's close-knit kin, she didn't recognize any of the somber faces and she quickly became overwhelmed by it all.

Marcela noticed it and looped her arm through Semaj's as they made their exit from the church. "There are so many people. Who are all of these people?" Semaj asked as the cold caused her breath vapor to hit the air.

"This is your family. The other people standing out here are just our associates coming out to pay their respects to our family. Paulie was a powerful influence, and he is the reason many people could live a good life," Gio answered as they stood at the top of the church's steps and watched as the pallbearers brought out both caskets and loaded them onto the black, horse-drawn hearse as white doves flew around in the sky. Gio made sure he spared no expense when sending his loved ones off. He helped Semaj into the car, and they prepared to follow the bodies to the gravesite with a diplomatic procession of vehicles following closely behind them.

Quasim sat behind the dark tint in the black Mercedes-Benz as he watched the burial proceedings from afar. People thought that he was dead after the nightclub shooting, and he went all out having his childhood friend, Al-B stage a cremation memorial for him. Quasim knew that there was no doubt that Gio would send his goons after him. Even with his aunt Sabrina dead, Gio was from the old school and played by the rules of family: harm mine, and I harm someone in your lineage. Quasim was certain that if Gio hadn't thought he was dead, he would have stopped at nothing to see him buried.

Quasim peered out at the many familiar Dominican faces, and it brought back great memories. Having moved a lot of bricks

for the Family, he had once been a part of the dynasty. *This shit is fucked up*, he thought. He had never been a scary nigga, but a foolish man he wasn't either. So, he had to put a great distance between him and Gio. Besides, he knew more than likely people would be after him after Block's death, and he just wasn't willing to chance his life—at least not until he formed a new goon squad.

A slight grin crossed his face as he noticed the Milano Hitters step from the back of the car and waited for Semaj to exit the vehicle behind theirs. He knew exactly who the beautiful women were. Gio had sent them to wipe out niggas for him plenty of times. A lot didn't surprise Quasim, but he had to admit that the murderous ability of Gio's nieces amazed him.

A crowd mobbed around the burial plots, and the priest began to deliver the Lord's Prayer.

Quasim noticed one of the henchmen who appeared to be speaking through an earpiece communicator rush over to a sedan and accept an envelope from the driver.

Under any other circumstances, Quasim wouldn't be caught dead in the States, but when he saw coverage on CNN news, he caught the first flight out. He had to pay his respects to Paulie, but what he didn't admit to himself was that he actually wanted to see Semaj. He truly missed her, and there was no denying it.

A small smile flashed across his face as he noticed her looking around, as if his energy was sent through his faraway stare and tapped her on the shoulder. He knew that she unknowingly felt his presence, and the thought made his heart flutter. *Damn, ma!* He shook his head. *Why?* Although Semaj was no longer his, the sight of her with another man caused a streak of jealousy to pulse through him. *She really married another nigga.*

Semaj had moved on and made a family, and even though the little boy that bonded them together was gone, Quasim knew that what they had, ended a long time ago. *Why that shit had to happen to us?* he thought glumly as he watched the gravediggers dump dirt on top of the caskets.

Quasim noticed that the henchman had walked back up and pulled Gio and Emilia to the side.

With Gio around, we'd never be able to be together again, he thought as he engaged the ignition and looked at Semaj one last time. He reluctantly pulled away in the S600 and headed to the airport to catch his international flight back to the United Kingdom.

"Ms. Emilia," Arturo said as they walked away from the crowd. "One of your sources gave me this envelope to give to you." He handed it over and she immediately unsealed it.

Semaj watched as Emilia attentively opened up the envelope and pulled out what appeared to be a sheet of paper. *What's going on?* she thought as she continued to read her facial expression.

"Ay, Uncle Gio. Ain't this the boy, Gabe that you used to deal with? You sent us to get at his people, right?" she asked as she thumbed through the pictures of Gabe boarding a U.S. plane with a gang of Jamaicans, and then looked at another one where they had arrived at JFK airport. Indeed, Emilia's resources had come through once again.

Gio's brow furrowed deep, but he held his composure as he put two and two together. "Gabe must've linked up with Ox," he said as he stared at the ten-by-thirteen photograph. Each dude had on an enormous piece that spelled "Warfare", and that alone was the only confirmation Gio needed. It was a term Ox called his organization. "There aren't many people bold enough to bring problems to our family."

"What's going on, Poppa? Emilia?" Semaj asked as she walked up with the rest of the girls on her heels. She looked in between the two of them. "Did something happen?"

"I believe the Jamaicans are responsible for this, because Ox has been very angry from the Milano Hitters' killing of his soldiers. It isn't coincidental that Ox's people were killed at the nightclub, and all of the sudden Gabe has connected with some dreads."

"Gabe?" Semaj yelled out in shock. "This is the guy that beat

me the night Quasim was shot! Vega didn't check to make sure he was dead!" Her hand shot over her mouth as tears slid down her cheeks. "Oh my God! He killed my baby! He is the reason my son is dead!"

What Semaj didn't know was that Gabe not only had a score to settle with her, but her grandfather also. She had no idea that when she was setting Gabe up to be robbed by her father, that she was actually responsible for Paulie's only son's murder, and now, Gabe had one up on them. He had gotten information from Ox, and it all made sense. He was aware that Gio had discovered that Semaj was his granddaughter, and his sister had killed two birds with one stone.

"I promise you we will handle this guy, Maj," Gio said as he pulled her into his chest. Nothing else had to be said. He knew what had to be done. He whispered something in Emilia's ear. She quickly told her sisters that they had to go, but before they hopped inside the car, Sosa turned toward Semaj. "There will be a lot of white chalk drawing, white sheet laying and toe tag labeling. You ain't gotta worry about shit. We finna find these cowards and get it popping. Believe that," she winked. "And I'ma make sure he sees your face before we end his life."

Semaj nodded her head weakly and folded her arms across her chest as she watched the foursome enter the car and pull away from the cemetery.

Chapter 3

Semaj lay beneath the crumpled satin sheets with her son's soft blanket snuggled against her heart. Her head spun in guilt, and her mind raced in regret, sending a heartache that was so extreme that she felt as if she was suffocating.

Knowing that she had done so many grimy things to so many people, and the fact that someone had actually come back to retaliate let her know that karma was real. The weight of bricks had burdened her spirits, and there wasn't anything that could ease her pain. Wrecked with grief time and time again, she wasn't sure if she would ever be able to let her baby go. Night after night, she prayed for his soul, but she wasn't sure if her prayers would be accepted with all of the bad she had done.

Eyes rimmed pure red and dark bags beneath made it obvious that she hadn't slept in days. Sleep was evasive, and rest was something that she couldn't attain. Never leaving that spot, she hadn't moved. She couldn't move. Heartbreak had paralyzed her, and hollowness had taken over her normal state. She was empty. The fighter in her had disappeared, and only a small fraction of her former self existed, and it was as if she was close to hitting rock bottom.

Semaj no longer felt worthy to live. Her life was now empty. Her son's joyous sunrise had quickly become a devastating sunset. Without baby Niran in the world, she was no longer complete. Not a single fiber in her body wanted to move on with her life. How could she?

The one person that she changed her life for had forever changed her life again—this time for the bad. The one and only human being she had ever lived for had died, and yet she remained on Earth. How could that be so? Her baby was innocent, but yet she was very far from it. Semaj felt that God had performed a cruel act and should have left her accountable for her own wrongdoings. *If this is what He has for my son, I can just imagine what's in store for me.*

Images of her son flashed before her eyes, and she felt like it had all been a bad dream, but the multihued laminated obituary that sat on the nightstand was almost magnetic, allowing reality to hit her. Her baby was gone. There would be no celebration for his first birthday, no terrible twos, or no know-it-all three year old. Only short memories of the little time that they had spent together.

Baby Niran's short stay on Earth had showed her that she could love someone more than she loved herself, and the thought of missing the biggest piece in her life was enough to let her know that she would never be whole again. Life's puzzle for her would never be solved, and knowing he was no longer in existence was slowly turning her heart completely cold.

Semaj heard footsteps move across the hardwood floor as the bedroom door squeaked, but she remained unflinching. Although she knew it was probably one of her cousins coming to check up on her, she hated that the two men in her life were not with her. Their presence seemed to slightly ease some of the pain, and without them she felt as if she was facing the anguish alone.

For the past couple of days, Vega had been in Baltimore to make sure business was right, and Gio had taken a flight to South America to have a meeting. Paulie's seat had to be filled immediately, and it was Gio's obligation to discuss it with the 16 Tent who he had decided to fill his shoes.

The 16 Tent was a governing body of Mafia families that were responsible for forty-six percent of the drug distribution across the world. Only top ranking members of the cartels knew about this connected group of people, and that's the way they preferred it.

There were no loose links to each other just in case one of the families got jammed up, and everyone would take their own heat.

Sixteen members sat underneath a tent, and the commission would all have to vote on the next one in line to effectively run the business stateside. Everybody knew that Bonjo was supposed to be the successor, but some of the members weren't sure if they wanted the ruthless man to become second in command of the commission. That, along with running the U.S business would be a sure way to head down a road of self-destruction, and the members didn't think Bonjo was best fit.

"Semaj?" Sosa called out as she walked around the bed, a chain dangling from her hand. The necklace quickly got Semaj's attention, and for the first time in what seemed like forever she sat up. Her heartbeat quickened and sweat formed on her nose as Sosa approached her with a gracious smile etched to her face. Her smile hid what she was really thinking about her cousin. *I can't believe this happened,* Sosa thought.

Semaj's face was swollen and ash-white, almost sallow. Sosa had been used to them being in friendly competition when it came to putting themselves together with meticulousness, so seeing Semaj's thick, luxurious mane matted to her scalp and her French-tips chipping was shocking. Semaj was a fading shell of her former self. The tragedy of life had defeated her. Her world had shattered into pieces, and she displayed a weakness that only a mother would endure after losing a child.

"Semaj, we found these cowards." Sosa dropped the chain on her lap. "I got this Gabe nigga up my ass like a thong, ma. Jah-Jah got word on dude and found out that he frequents this strip joint every Tuesday uptown."

Jah-Jah was from Harlem, and before she met Bonjo she used to rob niggas. So even though she was in a different position, Jah-Jah still knew every nigga who was getting money, and somehow Gabe had come up big time. They put Sosa on him, and their plans have been flawless thus far.

Semaj slowly grabbed the chain and held it up. It was a lettered charm filled with Jamaican-hued diamonds. She knew exactly where it had come from. It was one of the Jamaicans, and Semaj knew that her cousins had finally located the enemy. A boost of energy entered her body and she hopped out of the bed in slight relief. Although it was freezing outside, she needed a breather. She walked over to the balcony door, slid it open and welcomed the cold front. The crisp air hit her instantly, cooling her off almost right away.

Sosa grabbed the plush cotton robe and wrapped it around Semaj's shoulders. With tear-filled eyes, Sosa gently took her cousin by the hand and stepped out onto the balcony.

This is so relaxing, Semaj thought, admiring the snow-clad grounds.

"You know, Maj. I feel your pain," Sosa said out of the blue. "Deeper than you know. I understand it from a mother's standpoint." Sosa stared out into the distance as her eyes misted. Tears slid down her face, and for the first time she felt that she could express her to-the-grave secret with someone that could relate. *Semaj would understand the feeling that only a mother would embrace, no matter the circumstances.*

"I'm about to tell you something that I've never told a soul. Not even my sisters." The tears continued to roll down her face. "We all have to be so hard, tough and raw that we can't react on our emotions. Our father discovered the monster in us, and ever since then, we covered up with a hard exterior," Sosa said solemnly. "Me and my sisters don't know anything but murder, murder, kill and kill. Showing emotions is a reflection of weakness to us, so we never acknowledge the bad shit that happens to us. People like us don't have a conscience. Mu'fuckas like me don't 'pose to let shit faze them. We've been taught that shit happens, but just move on from it, no matter what it is."

She turned to look at Semaj. "I know you real, Maj, and I know this conversation won't leave here."

"No doubt," Semaj responded in a hoarse whisper, curious as to what she was about to be told.

"I know exactly how you feel, Semaj. When I was eighteen, I got pregnant by one of the men that aided in my father's conviction many years ago. We knew it was this man, because my father was only convicted on the murders he committed for him. The Family put me on this big time drug lord that used to pay my Poppa to murder people for him. That man was Ox—"

"Say what!" Semaj exclaimed, completely shocked.

"I was never supposed to have sex with him. I promised that I wouldn't. But I knew Ox had power just as well as Uncle Gio did. To get him where I wanted him, I had to take one for the team. Swallowing the enemy's cum and letting the man that helped send my father away for life pound me out was my only option. He never went anywhere without his goons. I already knew it would be hard to get at him, so it had to be done right. I didn't wanna take any chances," Sosa said as she wiped her face with her sleeve.

"I spent months with dude trying to get him where I wanted him. But he never told me shit. He kept his mouth closed. I didn't know anything about him—where the meetings were held, where his stash was, who his connect was—not even small shit. He never told me where we were going, and I could never take my phone with me. Nothing. He never allowed himself to get in a position that would fuck himself. He was one of the few smart ones that we've encountered."

"I never got the chance to end his life. One day he figured I was on some foul shit, and although he couldn't prove it, he still almost beat me to death. At the time, I didn't know that I was pregnant."

"But as I sat in a hospital alone in Jamaica, no family members, no sisters, no one, the doctors couldn't figure out why my blood pressure had dropped. But it only took them a few hours to find out that I was pregnant. I gave birth two days later. I was almost in my fifth month, and my daughter lived for three hours before she died. I know it is kinda different, Maj, but the pain I felt was a pain that I have never

experienced. It fucked me up, for real. Every time around the New Year, I become anti-social. It was around the time it all happened, and I really be depressed like I'm reliving it all over again."

"So, why were you afraid to let the family know that you had messed around with him?" Semaj asked.

"That, and the fact that I was actually grieving the death of my daughter that I created with a man that we all hated." Tears and snot mixed on her face. Her remembrance of everything was as clear as it had been the time it happened, and the pain within was just as great as the day her baby was born. "I felt so bad, and I tried my best to despise the tiny infant, but I couldn't. Though Ox helped me make her, she was my daughter… my baby. Every minute she breathed my head was bowed in prayer. I got on my knees and begged God not to make this be my punishment. I was rejected, and her life wasn't rejuvenated." She dropped her head. "Ox will one day pay with his life for my daughter's death."

Semaj was full of sympathy as she pulled Sosa in for a consoling hug, but before they could soothe each other, Emilia stuck her head out the door.

"It's cold as shit out here, and y'all…" she stopped mid-sentence, realizing that they were embracing one another. Figuring it was for Semaj's sake, she said, "We're getting at Gabe tonight, Semaj."

Releasing Sosa, Semaj unfolded her closed hand and looked down at the chain. "Tonight, huh? What's the plan?"

"Sosa ain't told you?" she asked, but was too anxious to wait on her response. "Dude been making major moves around town due to his new Jamaican connection with Ox. But we got all the information we needed on him. Tonight, Kanye & Jay Z are having a concert at the Garden, and Sosa is going as his date," Emilia laughed.

"Yup!" Sosa had quickly reverted back to her usual self. "Now, you need to hurry the hell up and throw on some clothes. We finna hit up the salon and catch it before it closes. We're getting you out the house so you can get your mind off everything. I p-r-o-m-i-

s-e, we'll have a ball!" she sang gleefully. "We're gonna have a lotta fun tonight, ladies. Fun seeing K. West and Jay kill the mu'fuckin' stage, and fun murdering this nigga like we from the Wild West!"

They all burst into laughter, and even though Sosa said it in a joking manner, they all knew she was serious… dead ass.

"Y'all bitches are crazy as shit!" Semaj continued laughing, and for the first time in two weeks she had cracked a smile. "But I'm game. Let's do it, ladies."

Chapter 4

People dressed in their best designer attire filed into Madison Square Garden trying to get a glimpse of the mega stars as Emilia and LuLu sat in the backseat of the chauffeured Town Car. It was popping on the brisk New York night, and everybody that was anybody came out to show out.

"There goes our main man," Emilia said as she closely watched the stretch limousine pull up curbside in front of the arena.

"I'm going to murder that man!" LuLu seethed as she screwed the silencer on the tip of her nine-millimeter. "This clown's really out here like shits for play, and don't even know he's walking with the enemy," she said, and focused her attention on Sosa and Gabe as they exited the limo.

To the average person, Sosa and Gabe were the ideal couple, but they had no idea that he was behind enemy lines.

Draped in a long-sleeved silk Versace knee-length dress it looked as if Sosa had been born with the fabric on, the way it hugged her shapely figure. The suede six-inch ankle boots helped her ass sit right, and Gabe held her hand as if he knew he had the baddest bitch as his arm piece. He had no clue that she sent her sisters to his trap earlier and murdered his Jamaican lieutenants.

Like most men, Gabe was a sucker for a pretty face, and after only spending four days with him Sosa knew where all his dope houses were, and with some serious ear hustling she learned that he was planning to takeover New York City with the aid of Ox's young

assassins, who he bred and called the "Warfare Clan". *Too bad dude will never reach his goal*, LuLu thought as he disappeared into the building with goons in tow.

"Arturo, follow that limo!" Emilia ordered from the rear seat. The two siblings remained silent and trailed three car lengths behind Gabe's driver. Heartbeat regular, breathing steady, adrenaline normal, the girls had no signs that they were about to commit murder.

When they entered the vacant gas station, Emilia cautiously looked around to make sure the coast was clear. She would hate to kill an innocent bystander, but would without a second's thought.

Once the chauffeur pulled up to the fuel pump the town car pulled alongside the limo. The driver must have been trained to be alert, because he tapped the window with a long pistol. "Back up, *bumbaclots*. Me don't know fuck you pro'blm is—" he stopped mid-sentence as the beautiful woman rolled her window down.

"Hey! I am so sorry, but I'm not from around here," Emilia said sweetly. "I'm looking for the Garden. I don't wanna miss the show." With a slow lick of her succulent lips and her soulful eyes batting, she had given him an instant hard on while her panties soaked in juices. Their reasons were totally different though, because her thang stayed wet when she was about to dead a motherfucker. While money made most bitches cum, murder made the Milano Hitters' pussies explode.

Lowering his gun was his biggest mistake, and his lust quickly turned into shock and then fear when she raised her burner. Emilia didn't hesitate and rapidly pulled the trigger, hitting him in the chest with four slugs.

Unsurprisingly, LuLu slightly leaned forward with her arm extended and hit him with two more shots to the head. She hopped out calmly and walked around the car as she surveyed her surroundings. Unflinchingly, she emptied her entire clip into the dead man. She didn't care that he was already lifeless. She was in a blood rage and she wanted to see as much of it as possible. Anyone could get it and no one was an exception. It was definitely murder season.

"Fuck is you just sitting there for?" LuLu barked at Arturo. "Get this body in the fuckin' trunk so I can drive this big mu'fucka."

"I just can't believe this dude has come up in a major way. I remember when the dusty nigga couldn't even bond his ass out the county jail," Semaj fumed as she stood on the side of the stage. Jewel-encrusted skinny leg jeans and a Fendi blouse looked as if it had been painted on her, and the red double platform stilettos made her shine as if she didn't have a care in the world; but actually she hid her emotional state behind large, wide-rimmed frames. From where they were standing a person in the crowd couldn't see their faces because they were so far back and hidden in the shadows of the abandoned area.

"Don't even trip, Maj. He'll be dead before daylight," Jah-Jah assured. "For now though get your mind off of things a lil' bit, 'cause he don't even know his life is on the death clock. But we do. Five of his people got murked today and three more are going tonight. No need to worry, we trying to dead everything with his last name."

"No doubt," Marcela added, her arms folded across her chest and a baseball cap pulled low over her eyes.

"Funny thing is he all over Sosa. Like he ready to jump the broom or some shit." Semaj shook her head. "Fuckin' idiot ain't learned not to trust bitches yet." She was referring to the encounter he had when she put her father up on game to rob him.

"Ain't this nigga on some straight wedding bells shit? Clown ass boy!" Jah-Jah stated. "And he been tricking on her something crazy. Laced her from the top of her head to the bottom of her feet. He just don't know his companion is the perfect fuckin' stranger."

"The perfect monster," Marcela corrected.

"Oh, I almost forgot to give you something, Maj." Jah-Jah reached into her clutch, pulled out a rubber-banded knot of money and handed it to her.

"What's this for?" Semaj asked curiously.

"When we caught them niggas slipping in the trap I found the stash. I too used to rob niggas before I became the dopeman's wife. These bitches might be killers first, but I'ma hustler first, killer second," Jah-Jah said seriously. She never went into a situation and came out empty-handed. She pulled up floorboards and snatched artwork off of walls only to crack open safes to get to the money. "You family, and when it comes to shit like this we split the money six ways."

"Bitch, you is off the chain!" Semaj laughed.

"I know, right?"

While most of the chicks at the concert were there to seek a come-up on a potential get-money nigga, the three girls were discreetly conversing about drug-related killings and imminent murders. Potential come-ups weren't their topic of conversation because each of them had came up long ago, and their finances were straight. They were world-class chicks where most broads in attendance weren't even first-class material. Their prime focus was on the situation at the front of the stage. This wasn't playtime for them, but Showtime.

After the concert was jumping, the streets and parking areas in midtown Manhattan looked like a foreign car show, as the East Coast's biggest ballers came out to rep their city. New Yorkers weren't the only people that were there. Cats from D.C, Virginia and some of Philly's finest graced the city with their presence.

Still inside of the building, Sosa stood off to the side as Gabe interacted with a couple 'hood fellas. *This nigga laughing and shit and don't even know I hold his life in my hands,* she thought ruthlessly. She impatiently shifted her stance. *Fuck is takin' this nigga so fuckin' long?* she thought. She began to move around jittery. Most people caught the jitterbugs when they were nervous, but Sosa was the complete

opposite and caught them out of eagerness to commit murder.

Fuck this! He gotta come the fuck on, Sosa thought as she made her way over to him. "I'm ready to give our favorite man a treat," she whispered in his ear seductively. She was simply trying to speed up the process. "And please leave the fellas behind." Sosa knew with them not around he would be powerless.

"I'm up, family." He slapped hands with each dude. "I'ma hit you shotta mu'fuckas up first thing in the a.m. We gotta get back to the money. Y'all niggas call Rude Boy to see about that re-up his people was 'pose to shoot through," Gabe ordered as Sosa stepped in front of him and rubbed her extraordinarily large ass against his penis. *Too bad you will never be able to tap this pussy again.*

As they walked out of the door the night air hit Sosa in the face. As planned, the limousine was waiting curbside for them. They made their way to the car, and before Sosa stepped inside she looked across the street where she made eye contact with her sister.

Emilia sat in the backseat and the window was rolled all the way down.

The other two should be out in a minute, Sosa subtly told her in sign language. Their mother was deaf, and they were taught the communication gestures when they were very young.

Emilia signed back, letting her know that LuLu was behind the wheel.

That's what the fuck I'm talkin' 'bout! Sosa winked and slid into the car where she got comfortable and was anxious to see the man sitting beside her dead.

"*Boom!*"

The gunshot blast caused Gabe to come to as his ears rang loudly. His head spun and the excruciating headache made him disoriented. His vision was blurry and the single bulb emitting above him gave little to no illumination to the darkened room.

Fuck am I? he thought as he attempted to wipe his tired eyes. He never got the chance to raise his hand to his face because he was restrained in the middle of a warehouse. With his legs roped to a wooden chair and his hands bound tightly on the armrest of a chair, he realized that he'd been set up.

Damn! Gabe thought as his vision became clear. He looked over and saw that both of his men were in the same position. The only difference was that they each had a single gunshot wound to the back of their heads, and blood oozed from the sides of their mouths. He frantically scanned the room and ferociously wiggled his body, but the chair barely moved.

It wasn't until the lights came on that Gabe noticed the figure sitting in front of him emptying the legal contents out of a swisher and replacing them with illegal herbs. It was Sosa. She had been waiting an entire hour for him to regain his consciousness. "LuLu, this bitch ass nigga finally woke up," she said as she filled the cigar with cush. She was a weed head and smoking was her favorite pastime. She never got high when things were serious, but this simply was red for her.

"Oh yeah?" LuLu asked, wiping her smoking gun as she emerged from the shadows. She had just sent the two Jamaicans to meet their Maker. Her finger was itching to dead Gabe, but she knew she had to wait for Semaj's arrival. Actually, she wasn't supposed to kill any of them yet, but murder was a bad habit of hers. While the others could contain themselves, LuLu was incapable of that control.

When Gabe saw LuLu's face, he shook his head. "You bitches gotta be playing. I know you ain't the one who killed my mans and 'em! This how you playing the game, Lace, huh?" he asked, referring to the fake name Sosa had given him. "What, you bitches want some money? This a robbery? Y'all on some ransom shit? What?"

"This nigga!" Sosa laughed and perched up from her seat as she lit the blunt. "I look like a stickup bitch to you, nigga?"

"Fuck I 'pose to know?" he replied with bravado. "That's

what I'm asking y'all bitches for."

"*Boom!*"

On impulse, LuLu sent a hollow tip through his knee. "I ain't gon' be anymore of your bitches!"

"Aghh!" he screamed.

"Fuck type of *bitch* you thought I was!"

"*Boom!*"

She didn't hesitate to pull the trigger again and released another shot through his uninjured knee. "Both of your knees is blown out. My next target is your head." LuLu stepped up closer and pressed the barrel of the gun against his temple. "Don't say shit else!"

Lights shone from outside and Sosa saw the car pass by. "LuLu, calm your trigger-happy ass down and go let them in while I cut his clothes off." The blunt dangled from the corner of her mouth as she grabbed a box cutter and petrol can. Gio had ordered him to be naked when killed, and unrecognizable. "You gon' dead the man before cuz he wants the opportunity to see the nigga alive. Yo 'ol loony ass."

Semaj sat behind the tinted windows of the black coupe in the middle of the night as she peered out at the warehouse. Headlights off, it was pitch black out and all she could think about was how Gabe was about to die. Outwardly she appeared fearless, but something inside of her couldn't help but to be fearful.

Her grandfather had ordered his death. One of the Milano Hitters was supposed to be the one to carry out the murder, but the thought made her heart unsettled. It was a deadly action that she had to commit. Like her cousins, Semaj's father had also been a hetman. While she was a direct reflection of his grimy ways, she hadn't been a representation for his murderous ability. It was like she had seen the art of gunplay up close, but never partook in it. Tonight that would all change though.

Gabe had taken her son's life, and Semaj felt that she should be the only one to take his. His blood was about to be on her hands and she was about to put in work herself. Hours ago she had told her cousins that she wanted to kill him and instructed them to leave. She didn't want any of them there.

At first Emilia protested, but the desperation in Semaj's voice convinced her to play by her rules. She understood. Semaj wanted his last breathing moments to be spent with her. She wanted her face to be the last face Gabe saw.

There was no plot, no plan, and no preparation. Moments like this didn't need any. Free styling was the way. Semaj was the solo artist of the street painting, and she was about to color in the work of art for the streets to recognize. Coats of destruction had splattered in both of their direction, but Gabe's slap this time around was uncalled-for... unjustifiable... unforgivable. The vicious beating that he had inflicted upon her that night was nothing compared to the death of her son.

You gotta do this, Maj. He killed your little man. He deserves to die, she told herself. Her hands shook terribly as she thought about taking a life. She had been in that same position for hours. There was no denying that she was completely terrified. She was almost ready to back out, but hearing the innocence of her son's coos in her ears to only hear his ear-piercing screams, Semaj realized that she was in too deep. It was all or nothing. Now or never. Her or her cousins. Gabe was going to die regardless, and it was too late for her to back down now.

Someone had always been there to rescue her, but the thought of her failing at saving her son fueled her courage. She felt that she let her baby down, and that fact incited a rage of bravery in her. She wasn't a killer, but she had been pushed to the limit. She had to put in work. Closure was what she needed and his soul taken was what she wanted.

Avenging their deaths motivated her, and she detached herself from her sanity. While sitting inside the car she turned her

emotions completely off, so that way she wouldn't feel any remorse at all. Disconnection from everything was her best option, and she had temporarily become out of touch with her usual self.

No longer able to wait, Semaj stepped out onto the blacktop and pulled up her jeans as she approached the warehouse. She walked down the staircase, and as she reached the ground level she was instantly hit with the putrid smell of human waste mixed with blood. The dead men had shit on themselves because of their relaxed muscles after LuLu had executed them, and the entire basement reeked.

As if all of her five senses where inoperative except for one, her sight was focused on the naked man bound to the chair. *I told them bitches to leave this nigga untouched.*

Semaj walked closer and the rise and fall of his chest sickened her as her heart filled with hatred. Gabe had passed out from the gunshot wounds and that further infuriated her. *Where do they make these weak ass niggas at?* she wondered. *Inga's gon' have to get up though. He'll have enough time to sleep in Hell, but right now he got to wake the fuck up.*

She snatched the gasoline canister and began to douse the liquid inside all over his exposed body. "Wake up, you bitch ass nigga!" she screamed as she continued to empty the can on him. "I fucking hate you! I'ma be the bitch that takes you out of this muthafuckin' world!" she fumed as tiny sweat beads covered the tip of her nose.

The flammable liquid splashing over Gabe's bare body woke him up. His open wounds caused his flesh to sear. His vision was blurry, but he managed to see a woman looming over him. *Who the fuck are these bitches?* At first he thought urine was being poured over him, but as he slowly regained his consciousness the strong smell of petroleum overtook his smell senses. His eyes and nose burned badly, and it didn't take long for him to realize that one of the chicks had soused him in gas. His eyes felt like they were on fire, and his kneecaps felt as if they had been sliced off in individual

pieces. "What do you bitches want," he managed to force a whisper. He was lightheaded and had little to no energy left in him to speak. All of the blood he had lost was enough to donate to the blood bank, but Semaj was there to clear him out... wipe him dry.

"You could have done anything to me, but you crossed the line harming my baby!" Semaj picked up a steel spiked bat and began to circle around him.

The voice sounded so familiar to him. He had heard it many times before, and as Semaj walked around him he lifted his head weakly. *Couldn't be!* he thought in disbelief. Through his virtually obstructed vision he saw her, but before his shock could settle in, Semaj had swung the bat as if she was the female Barry Bonds.

"Whack!"

"Agghhhhhhh!" His blood-curdling scream was enough to incite fear in the toughest man, but Semaj's mental state had been taken to another place. She was determined to put an assault on him that was crucial. While his physical pain would be temporary, her emotional pain would last forever, and she wanted him to feel her before he died.

Several stab wounds had formed on the right side of his face where the baseball bat had got stuck and cut through his skin. "You killed an innocent child for something that had to do with me and you! He was just a baby! He didn't have shit to do with this! You could've done any fucking thing to me. I could have even given you a pass, but you took my baby's life! You have to go!" Semaj screamed. She was so angry that she brought the bat all the way back and swung it with as much force as she could, this time connecting with his mouth, knocking his front row of teeth out and blood spurted everywhere.

Gabe cringed as blood gushed out of his mouth, and if before he hadn't thought he'd die, he knew it now. His blood pressure dropped to its lowest from the loss of so much blood, and he could feel every inch of his body throbbing. Slobber mixed with blood dripped onto his chest. He was in excruciating pain and he felt

himself slipping out of consciousness, but he couldn't allow himself to black out just yet. He was dizzy and weak, but he mustered up every bit of strength he had left to speak. "Every day you are out there you will have to watch your back, bitch!" he whispered. "Even with me dead you will never accomplish what we did. We got to your son so you aren't untouchable, Semaj. I have a little sister out there that will make you wish you were dead. Every day you will need to be worried that she's coming for you."

"Fuck you and whoever the fuck your little sister is, nigga! You better know when I find out who the bitch is I'ma send her ass right to hell with you, pussy!" Semaj wasn't intimidated by his antics, and his empty threats only intensified her rage. She was about to let him have it. "Bitch ass nigga!" she sat through clenched teeth as she hit Gabe repeatedly with the pointed steel, swelling him up beyond recognition.

The savage beating continued for ten minutes until she was totally out of breath and sweating profusely. Sweat dripped from her forehead as she staggered backwards. Her chest heaved in exhaustion as she stared at his battered body. *Weak ass nigga!* she thought as she looked down at her blood spattered clothes. She was covered in crimson. Perspiration mixed with blood was on her face. Unable to take the sight any longer, she pulled the book of matches from her back pocket. She struck the whole book, igniting an orange glow. "Burn in Hell!" She tossed the matches on his lap, and quickly the amber flames spread all over his body. Flesh burned, and the smell was horrendous.

After she watched him burn to the crisp for a few minutes, she pulled out a gun and then put two bullets through his skull, rocking him to sleep forever.

Chapter 5

Semaj took a deep breath as she entered through the gated community. She had driven through the city streets in a big blur. Pleased that she had made it back to the family mansion safely, she exhaled.

As she turned onto the long driveway she noticed a fleet of luxury cars lining the front of the house. Gio was holding a meeting for the family in the conference room. *I didn't know Poppa would be back already.* She continued to drive around to the back and headed inside to clean herself.

As soon as she stepped foot in the house, she headed straight upstairs and walked into the spacious whitewall and chrome décor bathroom. Turning on the knobs, she stepped beneath the hot water, and for a brief moment her worries washed away. Closing her eyes, she tilted her head back, but the minute she opened them and saw the blood rinsing off her body, her tears fell.

I killed him because he took my baby, she reasoned with herself. She cried silently, but it wasn't exclusively for what she had done but for all that she had lost. After everything that she had been through when she came in contact with Vega, her baby, and her family, Semaj felt as if things had finally become normal for her. She felt as if she had found safety, but her disillusioned view had shattered into pieces the moment her son had been murdered.

Seeing Jah-Jah for the first time in a long time, Semaj thought

about what her life was supposed to be. What her dreams had been. While she should have been starring in more movies to build a promising career for herself, she had a feeling that she would be living out an old gangster movie, and the fairytale life just wasn't meant for people like her.

In actuality, Semaj didn't have it in her to step back into that life. The energy of wanting to produce good deeds and follow dreams didn't live within her anymore. It was as if she had gotten a fleeting moment of the "normal life"; a glimpse of a "different world"; but the forces surrounding her were plotting against her, and every time she considered going back to the honest lifestyle, tragedy showed up. In reality it hadn't been for her, and she was learning to accept it.

Semaj sighed as she stepped out of the shower and wrapped herself in a towel. She thought she'd be satisfied after killing Gabe, but dissatisfaction plagued her. Taking Gabe's life had made her content during the moments, but it hadn't given her the fulfillment that she desired. She couldn't help but feel that there was something else out there; someone else out there to get her.

"*Knock! Knock!*"

"Bay, you cool in here?" Vega asked as he walked through the door.

Semaj was sitting on the edge of the bench embedded in the travertine stone floor in front of the fireplace. She picked up the soiled clothes and tossed them into the fire.

Vega walked over to her and sat down as they both watched the items burn. Although she had just showered, she was blazing hot, and for some reason, she couldn't understand how Vega was able to keep calm. Their baby had just died and he had been away, and was as composed as if he had not been affected by the death of their son. He kissed her on the forehead and put his arm around her.

Emotionally drained, physically exhausted and psychologically overwhelmed, Semaj turned to face her husband with her eyes ablaze with anger. "Get your fuckin' hands from around me!" She

threw his arm from around her neck and stood up. "Fuck can you just sit here and be all cool like everything is all fucking good? Your son is dead, Vega, and you ain't shed not a fucking tear!" she screamed as the tears ran down her cheeks. "You don't care about us! You didn't care about your son!"

"What!"

Images of Gabe flashed in her head, but she pushed them out. Without anyone else to lash out on, she began to flip on her husband. He became her worst enemy. "Our son hasn't even been in the ground for a full week and you off back into living your regular life. Fuck they do that shit at? How can you just be gone like shit didn't happen? Huh? Like our son didn't get killed in that explosion?" She lunged at him in full attack mode, taking all of her frustrations out on him as she repeatedly beat him in the chest with balled fists.

Vega grabbed her wildly swinging arms and turned her around so he could hold her with her back facing him. "It's going to be a'ight, Maj." He planted kisses on her collarbone. "We all we got now and we can't be going at each other," he whispered in her ear as her stifled sobs caused her body to shudder. "You probably thought I got back to the basics, but baby, I was out searching high and low for that nigga."

"That's my son. You carried the child that I created, but he was my seed too, Maj. You thought I didn't care, but I know I have to be strong for us. If my resolve breaks, then we'd be broken. I'm your other half... your stronger piece. You know I love you and our son more than anything. I miss my little man too. We both do."

The fact that he confessed his feelings, Semaj realized that she had overreacted and stopped fighting him. She was unable to hold back and cried loudly, but Vega continued to hold onto her. He was her husband and he was slowly calming her down, and the tension was leaving her body as if his confession was the therapy that she needed.

"Now, there is something really important that I wanna

discuss with you," Vega said. "I was downstairs attending the meeting, and Gio is pissed. The members at the Tent don't want Bonjo to become a part of their commission. You know he's more of an in the field nigga anyway and said fuck 'em. I agree that he might be too ratchet to be the representation for the States. He suggested that you fill Paulie's seat."

"What?" Semaj turned and faced her husband. "Me?" she asked, bewilderment flashing across her face. "Why me? I don't know how to run a drug enterprise. With all that I've done in my past, drug dealing has never been one. I can't do this, Vega. I just can't."

"You can only be involved in this organization by blood relations or by marriage, and Gio's only gonna let an heir lead the family. You have to," he said convincingly, only for his own ulterior motives.

Vega knew that women were loyal to their men above anyone else, and would practically do anything their man asked of them. He figured that if he played his role as the supportive husband, it would be easy for him to call the shots from behind the scenes, and sooner or later he'd be able to coax himself into a leadership position. It was the opportunity he'd been waiting on his entire life.

"I'm not fit to play this position. And since Bonjo is a part of the Family already, what harm would he bring to the overall organization?" she asked, confused.

"He assisted well with his acting role as Paulie's right-hand man, but if he got promoted to boss he could change the rules. The 16 Tent is afraid of that."

"Why can't one of the girls do it?" Semaj whispered.

"C'mon now. You know Gio's already got them placed. Besides, if Bonjo brings the Tent hell, what do you think one of them will do?" His thick brow lifted as if she'd asked a ridiculous question. "Gio ain't sure about it, but everyone else thinks you'd be perfect."

"I think my grandfather is right about this, baby. I'll have to bring my A-game, and I don't think I can bring that with the dope game."

"Where is the money go getter from Brooklyn at? You know

how to boss-up. That's all you gotta do," Vega coached. "You done seen and did just about everything. It's time for you to get your own power. You ain't green to this shit, Maj. With this, the sky is the limit."

"I just can't do it," she whispered.

"If you want everybody to be straight, you have to. With you running the family business I know you'd make sure everything is done smoothly. Thing is, you'd only be worried about the whole selling market and ain't gotta break shit down. You'd be moving weight. Brick by brick. Basically you'd be supplying the suppliers," he explained encouragingly. "With this you'd be right where you always wanted to be. We all gon' hold you down. We just gotta know if we can count you in. Feel me?"

Maybe I should step up to the plate. I gotta do it for the Family. I'm the last of a dying breed. It's all on me. I can't let my family down. They're all I got. I'ma do it, she convinced herself. Semaj nodded and said, "A'ight… fuck it! I'm with it."

"That's what I'm talking about! We finna make it happen." Vega kissed her on the top of her head and tapped her playfully on her ass. "Let's head downstairs to join the meeting, Boss!" he joked.

Gio sat at the head of the table as he leaned back in his oversized chair contemplating the situation at hand. His heart was burdened, and as he stared at Paulie's empty seat he noticed everyone else doing the same. The recent loss of his son had made circumstances difficult, but he knew business had to go on. Paulie wouldn't have wanted it any other way.

As the key members of the Milano Family drug organization sat in complete silence, Gio thought about the meeting he had with the associates of the 16 Tent. The fact that he was outvoted by the rest of the commission had him stuck in between a rock and a hard place. The suggestion Bonjo made about letting Semaj

head the operation, Gio felt was absurd. She was inexperienced and didn't know anything about handling drugs of a large quantity. She may have understood and comprehended the underworld on a low level very well, but this was the major league, and it wasn't for her.

"On some real shit, Poppa, I don't think it'd be a problem. When Paulie had gotten shot during the first drug war with the Jamaicans the Family was under the leadership of Kasey, and she added value to the organization. She is one of the main reasons we are where we are today. If Semaj is anything like her mother, baby girl gon' bring something valuable to the family business," Bonjo stated surely. "I know she is capable of running shit, and now is her time."

"I'm sure I'll be able to handle it, Poppa," Semaj said as she entered the room. "Tell me what needs to be done and it's done," she assured with confidence.

The eyes of everyone in the room shot to the door where Semaj was standing, and for a brief moment the room went mute.

Gio finally broke the silence. "You tell me what you think needs to be done, Maj," he said as he looked up at her. "Do you even know how the family business is run?"

"I know I will handle all major transactions and discuss business quarterly at the 16 Tent meetings, assisting Uncle Ortiz so we are aware of all the underworld handlings from an international perspective. There are eight families with two members from each family seated at the table. Each family is from different regions across the globe, and is an asset to this organization. Uncle Ortiz's job is to make sure that everything is right from the quantity to the quality and getting it over here. I'll be responsible for getting it out to top buyers. I will only discuss business and have others deliver the customers the work. I know this is an exclusive organization and I can handle it, G-Poppa."

Gio smiled slightly at Semaj. It was obvious that she was built for the family business. He figured that she would blow her chances and he would close the door on her opportunity to assume

leadership position, but unexpectedly she had won him over. As he looked his granddaughter up and down it was obvious that she was Kasey's daughter.

Semaj had paid attention to her surroundings and listened well. She was extremely knowledgeable on the game like Kasey had been, and it was unbelievable how she reminded him of his daughter. Like Kasey did when she first wanted to be a part of the family business, Semaj too proved that even in silence she was studying. Her demeanor was even the same. He watched as Semaj clasped her hand onto her arm and lifted her index finger to her chin just as her mother used to do while impatiently waiting on his response. Nonetheless, she had what it took to run a sophisticated operation—intellect.

Without further consideration, Gio knew that the Milano family business was under new management. He arose and walked behind his son's former chair. He pulled the chair out and rested his hands on the back. "Semaj, take your seat as the new head of this Family. But first I have to know: Are you ready to embrace this world completely?"

Semaj nodded her head assuredly. "Yes, I'm ready Grandfather."

"In the coming weeks you will be attending one of the most important summits since the Dominican Republic Conference in 1993. It will reflect on the future of the underworld and the future direction of the families. This convention will be held in London, England as the European Union Conference, 2012. You will accompany Ortiz, and he leads all meetings. Are you sure you're truly ready for this world, Semaj?" he asked one last time to make sure.

"I'm certain of this, Poppa," she reassured him with a convincing wink.

Gio clapped his hands as he welcomed her as leader of the Family. Everyone at the table joined in on the applause, and then Gio went around the table and explained everyone's role.

"Jahnni Yates, as you know as Jah-Jah, is the accountant for

Milano Enterprises. She's half-crazy, but she's a genius when dealing with numbers and technology. She keeps this family afloat as far as legitimacy goes. She is in charge of money laundering for our entire operation. Her job is to keep the Internal Revenue Service off our asses and to keep things in order. She pays off a lot of bigwigs in this country, from local to federal to keep us untouchable. She only comes out when needed, but has no problem doing so."

"Welcome to the family business," Jah-Jah said politely.

"Bonjo, the man responsible for your position, is something like your advisor. He's the Family's underboss and enforcer all wrapped in one. I've been in the game long before he was born, but I still find myself learning something new from him. He has all of your buyers lined up for you. You basically meet with the chiefs monthly and our clients annually to discuss all business for that year. That only changes if I give you the okay on it. Our operation is thorough and only we are aware of the locations where the sit-downs take place. The customers will only learn that once you're on your way to the destination."

"Bonjo sets up all your meetings. You don't have to worry about moving the heroin or pricing it. Bonjo does all of that," Gio said. "His distribution skills are better than anyone I know, and he runs business with an iron first. Though he is not the one to represent us for the U.S. side of the business, he controls a lot of the black market here on the East Coast. He has his hands in just about everything and he will be the one to introduce you to our organization's chiefs."

Gio looked over at his nieces and said, "Finally, The Milano Hitters. This is your protection, but as you know there are only four of them. Their role is simple; to shoot and to recruit soldiers that won't hesitate to shoot. Their shooters have shooters, so you do not have to worry about having a hit squad. Everyone knows about our most valued murderous crew, but very few know that four beautiful women are behind the name. Many assume it's a large group of Dominican men. That belief suits us just fine."

"Now that you know that," he said as he returned to his seat and then leaned back in the chair, "I know about your issue tonight. I know about your father murdering Ortiz's son the night you all set up Gabe. I know all about it. That's what's really making me believe that you have what it takes to be the leader of this Family. You have heart."

Semaj grew a look of confusion on her face. *How the hell does he know about that shit at Gabe's spot, and how does he know about tonight?* she wondered.

"I have my ways of reading you and my ways of finding things out," Gio said as if he had read her mind. "I know everything. If I don't, it won't take me long to figure it out."

"I never even knew that I had a living maternal grandfather, let alone knew that I'd had a cousin there the night that my father killed."

"I know you weren't aware. I don't blame you. But know that you can't blame me for anything I've done either. Everything we do is for the belief in the Family rules."

What do he mean? Semaj asked herself.

"Now, what it basically comes down to is that I don't want you getting your hands dirty. You have people to handle that for you. You are stepping into a much bigger arena now and you have to act accordingly."

"I understand," Semaj replied as she clasped her hands and leaned into the table to look at them closely. "And just so you ladies know how serious I am, your first assignment is to deliver a message to our enemies. They need to know that this is still a family, and anyone that has the balls to try and go against us will suffer the consequences."

Marcela smiled at her cousin's authoritative approach and knew that it was only a matter of time before she stepped up and claimed the position that was rightfully hers.

No one knew if it was the death of her son or the fact that she had murdered a man that cracked Semaj's shell wide open, but

either way she had surfaced. It was the day Semaj took over the family business, and the day a "made bitch" was born.

Concealing her identity behind a black Hijab headscarf and oversized dark shades to keep a low profile, Paris stood in front of her brother's casket as Gabe had now joined their sister in death. As the pastor spoke the words, "…Ashes to ashes, dust to dust…" it signified his finality and threatened her knees to give way. She and her brother were as thick as thieves, and she couldn't believe that he was gone. *First Egypt, now him,* she thought somberly as she looked over at the two-dreadlocked goons. They stood beside her quietly.

Paris could barely pay full attention to the preacher reading from the Holy Bible as she looked around apprehensively. Something told her that she shouldn't attend, but her loyalty to her brother outweighed everything and her presence had to be felt.

She wasn't sure who was responsible for his death, but had a pretty good idea who contributed to it. It didn't take a rocket scientist to figure it out. *It ain't coincidental that the soldiers Ox sent with Gabe are dead too. But how did they know Gabe had affiliations with the shottas? They killed them and Gabe within twenty-four hours of each other.* She was completely lost, and the sequence of murders let her know that they had found out vital information. *I know they couldn't have found out we're related,* she told herself.

Fortunately for Paris, she and Gabe had been separated during early childhood, so there was no way to link the two together.

As the preacher continued to read his message from the Book of Ezekiel 28:18, Paris peered out into the overpass. The stretch limousine with tinted windows didn't go undetected, and she watched closely as it came to a slow halt at the end of the bridge. She knew exactly who it was and assumed they were there to confirm her brother's death. *How y'all killed him, y'all shouldn't have to see if he's dead,* she thought. But as she looked at the coffin

everything became clear to her.

Her face dropped in shock as she noticed several red dots appear on the casket. She stepped back in disbelief, but when she saw the red beams form on the back of the goons' heads, she dove to the ground. *What the fuck!* she thought, and didn't even bother pulling her pistol because her thirteen bullets were no match for what she knew was to come. "Fuck type shit!" she mumbled.

There was no sign of any shooters nearby when she looked around to check the area, but yet the people on the ground were targets. She wasn't stupid by far. Posing as an innocent bystander would give her a better chance of surviving, and she scrambled as fast as she could on her hands and knees to flee away from what she knew would become pandemonium.

The fifty caliber bullets sounded off like soft door knocks as the Milano Hitters lit up Gabe's coffin in broad daylight. The small eruption from the muffled silencers didn't gain immediate attention, but the hail-sized bullet-riddled-casket and brain matter that flew everywhere got everyone's attention. Bystanders screamed and scattered as they frantically looked around, trying to get out of the shooters' way. Nobody knew it, but Paris had hidden in the reserved tomb.

Releasing her clutched-hand from the fence, Semaj glanced up at her cousins a block over on the rooftop of a high-rise building. They slung the rifle cases over their shoulders, and from a short-distance she peered out at Sosa. She was the cockiest of the foursome and saluted her cousin. In exchange, Semaj flipped the platinum coin in her hand into the air as she watched them disappear as if murder hadn't just occurred, and slid into the awaiting car. The coin toss was Semaj's way of saying, "Mission accomplished."

As Semaj rode in the backseat, she knew that she didn't really want to cause any more bloodshed, but it was all in the game

and she had to make an example by having everyone of Jamaican descent touched at the graveyard. She had chosen this life, and there was no half-stepping. She had to either go hard or go home. Shit or get shitted on. Power was alluring, and she recognized that as her adrenaline pumped furiously at all that she had come into almost overnight. "Reign supreme" was the best way to describe her position, "gangster" was the right way to depict her demeanor, and "bad bitch" was the only way to explain her persona. Semaj had arrived.

Chapter 6

London, England

Semaj got off the international flight as she tied the belt tighter on her cream wool trench before stepping into the airport. Huge coal-black tresses framed her face and a brown silk headscarf wrapped around her neck. Her French manicured hands gripped the gold handle on her Louis Vuitton luggage as she wheeled it through the terminal. Heads swiveled from both female and males alike as she confidently strode across the tiled floor as if it were a runway. Although she hardly got recognized from her one-time movie role anymore, her appearance gave her an aura of being a superstar.

As she departed Heathrow Airport, she saw the limousine waiting curbside that Ortiz had arranged for her to be picked up in. She walked over to it and smiled slightly as she greeted the driver with a nod. He opened the limo's door and she slid inside the vehicle. A full vintage wine bar was set up for her inside, and she decided to pour herself a glass of white wine.

Semaj was silent as she slowly sipped from the crystal flute and watched the city streets pass by. She had been many places in her days, but never had she been in such an unfamiliar setting. London was a far cry from the destruction she'd seen back in New York. As they headed into city limits, she looked around in awe. Everything was so beautiful, so lavish and so rich.

A day earlier, Semaj had witnessed a hit that she'd ordered,

but today she was in a scenic city that tourists frequented. It was crazy, but it was the life of a person in her position.

As the driver pulled up in front of the gorgeous hotel, Semaj pulled the snub .380 that Ortiz had stashed for her from the console and put it in her purse. He never traveled unarmed and was showing his niece to move accordingly.

She glanced up at the 18th century-styled hotel that was owned by the Abbott Family. The British family was a part of the commission, and they had arranged for her to stay in their suite. The atmosphere was friendly, and as she stepped out of the car a bellhop immediately assisted her.

"Welcome to London, Miss Semaj. Mister Ortiz Milano is waiting for you inside the lobby," the young man said in a British accent. "Here's your room key, and I'll take your luggage up while you dine in our private dining hall with Mister Milano. Enjoy your stay, ma'am."

"I will. Thank you," Semaj replied as she walked through the doors. Her stilettos echoed against the floor as she causally strolled in the direction of the man who arose, and she immediately knew it was her uncle before she even got closer to him. He was accompanied by three bodyguards draped in overcoats.

"Hello, princess," he greeted in a heavier Dominican accent than Gio's. "You are just as beautiful as your mother was. Exquisite!" He reached out for her hand and kissed it graciously. He was much thinner and taller than her grandfather, but his handsome features were similar. "Niece, you should have traveled with some sort of security. You are royalty and a Milano successor."

"I didn't think it was necessary now," she replied, but had no idea that she was under protection anyhow.

"After this meeting it will be essential that you always be escorted by a guard." Ortiz led her into the dining room and pulled out her chair. "I know your flight was long. First let's eat and get acquainted with one another. Then we can get down to business. Is that fine with you, *Señorita* Semaj?"

"Of course, Uncle Ortiz." Semaj smiled as she picked up the menu. She was looking forward to learning more about the family business from Ortiz.

Kingston, Jamaica

Oversized Prada sunglasses shielding her eyes from the intense Jamaican sunbeams and linen pants covering her plumped ass, Paris emerged from the large black tinted casino building and entered the back of the black town car. She arrived on the island earlier that morning, and as scheduled things was moving accordingly. Her glamour girl attire was a facade for the destruction she caused wherever she went.

She reached into her purse and pulled out a small M.A.C. compact mirror and removed a Ziploc bagful of cocaine. The white powder was so pure that it gave off an incredible sparkle, and the sight of the potent substance caused her nose to itch in anticipation. She didn't hesitate to sniff the fat lines of blow, using her nostrils as a vacuum cleaner. She quickly jerked her head back so that her nose wouldn't run. She took a deep breath as the drug entered her system, allowing her to feel as if she was flying in the sky.

The recent losses of her siblings had increased her coke intake and she snorted so much snow that her nose should've been diagnosed as glacier. Her heart was cold too, and throughout the last two years she relentlessly revealed her murderous nature. Her shoot 'em up, bang-bang mentality had slightly died out though, and she had graduated to bomb hits. Whereas before she breathed to bust hollow tips, Paris now lived to blow shit up.

After linking up with Ox, she had succeeded in numerous bomb hits. Most were business moves but a few were personal, in particular the bomb plots against Semaj and her family. She was out to get revenge.

Paris knew Semaj from around the way and never liked her, but after learning how she set her brother up, Paris befriended her. Coincidentally, the day she planned to murk a major cat she was dating at the time, Semaj's father came to rob him, and unknowingly Murder Mitch had allowed an enemy into the circle. From setting Tala up to be killed and snitching to Quasim about her involvement with his father's murder, Paris had already made Semaj's life a living hell.

Paris couldn't stop the devious smile that crept across her face as the vibration of the ground shook the car violently. Her wicked grin faded when she thought of all the times Semaj had bounced back. Everything about their interactions was like a game of chess, but every time she knocked one of her pieces off the board, Semaj didn't stay behind for too long and strategically gained one up on her. Their moves seemed to be equal and balanced on a delicate scale. When Paris struck, Semaj struck back harder.

"On my life, before this shit is over I'ma make sure to make this bitch feel me!" Paris vowed.

Her lazy eyes stared out of the window as she watched busy roadway turn into sandy beaches as the driver drove along the island's coastline.

In less than an hour, she was on Ox's property. Armed Jamaican henchmen walked the perimeter while the others stood their post from high towers. Ox's property was guarded like a fort.

"Hello, Ms. Paris. Mr. Oku Oxlade is expecting you," the dark-skinned heavy-set housekeeper stated.

Paris followed the woman into the opulent mansion and through the sliding glass doors where Ox sat outside on the white limestone lanai. His daughter, Nyala sat on the ground playing with Barbies. She was adorable and her hair was long and silky. Her skin was the color of butterscotch, and although Ox never discussed her mother, Paris figured that the woman had to be exotic because Nyala was too pretty.

Ox kissed his daughter on the top of her head and excused

her before facing Paris. "Did t'ings go as planned today?" he asked.

"Of course." Paris picked up the remote from the coffee table and breaking coverage was on TVJ news:

"...Late this evening, cops are on the scene of an explosion that has killed countless people, including casino owner Bark Lansky, a Jamaican native for over forty years. Local authorities are gathering up as much evidence as possible to see if there are clues to who may be behind this heinous act at this popular casino. More details on tonight news as this story develops..."

Paris turned the television off and nothing needed to be said. The job had been done.

Ox poured himself a glass of water and looked over at Paris. "Me sorry 'bout what happened ta you bredda. Me didn't mean fo' dat, ya know."

Paris dropped her head. "Yeah, I know, but I just want you to send me back to the States with more shooters so I can get at them mu'fuckas—"

He cut her off mid-sentence. "We have to be more strategic when going after dem," he told her. "Gio has equal power as me. So me must t'ink 'head. Strike when dey are unaware." A man who hardly spoke to others on his business, Ox felt that Paris was one of the few loyal ones. They had established a level of trust long ago.

Before Paris could respond, Ox's cell phone rang. It was his son, Rude Boy and he had been waiting on that particular call. "What up, me son?"

He remained silent for a moment, getting details from the other end of the phone. He smiled and then ended the phone call. He looked up at Paris. "We just landed in London and our main focus has arrived in a whole 'nother continent for unknown reasons," Ox grinned. "I t'ink we'd be able ta get de Mafia's princess sooner 'dan me t'ought. Me hear she traveled alone. Meanwhile

me have ta catch me scheduled private flight to the U.K. too and discuss other issues."

"I'm coming."

"Me have her shipped down here ta you so they will discover her body on me turf. Me want de Dominicans ta know we posse work as fast as 'dem squadron," he explained. "Chu two a share a lot of time together soon doe. Me promise."

Westminster, London Borough

As the black Benz truck came to a complete stop in front of the Greek restaurant, Quasim got out and stepped underneath the umbrella one of his goons held up for him. It was drizzling outside, and that was one thing about London that Quasim could never get used to. He had been there a little over a year, and he was already deep in the dope game. Unlike back home, he decided before he stepped back into the game hard he would be about his gunplay to instill fear in the streets. He learned that it was the only way niggas would respect him, and he would have it no other way.

Quasim knew there were ghettos across the world, and East London was just as rough as Yonkers and he took advantage of his surroundings. Where he was from, many people wouldn't have thought about hustling in the U.K., but his back was against the wall after Block showed him shade. Quasim had lost everything, but it didn't take long for him to start eating and getting a piece of England's pie.

After a street doctor on his payroll nursed him back to health, Quasim jumped on the next departing flight to start anew in a city where royalty reigned, confident that eventually he'd reign again as king of the streets. Dead on paper, he left the States behind and had documents under an assumed name. He had all the makings of a new life, but even so, without the only woman he loved enjoying it

with him it all meant nothing. He hustled tirelessly in the streets, only because it was the one thing that was a distraction from Semaj. In moments like this, meetings with his connect was the perfect interaction to keep his mind focused on the money.

Looking down at the chrome briefcases in his hands, Quasim refocused and briefly waited as his goon opened the door. He entered the restaurant escorted by two Black British henchmen who remained at the front entrance. As he made his way up the black porcelain wraparound stairs he was instantly hit with the smell of cannabis, widely known to people in the States as weed.

As he reached the second level of the empty establishment, Quasim noticed that the décor had changed. The well-lit, spacious room had an all white plush carpet equipped with black leather couches. A huge flat screen television hung on the wall and a soccer game was airing. Everyone except the bodyguards was tuned to England versus Spain. Soccer over there was like football to fellas in America. They even called it football.

"Are you niggas gon' keep watching this game or handle this BI, family?" Quasim joked and walked over towards his people, ready to get down to business.

"Oh shit! If it isn't me my man, Quasim!" Ox stood to greet one of his largest customers. Neither of them knew that Ox had assisted with the hit on Quasim the night he was shot. With his affiliation with Block's family, Ox didn't need any names or ask any questions when sending Block some shooters. The only question that he wanted answered was how many soldiers were needed.

Both Quasim and Ox were veterans in the business and they lived by the golden rule: *Mind your own business if it ain't about business at hand.* Everything else was irrelevant and they never discussed anything outside of their business dealings, but it would be a mistake that would cost them dearly.

"What up, me fuckin' bredda?" Rude Boy said with a blunt in his mouth. He was the reason Quasim had made the connection with Ox.

72

When Quasim first arrived in London he wasn't too familiar with the pace of the city and how the drug market operated. It didn't take long to find out that Rude Boy was one of the few go-to men though. The streets talked and Quasim learned that his father had a hand in London, Miami and Kingston's drug trade, but Rude Boy was behind his operation in London. Like a man, Quasim approached him and the rest is history.

"Same shit fam," Quasim replied in a light cockney accent as he set the briefcases on the table and popped them open. He had picked up a slight British accent. "Let's get down to business. There is eight hundred and seventy-five thousand in each briefcase." His cell phone began to vibrate and he pulled it off his hip. He ignored the call and set the phone on the arm of the couch. "Rude Boy tell you about me wanting to go up on my quantity?"

"A hunnid squares of raw, right?"

"Yup," Quasim said. He was originally moving through fifty bricks a month, but business had picked up drastically ever since Rude Boy had forced the competition out. "I think since I upped the amount we could work out a deal for a lesser price. I'm getting 'em for thirty-five a pop. What are you willing to give them to me for now?" He knew he was pushing it because he was already getting Afghan's purest heroin for dirt-cheap prices, but Quasim knew it never hurt to negotiate a better deal.

"De price remains de same fo' de first fifty, but each kilo after dat you can get 'em fo' thirty. Deal?" Ox extended his hand out for a shake. "You shipment is already in de car."

Quasim shook his hand and perched up from his seat. "I'm finna get up outta here, Rude. I'ma catch up with you later so I can rap with you about expanding. Since you got all of Pelpa's block lieutenants out the way we might as well expand now."

"I'ma be wrapped up fo' de next day or so, but us gon' handle dat, family," he said. "Matter fact, me finna get up outta here, too. I got some unfinished business to tend to on behalf of one of me peeps. Me man is watching she as we speak."

"She? Nigga, you on settling scores with bitches? Damn, my man! I'd hate to see what you'd do over some American pussy!" Quasim joked, assuming he was referring to one of his British chicks.

"Dis is American pussy, me bredda."

"You's a fool nigga!" Quasim chuckled. "I'm up, fam."

They slapped hands and Quasim gave his goons a head nod, indicating that it was time to go. When he emerged from the restaurant he unfastened a button on his Armani shirt and smiled once he saw the gray sedan parked in front of his truck. He nodded at the middle-aged female driver, knowing there were a hundred kilos of Saran-wrapped heroin in duffle bags in the trunk.

Darkness crept over the horizon as Quasim's driver took leave. Raindrops pelted the windshield as he thought about how he had come to town and got right back at it. He was a strategic, intelligent man and moved like a businessman. He had already bought into the real estate market and invested in a nightclub in an attempt to get business back to usual.

The truck stopped at the light and Quasim watched as two females in maxi-length fashionable raincoats crossed the crosswalk. Thin fog made it almost hard to see clearly, but even through the mist Quasim distinguished the red bottom high heels stabbing the pavement with each confident tread. The hoods on the raincoats were pulled over their heads, and he wondered why the women were out in the middle of a rainstorm. The light turned green and he quickly brushed the oddness out of his mind as a peculiar feeling swept over him.

LuLu and Marcela walked in between the white strip as if they were regular pedestrians and watched as Rude Boy stepped out of the restaurant with several goons walking in front of him. Simultaneously their killer instincts kicked in and they both pulled out twin Desert Eagles. Gunshots were not a common occurrence around those parts, but the Milano Hitters didn't care. With one gun in each hand the Hitters unloaded their semi-automatic pistols

on the men.

"*Boom! Boom! Boom! Boom!*

They caught each dude in their chest. They were extremely skilled and handled the guns with precision. Even with the downpour partially obstructing their sights the female shooters knew how to hit moving targets and aimed for the kill.

The melody of their gunshots harmonized as the girls popped off one shot after another, over and over again. Glass flew everywhere as bullets rained down on the unsuspecting men.

The Milano Hitters didn't know much about the Londoners, but they wanted to leave a bloodbath behind and send a clear message to Rude Boy's crew. Although outnumbered in people, the Milano Hitters were well aware that a lot of London cats knife-toted, but with ease they continued to fire hollow points while walking in their direction until all of their extended clips were empty.

On cue, Emilia pulled up beside her sisters and they quickly hopped into the car and pulled away smoothly as they disappeared down the road before anyone could witness them.

Westminster House Hotel, London

Wrapped in an oversized bathrobe, Semaj sat on the windowsill and stared across the River Themes as nighttime fell over the city. She couldn't believe the direction life was taking her. If anyone had told her a year ago that her life would have shifted to this she wouldn't have believed them, but as she looked around she felt exalted. After speaking with her uncle, she knew that hustling was in her blood and her involvement in the family business was inevitable.

Semaj called room service and ordered a bottle of champagne. She figured this was the last night that she'd be considered regular.

Besides, she wanted to toast to beginning a new chapter in her life. For the first time since the loss of her son there was a twinge of joy instead of complete sorrow. London had actually put her in a good mood. It was something in her soul that felt so right.

What she didn't know was that God had connected her and Quasim spiritually, and she was feeling exactly what he felt as the truck he rode in passed by. Semaj began to think about love, but had no idea that Quasim was the reason for her emotions.

"Knock! Knock!"

"Room service!" a butler announced with a heavy British accent.

She heard the sound at the door and walked barefoot across the cold floor. *That was quick,* she thought as she opened the door. Her eyes bugged wide in shock as she scrambled backward, away from the huge broad-shouldered masked knifeman. Before she could snap out of her daze, the assailant came barreling into her, causing her head to crash into the floor. She grimaced and closed her eyes. The impact was enough to make her dizzy. She was so disoriented that she barely felt the man grab her up by her hair and fling her violently across the room as if she were the size of a ragdoll. "Hmm!" she moaned.

Like a giant, the goon stormed over to Semaj and wrapped his hand around her throat. He straddled her and choked her out. He was squeezing the life out of her and Semaj tried clawing at his hand in a desperate attempt to gasp for air. He gave a sinister smirk at her effort as he poked her in the face with the tip of the knife, tracing her cheek with it as blood trickled down her face and he lapped up her blood as if it was juice. The goon had been sent there by the Jamaicans, and although he had specific instructions to simply be a lookout, he had taken it upon himself to rape her first and then kill her himself. "I'm going to have fun fucking you before I kill you, bitch!" He released his grip on her, letting her fall to the floor, panting for air.

"Cough! Cough!"

Semaj held her neck and her lungs burned with desperation.

Who sent him? She thought as he picked her up and tossed her onto the bed. He quickly pulled his pants down, exposing himself as he parted her naked legs roughly. Semaj couldn't believe what was about to go down. She couldn't let him take her out so easily, not after everything that she had been through. *This mu'fucka got me fucked up! Think, Semaj! Think!* she thought as her eyes focused on her purse. *The gun!*

Her heartbeat quickened as she tried to form a plan in her head. *All I have to do is get to my gun!* She knew she only had one opportunity for a potential escape, and as the large man focused in on her ripe body, she noticed the excited look in his eyes, and in the split second that he took to look at her body the lamp that once sat on the nightstand had been slammed against his head. She jumped up and scrambled across the room and pulled the gun from her purse. As soon as her fingers wrapped around the trigger, she turned around and fired twice:

"*Pow! Pow!*"

She didn't bother checking to see if the dude was dead as she raced out of the suite and into the hallway, bumping right into, Sosa, gun already in her hand.

Fuck I leave my phone? Quasim questioned himself after patting his pants pocket again as old school Marvin Gaye bumped through the speakers. He had the wits of an OG and the soul of an old head and often listened to the legendary musician. He took a deep breath in slight annoyance as they headed back to the restaurant. As they pulled onto the block, he noticed flashing red, white and blue lights flashing everywhere as policemen blocked off the murder scene.

Fuck happened that damn fast? I was just here, he thought in pure disbelief as he peered out at several paramedic vehicles and a few coroner's wagons. More than fifty number markers were put

down as evidence for each bullet shell casing. Sheets had been placed over dead bodies and black bags were being zipped and loaded onto the back of the wagons.

Quasim made sure he tucked his pistol underneath the seat before he got out of the car with two goons in tow. "I'm good, fam." He stopped them and grabbed the umbrella from his goon. "I see my people right over there. Y'all niggas can just pull the car back around" he instructed and walked towards the small crowd of henchmen surrounding Ox. It surprised him to see Ox on the set of a homicide, but when he noticed the mixture of distraught and rage on his face, he assumed the worst.

"I blow de bumbaclots skulls open and scatter dey brains like popcorn!" Quasim heard his threats as he approached Ox.

When Ox saw Quasim approaching him he stopped talking and met him halfway. "Me know who put the hit out on me son. It was de Abbott Family. Rude tell me out of nowhere pussyclots come out and start blasting right when you leave."

"It was them bitches. That nigga, Pelpa sent some bitches at Rude," Quasim figured, immediately thinking about the two chicks that he saw earlier. "Where is he?"

"Him managed ta rush back inside without being hit. Since him da only one who survived de police is questioning him," Ox answered. "But him be free in a minute. What me need chu to do is set somet'ing up and get Pelpa taken care of. If not, these will cause chu both problems and chu don't want that. Get him out de way and you problems disappear." Ox handed him his cell phone.

"Say no more." Quasim walked away and got into the car. He pulled out his BlackBerry and put in the order to have Pelpa hit. He was tired of bullshitting with cats and wouldn't make the same mistakes he had made in the States. He wasn't sure if the British drug family was hipped to him or not, but Quasim wasn't willing to chance it. Pelpa had to go and the rest of his crew that was left if need be.

Sosa ran out of the elevator, her feet barely touching the floor as she raced down the long hallway and collided into Semaj with full force. She had heard the gunshots on the elevator and had a feeling that something was horribly wrong. She had been left behind to keep an eye on Semaj, but in the second that it took her to get something to eat from the diner, Semaj had been attacked and the devastated expression on her face revealed guilt.

"Oh my God!" Sosa shouted as she examined Semaj, trying to figure out why blood was seeping from her face. "That's why it's mandatory that you always travel with some sort of security. What happened?"

"This guy… I… I don't know. I thought it was room service, but the guy rushed me. He was about to rape me." Semaj was out of breath and her face throbbed in pain.

"Ox's son was watching you, Semaj, but I immediately noticed who he was when he boarded the plane right behind you. Luckily we decided to follow you over here, but he still must've had someone else on you after we landed," Sosa concluded. "We were so busy concentrating on watching you and plotting to catch Rude Boy slipping that we didn't know he had put someone else on you. I've been on this hallway all evening guarding it and wished I would have never left. Where's the guy?"

"I shot him, but I'm not sure if he' dead or not," Semaj whispered.

"If he's not dead he's gonna be!"

Just then the rest of the girls had stepped off the elevator laughing as if they hadn't just committed murders.

Sosa looked down the hall and then back at Semaj. *She's definitely Kasey's daughter,* she thought. Although she hadn't said it, she was glad that Semaj could handle herself when danger showed up at her doorstep. "Tell Emilia to call Pelpa's clean-up crew, and get you some rest, ma. You have a big meeting to attend in the morning."

Chapter 7

European Union Conference, 2011

The wind blew wildly as Semaj stood nervously beside her uncle as she watched the limousines arrive. They were at a secret location, and for miles and miles all Semaj saw was desert land and mountainous valleys below. The intense breeze made her white silk trousers flutter, giving them a rippling effect of tidal waves.

The drivers got out and opened the doors for their passengers, and each family was escorted by a bodyguard or two. As they approached Ortiz, he introduced Semaj to each family. The associates stood aside making small talk with the others while waiting for their introductions, and finally the two-members of all the families entered the exhibition tent, leaving their henchmen standing on the outside.

Each member in the tent took their assigned seat around the large roundtable, and Semaj followed suit as Ortiz took his seat at the head and positioned her to the right of him. Trusted black-jacketed servants placed gold dishware and cutlery in front of each member with a glass of Montrachet *1978* wine, complete with a Gurkha Black Dragon cigar. They ate and spoke like the old acquaintances they were, and after awhile the nervous energy in Semaj's stomach finally subsided and she listened in on their casual conversation, paying close attention to everyone.

Ortiz usually opened up the meetings with a statement, but

today would be different. He arose, and out of habit he grabbed his wine goblet and took a sip before speaking.

"Families, as we all know we have suffered the loss of a very great leader, Paulie Milano. My nephew was murdered and his death is what brings forth this meeting and the reason my niece will fill his shoes. It is a new decade, a new day, a new era. Things have changed a lot for modern day Mafia families as opposed to the golden age when my people headed this Tent. Recklessness is at an all time high and these fucking pricks have no respect for the golden rules. My grandfather, Marriano put these Families together exactly fifty years ago. Those times were when honor was above all others and disrespect wasn't tolerated. Things have changed over the years, but business must go on."

"I agree with you, Ortiz," Nikolai Gurko, the faction leader of the Russian mob and one of the deadliest women known to humankind said. Her family ran one of the most lucrative gun importing operations in the world and supplied the families with the best artillery. Confidence spilled from the young woman and Semaj knew that she had been a member for a while.

Semaj assumed that she'd be surrounded by old, big bellied gray-haired men, but there were three other females in attendance. But, there was just something about the Colombian woman that had her intrigued. Semaj caught herself staring at the woman and looked away.

"I say then, do something about the problem," Jorge de la Espriella added in a low baritone voice. Colombian-born, the Espriella Family was one of the most resourceful at the table. They had cocaine fields all throughout Colombia and Peru.

"We hear that the Milano and Abbott Families have been having issues with the same Jamaican mobster." Marko Dedaj laughed unnecessarily loud. He was the underboss of the Albanian Mafia and was the craziest at the table. Calling him psychotic would be an understatement. The term "psyched the fuck out" had to be meant for him because he was a nutcase.

"The Abbott Family is doing their best to gain control over our situation," Ingrid, Pelpa's mother said in her family's defense. "I agree. We will handle it," Pelpa added.

"Just kill 'em all. I've told Gio to knock the head off a long time ago. Once he does that the body cannot survive and this ongoing problem with Ox will be nonexistent," Julio Ordóñez said. He was Cuban. "I'll murder the prick myself and take over his territory down in Miami. It's a very lucrative area. My cousin lives there and his biggest competition is Ox's organization."

"I don't know why the entire Jamaican gang hasn't been killed yet. If it was me I'd have wiped out the entire fucking island. I'm starting to think them Negros got your Family shook, Ortiz," Marko said with a teasing stare.

"Ahem!" Semaj cleared her throat, offended, and arose from her seat. "I understand what you all are speaking upon, but far as the Milano Family goes we're straight. I understand everybody is concerned, but if we need your assistance we won't hesitate to let you know." Every word Semaj spoke was with authority and surprisingly she had everyone's attention. "In the meantime, let's get to what we all came here for. The families' international drug businesses and everything else will fall into place."

Silence filled the room as if she was a judge demanding order in the courtroom. The members at the roundtable looked at her straight-faced, hard, intensely, but realized that there wasn't an intimidated bone in her body. She stood her ground. She spoke up when most wouldn't have. Her expression was serious, her body language poised and verbal interaction balanced. Semaj was fearless and ready for whatever response they threw her way.

Sixty seconds seemed like sixty minutes and as time moved forward, Semaj saw Nikolai wink at her, indicating that she had handled herself well. She nodded her head slightly, accepting the girl's power move, but didn't lose focus. *What the fuck is everybody so damn quiet for?* Semaj wondered irritably as she waited for someone to speak. *I said what I said and it is what it is. Now let's get*

down to the damn point, she thought as she matched their stare as she resumed her seat.

Finally, Jorge's older sister, Valentina broke the silence. She headed the Colombian family. "She's definitely Kasey's fucking daughter!" she laughed heartily, breaking the awkwardness as the rest of the members cackled agreeably. The Espriella cartel didn't deal with black people too often, and since Semaj was half African-American her kind would usually be off limits, but there was something different about Semaj... something unique... something special.

"Damn right she is!" Marko added with a slick grin. "Maybe she'd enlarge your fucking balls, Ortiz," he said only half jokingly and the table fell into a fit of laughter.

Ortiz never paid Marko any mind and waved him off dismissively. He glanced around the table, and at that moment he knew Semaj was truly fit to represent their family. He could tell they liked her and liking her was respecting her. It was definitely a new day for the Milano Family and it was just a matter of time before Semaj took the family business to new heights.

"The fact of the matter remains," Ortiz stated confidently. "There are a lot of changes that need to be made, and once we all bring each other up on what's going on around the world I think everyone will be comfortable enough to meet in the center and all issues and concerns will be addressed before this meeting ends." He picked up his reading glasses and placed them on the tip of his nose. "Let's begin with you, Ang Wong Won," he said to the Asian man, and then looked at the Nigerian couple. "Ezra Naoroji, you and your wife can take it from there, and it continues clockwise as usual."

Semaj sat back silently and paid close attention as everyone added their input. She really didn't do too much more talking and just observed. They had all been around a while and she didn't want to come off as inexperienced. She had to prove herself in the business and earn her stripes, and once that happened she'd have their full respect. She was sitting amongst veterans of the dope

game; the ones that weren't expendable and she took mental notes as they went over mob policies, rules and other interests. The power that sat around the table amazed her and learning that their reach was so long—hitting all continents except for Antarctica—put her in a new place, and she was honored to be one of the delegates that represented her family.

The conference lasted for hours, and after discussions ranging from coordination and diversification, the meeting had finally ended. Some drank and others chatted before clearing out. One by one the families left until there was only one other family left.

"You handled yourself impressively today, Semaj. I thought that you'd be naïve and timid, but I think that you was born to be a part of something so superior. You are more than what meets the eye," the conservatively dressed Colombian woman said as her delicate nails tapped against the marble table.

Semaj's eyes were closed, but hearing the feminine voice caused them to reopen. As she peered closer, she realized that the woman that she had been admiring was where the compliment came from. Valentina was heavy-set and kind of reminded Semaj of Griselda Blanco by her weight and the dark look in her eyes.

"Thank you, Ms. Espriella," Semaj said. "My grandfather told me a lot of good things about you."

"Call me Valentina," she insisted and leaned back in the chair. "Gio's a great man and as I can see his granddaughter is his equal. See, I like you, Semaj and I don't usually like your kind," she admitted truthfully. "I'm going to be honest. I was one of the few that voted for Bonjo to become a part of this tent. But after you put that prick Marko in his place, I knew then that you would be able to run the States with more than an iron fist. You have heart and I could see it in your eyes as you spoke up. But I'm going to tell you this, Semaj. This is not a game meant for women," Valentina schooled. "In this deadly game you have to be a perfectionist. You have to be extra careful and precise. Emotions have to be thrown out of the window when it comes to the drug trade. My number

one rule is to get before you're gotten. It's personally my favorite one. You must take heed to that rule."

"I feel you, and your outlook on the game must be what got you to where you are," Semaj said. She couldn't believe that she was actually chilling with one of Colombia's biggest cartel boss's by herself. It wasn't an obligation but Valentina was voluntarily putting her up on game and Semaj was appreciative.

"Now understand me, dear. I am well aware of the beef that your family has had with the Jamaicans," Valentina said. "For years I have offered my assistance but your family has always declined. I must extend that same offer to you."

Semaj was built like every other Milano. She didn't need anyone to feel sympathy for her family. Pity was a sign of weakness and she knew that eventually her people would put a cap on Ox's madness. Although the eight families were part of the same movement and rode on the same drug train, each cartel was independent, and Semaj didn't need their services during war.

"If you need shooters, I have them readily available," she said, offering her soldiers. "All you have to do is give me the word."

"I appreciate it, Valentina, but we will handle it. Your cocaine supply is service enough to my family." Semaj looked at Ortiz engaging in conversation with Jorge and watched as he put one finger up to pick up his cell phone. Her phone began to ring simultaneously and she answered while looking at the disbelieving look etched to Ortiz's face.

"Maj, Pelpa was involved in a fatal car accident!" Sosa spoke through the phone. "We're down here at the scene. This shit wasn't accidental but an intentional murder, fam. Get down here ASAP."

Semaj's face scrunched up as she pulled through Brixton, a dilapidated community and one of London's seediest areas. From the graffiti covered walls to the condemned buildings, she realized

that this was the side of London where tourists didn't visit and the cameras didn't show. *I guess every city's got 'hoods,* she thought as she turned onto the block. Her mouth fell open in disbelief and her head whipped wildly in shock.

Metal pieces and glass fragments were scattered throughout the street, and all Semaj could do was shake her head. It was tragic. Yellow crime scene tape circled around the wreckage as investigators stepped through the remnants while local news reporters snapped pictures. British bystanders gathered around gossiping, and from what she could see it appeared that the entire London Police Department was on scene. There were policemen and paramedics everywhere, and all she wanted to know was how all this madness came about just that quickly. "This is crazy!" she uttered in pure disbelief as she stared out of the limousine window. She had never seen anything like it. There was barely a car left.

Semaj put her cell phone inside her handbag as she continued to look out the window, searching for her cousins. She saw them standing by a red telephone booth, speaking amongst each other as the police officers attempted to question witnesses. But like in American ghettos, the people didn't know shit.

Semaj got out of the vehicle and quickly made her way over to them. When the girls saw her, they immediately met her halfway.

"Where's Uncle Ortiz?" Emilia asked as she watched a black Mercedes parked down the block.

"You know he feels he too big to come down to a crime scene. He didn't even want me to come, but I had to see what Sosa was talking about. And this shit is really unimaginable." She shook her head, perplexed. "I just saw that nigga a few hours ago and now dude's dead. What the fuck happened?"

"They said Pelpa was being chased throughout this bitch, and out of nowhere this big ass 18-wheeler came flying down this block and *Boom!*" Sosa said, being overly dramatic as she punched her palm. "Smacked fuck up outta Pelpa and sent the car flipping over. Look at this shit, ma." She waved her hand through the air. "It

86

don't even look like a car even existed."

"Man, I swear to God that Benz looks suspect as fuck," LuLu seethed in suspicion.

"You peeped that shit too?" Emilia asked, her eyebrow arched in certainty. "I thought I was buggin' for a minute."

"Ain't nobody gon' do nothing with all these fuckin' cops out here," Sosa said surely. "It's time for us to shake this shit anyway. Our redeye flight takes off tonight."

"We may as well cancel that flight 'til first thing in the morning, because we gotta at least pay our respects to the family. We ain't gotta wait until the funeral, but we can stay overnight so that we can set something up to have a flower arrangement sent to the funeral home on the day of the memorial service. That's the least we can do," Semaj stressed.

"Well, whatever it is we gonna do, we need to shake this shit," Marcela said. "That black car is the only car that still has occupants inside. Shit's looking mad suspicious to me. We ain't strapped and I ain't feeling it. Let's go."

"Y'all bitches always paranoid," Semaj said jokingly. She commended them for always being on point, and today was no different.

Rude Boy sat behind the tint of the CL-65 coupé as Quasim sat in the driver's seat of his car, completely flabbergasted. His forehead furrowed in confusion, almost causing his eyebrows to meet. *Fuck is she doing out here?* he thought as he stared at Semaj attentively. He watched her closely as she stood near the crime scene. His heart fluttered at the sight of her alone, and then he frowned when he noticed the Milano Hitters. The only way to approach her would be to go through them, and that wouldn't be an easy task to accomplish for a ten-man army, let alone just him.

"Fuck is her doing 'chere!" Rude Boy fumed.

Taken aback by his sudden outburst, Quasim turned and looked at his man. "You know her, fam?"

"She de American bitch me tell ya dat me had ta handle. Me had me people watching she but me ain't been able to contact de nigga since last night. But 'dere she go." He leaned back in his seat and pulled on his blunt. "Me kill de bitch right here."

"*What?*" Quasim's heart dropped and rage pulsed through his veins. "You playing, right?" He shot Rude Boy a look that would have bodied him in his seat if looks could kill. His heart beat rapidly as he stared at Semaj and wondered what the bad blood between the two was for. *Did she set this nigga up?* he questioned himself. He looked through his rearview mirror and gave his goon a look that only the two of them understood. It was a gesture that worked affectively for him, and Quasim was simply implying to his man to stay on alert.

"Chu know dis bitch or something? Fuck chu so defensive fo', ock?" Rude Boy pulled out the .40 with the silencer attached and engaged the ignition. "Me finna pipe on 'dis bitch!" he said determinedly and cocked the gun back. "Me can't find me people and 'dis bitch is still breathing. Me can't have dat. De bitch is dead now!" he seethed with spit flying out of his mouth. He couldn't wait to put some holes through her white blouse.

Quasim's temple throbbed in anger. *Fuck type of shit Semaj done got herself into now?* he thought. He was in a very compromising position, being that Rude Boy gave him a paddle when he was stuck in the middle of the sea. But on the other hand, this nigga was going to kill Semaj... the only woman he ever loved... the woman who held the key to his heart. What type of nigga would he be?

Peering at Semaj closely, Quasim knew he didn't even have to think any further about taking a life in order to save hers. Without warning, he took a glimpse through the rearview mirror and a simple nod of the head finalized Rude Boy's death. Just before a single slug could spit, Quasim leaned back, and said, "That's the wrong one, my man!"

As he felt the cold steel press against his temple, Rude Boy's eyes grew wide, but he had no time to react because Quasim's goon hit him with two hollow points to the head.

"Psst! Psst!"

There was hardly a sound as two back-to-back slugs went flying through Rude Boy's skull. His brains blew out of the other side of his head, and the tinted window suddenly looked like it had dark red tint. Rude Boy's head slumped over and rested awkwardly on the door.

There were several passersby trying to get a close-up on the vehicular homicide scene, but due to the darkly tinted windows no one knew what had happened.

Quasim threw the gear in reverse and backed all the way out of sight and pulled away in the opposite direction.

With Pelpa and Rude Boy both out of the way, London was an open field, and he knew that this was his chance to take over the town completely. He was going to bring something new to the city, do something different, and not only wanting London, Quasim knew he wanted the whole thing and he was going to expand his operation all throughout England. They had let an American drug boss enter the U.K., and he was tapping into an unclaimed market by default.

Quasim was back on top and he had learned from his mistakes, and this time he was sure to build an empire that was untouchable. He was about to show 'em how a New York nigga's get-money system worked and how cash flowed endlessly for all the hustlers on his team.

But in the meantime, he had to dump the body and call Ox to offer his services in the honor of his dead son.

The Next Day

The sun began to set creating a rosy backdrop as Quasim stood

on an overpass near the beautiful Westminster Palace. The sound of the water flowing was the only noise that could be heard, and the lights from the palace along with the sunset glint illuminated the area. With one hand tucked away in his white linen pants pocket and the other hand holding a freshly lit Cuban cigar, he toked from the wrapped tobacco-filled leaf. Although he didn't really smoke, lately he had developed a habit for it.

Looking out at the stream, he stared blankly into the watercourse. The night before he had Rude Boy's corpse thrown into the same river and the authorities had already recovered the body. Quasim felt that his death was worth it in order to save Semaj's life though, but it left him with unanswered questions. *How did he know her? What did she do? Why was he trying to kill her?* All sorts of questions ran through his mind, but none of the specifics were answered. *Yo, I gotta figure out a way to get to her. I gotta see what the fuck shorty is up to.*

Past memories flashed in his mind and old feelings flooded his heart. Quasim hadn't had a steady companion in his life since Semaj. She had been everything that he needed, wanted and yearned for in a woman. No matter how long it had been since they were one or how much he remembered her betrayal, the strong emotions remained in the depths of his soul. He couldn't shake her, and ever since he saw her the day before, every time he inhaled he caught a whiff of her natural scent, and each time he shut his eyes he saw her beautiful face. Not being able to get to her broke his heart like the day he learned of her betrayal. And even with all that she had done, he couldn't help but still love her. His heart would heal fully, and out of nowhere shatter into tiny pieces all over again. It was as if he had mourned the death of their relationship one too many times.

He missed her tremendously and loved her beyond logical reasoning. Semaj had allowed him to love a woman unapologetically and show affection for her like he had done for no other. Although she was far from perfect, he had yet to meet a woman that could

hold a candle to her.

But it would be just too dangerous to reveal himself to her. Yet then again, he didn't know how much longer he could stay away, especially with her sudden trip to his new hometown.

Quasim took one last pull from the cigar and thumped it into the water before walking to his car. Just as he reached his Benz, a car slowly pulled down the street. He looked at the end of the road and noticed the police cruiser coasting up. As the car came to a stop, he reached for the handle to the passenger side of his car and opened the door. He reached in to retrieve the bulky small manila envelope from the glove compartment. He tossed it onto the police officer's lap quickly, and just as quick as the squad car pulled up, it disappeared.

Over the years Quasim had saw his ex-mentor wash one hand with the other in this business, and he knew that he too had to be a strategic thinker. He made sure that he let everyone eat, and with the handsome pay he was dishing to local policemen, he was sure to keep them out of his business, and this time be even more successful in the game.

As Quasim leaned up against the front of his hood he felt his phone vibrate on his hip. He looked at the caller ID and noticed that it was his man, Nasah. Nasah was a straight goon, but had a "Rico Suavé" look that fooled even the most experienced. Not the rah-rah type, Nasah let his actions speak for him. "'Sup?" Quasim answered.

"Yo, I'm looking at Pelpa's mother as we speak, my nigga," Nasah said with the hostility showing in his cockney accent. "Niggas is saying the old bitch is tryin' to find out everyone involved in her son's murder and she put some niggas out in the streets to be gunning for whoever."

"Is that right?" Quasim asked, unfazed. He was well aware that a few feathers would be ruffled behind Pelpa's death, but to kill two birds with one stone, he knew what had to be done. Taking out Ingrid would eliminate any beef she would bring him, and it would

appear as if Quasim was avenging Rude Boy's murder. "You already know what to do. Handle that," he told Nasah.

"Handle it like it's already been taken care of, fam," Nasah said right before hanging up the phone.

Without saying much, Quasim had ordered the woman's murder, and he was ready to put all the bullshit behind and take over London's unclaimed drug market. He didn't like war and preferred the money, but he had to do what needed to be done.

As he pocketed his cell phone, a black limousine pulled alongside the Mercedes with a sedan behind it. Ox stepped out and nodded his head for Quasim to come and take a walk with him

Quasim slipped his hands inside his Prada pockets and nothing was said as they casually strolled along the boardwalk, and for a minute the men bird watched.

"De weather out here is much different 'den de weather back home," Ox said, looking out at the flock of black birds flying.

Quasim remained silent as he waited for him to continue, but when he didn't he decided to speak. "I know you didn't call me out here to talk about the different climates. What's up?" he asked modestly but getting straight to the point.

Ox slightly nodded his head. "Dat's why me like you. Yuh always ready ta get down ta de solution," he said still nodding. He wanted to discuss business too, but revenge was the main thing on his mind and he had to make sure that Quasim could handle himself before he left him to run the town. "Me want ta talk 'bout de market out here fo' ya, but first me want ta know how are you goin' ta handle de folk responsible fo' me son's death."

"You don't have to worry about that. Before you get your flight his mother will be wheeled into the morgue." Quasim knew Ox wanted an eye for an eye and was already two steps ahead of him, and every move he made now was carefully calculated. He had tried being Mister Nice Guy back in New York, and tried to be fair to niggas, but he had to learn the hard way that no matter how much you try to stay away

from the grimy end of the game it was inevitable, and he had to be treacherous and deceitful in order to stay on top of his game.

"De game is yours, me friend." Ox positioned two fingers to his mouth and whistled. Two dreads emerged from the backseat of the sedan, carrying two large duffle bags and loaded them into the back of the Benz. "Dere is two hundred bricks of raw kilos, and me do business directly with chu from now on. Me son isn't here ta run dis town so London is yuh territory to supply. Me can't stay here no longer. Me have problems me need to handle back home and I can't war with too many people at once," he said as they began to walk up the boardwalk. "Chu handle 'dis here and me tend to more intense issues. Me people was slain this morning."

"I'm really sorry to hear that, fam," he said.

Ox nodded his head and continued to speak, "Do as you please wit' dis town, me friend. Twice a month you re-up and de 'mall plane will always be waiting in de same jet hanger fo' you wit' pure product. Me supply, but the turf is yours. Me don't come back here, but if chu may ever need me help chu know where me at." Ox patted Quasim's shoulder and then hopped into the black limousine and pulled away from the riverbank.

Ox had just plugged Quasim directly into the game, and for the first time in a long time he secured a solid heroin connect. Rude Boy's death had been even more beneficial than he had imagined. He was now the ruling general of London and his kingpin status had just been upped overnight, literally. He was back on like before. Actually, Quasim Santana was back on, and it was better than ever.

Chapter 8

Back in New York City

During the weekend that Semaj was in London discussing the direction of the mafia families with the dons, Vega was having meetings with his top lieutenants in Baltimore, plotting and forming a plan. He played the supportive husband well, but his only reason was because he knew once his wife was above all he would too, assume high position. The dope game was a job for a man. A woman's place was by her man's side, not in front of him, and although Semaj was gangsta, to him, she wasn't gangsta enough. Her role was supposed to be his queen, but the responsibilities of the Milano family drug business would sure enough make her queenpin. Vega wasn't having it though, and knew it would only be a matter of time before he became king and Semaj would be on his arm like a bad bitch was supposed to.

Vega and his little man, Micah, was parked a block away from the mortuary and watched as Dominican henchmen posed as drivers transporting dead bodies to funeral homes. To onlookers it appeared as if they were engaging in legal activity, but Vega already knew what was up and the bodies being loaded onto the back of the hearses were filled with drugs.

"You see that? I bet you she about to fill those briefcases up with a couple milli, fam," Vega said, referring to Jah-Jah who climbed out of the back of a Cadillac Escalade and arrogantly

strolled through the steel doors. They watched as two bodyguards waited for her outside of the truck.

"Man, if that bitch walking out with a million, nigga, I'm robbing that bitch. Bottom line," Micah said. "Since they moving money like that on a daily you need to quit playing my nigga and put us on getting some of this Dominican money. You're in the family now. Fuck we ain't moving more bricks? I say, murk Gio and Semaj a be so shook over his death she'd practically force the crown on your head."

Vega shook his head. "It ain't that easy to air out a nigga like Gio, fam. The nigga ain't expendable, like most mu'fuckas. He ain't an average mark. It's hard to get close to him and when you are close it's about twelve men watching his every move and them Dominicans ain't gon' play, feel me?" he schooled.

"No doubt."

"I hope you prepared for this shit though, Micah. Money flows like water for this family and they got a crazy coke connect. That's why Semaj out of the country now. To meet the dons and discuss drug business with the cartel families. She gon' be getting birds for seven, eight thousand. Straight from the coca fields."

"Nigga, you bullshitting!" he exclaimed. "Seven racks?"

Vega remained silent.

"Yo, nigga you really are serious," Micah said in disbelief. "Fuckin' shit nigga. I'm tired of waiting. I know you gotta be, big homie."

Vega nodded as he continued to watch the private mortuary and then focused his attention on the transport vehicles as they took leave one at a time. He knew each vehicle was filled with bricks and all sorts of devious set-ups filled his mind.

"You can't just jump into a pool with sharks lil' nigga, unless you prepared. I gotta make sure all of my bases are covered before I double-cross the mob legend," Vega explained. "What I got in store for this nigga, believe me, baby, death ain't a part of the plan." He smiled and started his car so that he could follow the route of the hearses in an attempt to learn it.

"Over the weekend the body of twelve Jamaicans, eight men and four women were found in a Jamaican Island home, bound, gagged and shot to death execution-styled. Homicide detectives believe that these killings are connected to a chain of murders. From bomb hits to deadly shootings, the Jamaica Constabulary Force is devastated behind these heinous acts that continue to harm Jamaican communities. Recent murders here are believed to be drug-related and crime on Jamaica's Island hasn't reached this peak since 1998 and the cause is what authorities believe is the reemergence of a heroin epidemic that has been brought to the island. Stay tuned as we continue to deliver you with the world's latest news."

Gio sat behind his cherry oak desk as he leaned back in his executive chair in frustration and began to massage his temple. His head was pounding as exhaustion plagued him and he wanted nothing more than a Tylenol to ease the ache, but figured the cognac would do. He swiveled around and pushed the button on his office counter that prompted a mini-bar to rise from the glass counter. Although he had retaliated against the Jamaicans, Gio didn't feel the lives he ordered on Ox's mother and sisters were a fair exchange for the lost his family had taken.

Through all of the range of emotions that filled his chest, the losses, the regrets, Gio's most prevalent emotion was he ache for Semaj, and the thought of her vulnerability as a woman tugged at his heartstrings.

Gio couldn't stop thinking about Semaj. The rape attempt in London lingered in his heart for hours and every time he thought about it, it became harder to breath. The Milano Hitters were scheduled to catch a flight to Jamaica for Rude Boy's funeral proceedings to get at Ox, but there was no way that Gio could

wait on them to fulfill their duties in London first. Every since he got word, revenge had been heavy on his heart and retaliation was deeply on his mind, so he sent his personal hit squad out to do the job.

Gio loosened his necktie to open his airways as he continued to think about his granddaughter. It was evident that he was regretting the decision he had made for her to head the family, but knew he had to hold up his end of the bargain and wouldn't renege on his position. *I'ma let Semaj run this family business. But the moment I feel she can't handle it, I'm pulling my granddaughter out for good,* he thought. *I wouldn't give a damn who ran it at this point.*

Jah-Jah sat directly across from Gio going over documents, but was unable to focus on the paperwork. Gio never put his emotions on display and from what she'd seen over the years the only person that had been able to bring that out of him was Semaj, and from the worry in his scrunched brows and the bags beneath his eyes, Jah-Jah could tell he was stressing. Hearing the many stories about the special connection he had with Kasey, Jah-Jah assumed that the reason he was overprotective over Semaj had a lot to do with her mother's demise and his failure as a father to always protect her. Like Kasey had been back then, Semaj was his only weakness.

"Gio? You cool?" Jah-Jah asked with deep concern.

"Yeah, I'm fine. Just have something on my mind, dear," he replied, his usual hard exterior broken. He cleared his dry throat. "How's everything coming along? Is the money right?"

"The money is always right with me in charge," she flashed her infamous smile to brighten up his mood. Jah-Jah could bring light to darkness with her smile but Gio was one of the few that knew it could turn deadly with her very quickly. "But that's not what's really on your mind. I know you're concerned about Semaj."

"She's my granddaughter and she's been through a lot, so of course I'm concerned."

"You're right, Semaj has been through a lot and she's been

handling it all with such grace. Too bad I can't say the same for her husband. What's up with, Vega?" Jah-Jah questioned wanting to know if Gio shared her concerns. "I ain't ever told Semaj, but it's something about homie I don't like. You can tell he wants to be king and not play his position, definitely not a team player. I don't trust the way he move."

Gio nodded slightly, admiring Jah-Jah's boldness. She reminded him a lot of his nieces, except she had charm. He remembered when Bonjo had first gotten with her and at first glance he gave her a nod of approval and every since she'd been a part of their family. She was a female, but moved like a witty nigga and outsmarted some of the most brilliant hustlers. *She has never been afraid to speak what's on her mind.*

"I've noticed how he moves too and I don't like it either," Gio admitted. "I never liked him and I hope that we'd never have to cross fire lines for the sake of Semaj. I'll never want to bring pain to my grandchild, but if I ever even sniff funny business coming from him I would murder Vega without hesitation," he stated coldly. "I was willing to give him a chance, because I know their story, the history they share, and what he did to save my granddaughter. For that reason only is why I've accepted him and allowed him into my family. Do you have some street connections in Baltimore still?"

"Gotta 'em in the streets all day long," Jah-Jah replied.

"Keep lacing their pockets. I need your sources to stay on top of things with Vega. I haven't fallen in this game from foolishness and I won't let another man become my family's downfall. I will kill all before I allow that to happen."

Jah-Jah nodded in agreement and retrieved her vibrating cell phone from her purse. She smiled when she saw Semaj's name pop up on the screen, and got confirmation that Semaj was landing once she opened the text message. She was back in town and the Family was about to step into a new phase in the dope game.

"That was Semaj, Gio." Jah-Jah said and stood to her feet. "The jet will be landing in thirty minutes. Me and Bonjo finna

head over to the hospital. Maj said she gonna meet us there."

"Who is meeting her at the private airport?" Gio asked with concern.

"Vega and many of your men are already on ground waiting on her to arrive," she explained. "I'ma make sure to let her know that she needs to come see you once we leave the hospital." Gio nodded as Jah-Jah began to get her papers situated and placed them neatly inside her briefcase before leaving and slipping into the backseat of the car, where Bonjo sat waiting.

Remy Ma's "Secret Location" bumped softly out of the factory speakers as Semaj stepped out of the back of the town car and looked up at the beautiful architect of the private hospital. "Thank you, baby," she told her husband, who held her hand, helping her out of the car. She had just touched down in *New York City* and even with the bullshit in London and no sleep, Semaj was anxious to jump into the action of these very streets too, the city made her feel at ease.

Bonjo and Jah-Jah emerged from the back of the vehicle after awaiting Semaj's arrival. *Look at them*, Semaj thought with a smile. A sense of relief instantly washed over her when she saw her uncle's face. For some reason the men in her family made her feel protected while the girls made her feel safe, but with all parties around her, Semaj felt strongly secure and confident. Bonjo was genuinely happy to see Semaj, and knew that they were getting back to the business, but this time under Semaj's reign.

The helicopter that descended upon the hospital's roof landing pad grasped their attention and Semaj squinted her eyes. To onlookers it appeared as a usual medical care flight had arrived with a sick passenger, but instead of an ill patient being unloaded, a vast delivery of pure cocaine was on its way to align for distribution. On ground, the four of them knew exactly what was up continuing their stride and

greeting each other before proceeding into the building.

When Semaj entered the large room, her heart skipped a beat at the beautiful sight of all the white riches lining the wall. There were rows on top of rows of neatly wrapped kilos stacked against the brick wall. Even through the plastic you could see the crystal-like flakes, and it was without a doubt *fish scale* product. The reflective spark that danced off of the masses would let the most inexperience know that the blocks were pure Colombian cocaine. *Damn, that's a lot of work,* she thought as her hand instantly began to itch because she knew that money was about to flow like the endless seas.

The secret room was built beneath the hospital, and only a few knew about this secret location. It was not in the original floor plan and anyone that didn't know about it wouldn't be able to locate it. Semaj walked over and picked up one of the key's of coke, and with the razor blade sliced the saran-wrap at the center. The texture spoke for itself, but the Milano operation ran with so much perfection that they always tested the substance. Besides, Semaj wanted to see for herself and dipped her French-manicured pinky in the coke and rubbed it against her gums to see how numb it would get. The faster her gums got numb the better the product. Quicker than lidocaine, Semaj's gums numbed up instantly.

"That's the good shit, Maj," Bonjo walked up to also test the drug, but used a different method. He put a pinch-full into a tiny glass jar and shook it up as the cocaine mixed with the liquid inside, immediately transforming the color from dark green to light blue; meaning it was definitely good shit. Bonjo turned to Vega and then looked at Jah-Jah. "I'm finna holla at Maj privately. The worker will be down here in a minute to load some of this work on the delivery van," he said, referring to a small medicine truck that was one of their many fronts to move the illegal drugs out of the hospital and it worked efficiently. "I'ma be at the top if you need me, baby." Bonjo kissed his wife on the cheek before he and Semaj boarded the elevator that lifted them to the last floor of the twenty-fourth story hospital, and then he pushed the huge steel door open that

led them out onto the rooftop.

Semaj walked near the ledge that overlooked the big city and peered out as she watched as thunder clouds developed on New York City's beautiful skyline. The smell of fresh rain was every indication that a light storm was approaching, and Semaj inhaled the invigorating air.

Her Uncle Bonjo walked up right beside her. "'Yo, I heard about the shit that went down in London. Fuck goin' on with these dreads, yo?" He rubbed his hands over his neatly trimmed goatee in frustration, the anger evident on his face. "First he pulls the stunt with Paulie and yo lil…" His words broke off in his throat as he thought of the dire circumstance with her son. He couldn't imagine losing his child and prided Semaj for holding up well. "Fuck sending other mu'fuckas I swear to God, Maj, I'm ready to murder Ox myself. Shit is getting wilder by the day with this nigga and we need to dead that beef A' SAP. Wars interfere with niggas making money and bring unwanted attention. We don't want flashlights aiming down at us. The sooner we get that dreadless Rasta out our way—"

Semaj interrupted Bonjo. "I agree, Uncle Bon. But we gotta be smart… think wisely, play mental chess with this nigga, because these mu'fuckas ain't playing. We need to be on top of this drug business side first, and then that's when we get at Ox. Catch dude when he sleeping. When we dead the head, the body will instantly fall," she said, repeating the motto she'd been taught by leaders at the 16 Tent. "That way we'd never have to worry about them Jamaican mu'fuckas again. We'd cook and burn the beef for good then."

Bonjo nodded, pleased with her strategic thinking and gave Semaj a rare smile. He never smiled because he never thought much was funny, but he was soft with his fam, especially with Semaj like they all were. "A'ight. I really like how you move. You gon' be an animal in the game, for real. How you did the kid, Gabe was handled like a vet, Maj." he nodded his head, impressed, and gazed out distantly. "You know, you remind me of your mother so much?

Kasey was a wolf in the family business and she was loyal, but as treacherous as a female could get towards the opposition."

"Huh-uh. I know," she nodded.

"Loyalty was everything to her and I still can't believe how Sabrina killed her. Kasey always said they were sisters from a different mother, but unlike Gio, I respect your father for avenging his wife's death. I can't speak on it from a traditional standpoint, but I commend that man for that. He couldn't prevent it from happening, but like a man he stood up for what he believed in and took out his mark. I know we don't talk about your pops a lot, but he was a real nigga. One of the realest niggas I done ever met and if a mu'fucka didn't know shit about Kasey, they knew she loved Murder Mitch. I still remember her most famous quote like she'd said it yesterday."

"What's that?" she asked.

"In this world you come in on your feet but you leave out in a coffin. Me personally, wouldn't have it no other way. I breathe for the mob. This is my life," he retold one of Kasey's many quotes. "If ain't nobody ever told you I'm telling you, Kasey was one bad ass woman in this dope shit. She the reason I even considered you because I knew you had the same hustling traits in you as she did. I know you'd serve this family good." Bonjo kissed her on the top of her head and walked off, leaving Semaj standing there to her own thoughts.

The thin black cardigan she wore wasn't the best defeater for the blistering winds and Semaj rubbed her arms roughly, as she gazed around the city and thought about the life she was stepping into. She knew at that point there was no turning back for her and continued looking out at her surroundings. It was a big ass city around her and Semaj knew it was an even bigger world out there.

As she continued to glance around distantly, Semaj felt that she wanted the world and realized she wanted everything in it too. It was definitely Semaj's turn to rule the world. Semaj took one final look at her surroundings and before walking away, she

thought to herself. *It's time to get this money. Get on my grind like momma always told me and make this cake. The world is yours, Maj, and once I'm where I wanna be, I'll get Ox's bitch ass. No doubt about that shit!*

Chapter 9

One Month Later

Semaj stared out of the window as her driver coasted up to her twenty-five thousand square foot lakeside estate on the outskirts of Connecticut. It was the same home her grandfather had brought her to when they reunited, and since then she had made it her home. Semaj knew the rules to the game... don't shit where you eat. Since she was in so deep, Semaj knew that living out the way was best. She pressed the numeric keypad on the back of the leather headrest, and the twenty-foot-high brick gate opened, welcoming her onto the private grounds. The estate was under protection from a high-tech security system and an army of bodyguards. *A mu'fucka won't be able to get within a hunnid feet of my shit*, she thought as she observed the many men patrolling her home.

Two hulking Dominican sentinels exited the tall, massive sentry-booths and once Semaj confirmed her identity both men swung open the tan rock-stoned doors that led to the entrance of the mansion. The car glided smoothly along the extended cobblestone driveway and crossed over a short bridge that framed the face of her home. The lights that were set up alongside the lake mirrored across the water, shimmering the area and illuminating the estate. The beautiful trees and opulent garden lined the front, creating a flawless sight. Semaj's favorite fixture was the luxurious fountain that sat in the center of the estate. It was made up of a huge statue of her mother holding her in her hands when she was

a baby as if they were angels. The Greco Roman stoned mansion suited her taste perfectly. From roach-infested project housing to rented lofts to this, Semaj knew that she was now truly living every hustler's dream.

In only thirty days, Semaj saw her life change right before her eyes. She was no longer just the dopeman's wife, lost in Vega's shadow, but had come into her own quickly and was getting it. She had seen and dealt with Hefty trash bags full of money as wifey, but more money had went through her hands in under a month as acting boss of the Family than she had seen in her entire life.

Twice a month there was a boatload of bricks shipped from overseas by private jets, and the drug smuggling ring that she headed was ran with so much sophistication it was as if her organization was a legit business. The Dominican Republic doesn't have radars to track planes and the hidden airstrip her family had was undetected by U.S. authorities, so her operation fell under the radar. Semaj made sure to be careful and precise as she was establishing herself in the family business and was moving through the blocks faster than a full-time bricklayer.

Semaj pushed real weight and with the Milano Hitters behind her she was unstoppable. They made sure that Semaj was untouchable and in return she gave them absolute respect. Every since the incident in London her appreciation heightened for her cousins. She learned to follow their lead as far as her protection goes. She knew they would never steer her in the wrong direction. They each were given Caran d'Ache lighters that the men in their family had. But in place of the gold ones theirs were diamond encrusted. The gifts were a token of their commitment, loyalty and honor to her. Her cousins were loyal and their devotion was unmatched. Semaj admired them and got schooled from their street savvy ways.

Each of them had an eye for realness and they read men that she did business with as if they'd graduated summa cum laude with a Psychology degree. The girls gave the approval of the buyers and solved all problems while she sat on the throne and made the

connections. Fuck being a dope girl, Semaj was a queenpin and made hustling look too easy. Most men wouldn't know how to handle ounces and she was handling more bricks than any nigga she every fucked with had ever seen, with the exception of maybe Quasim.

Her uncle Paulie's set price had been twenty thousand per kilogram but she was in position now to set her own market value and sold them for $15.5 a pop. Whereas her uncle's bricks went for grown man numbers, Semaj decreased the cost and was selling 'em for teenage numbers. Dope prices were at an all-time high and Semaj knew that she'd lose big profit in the beginning, but also knew the cheaper she sold the work for, the faster the birds flew and the more her customers would cop. It didn't take long for her clientele to raise either. Because Semaj wasn't as skeptical as Gio regarding the 'hood, and unlike Paulie she fed the streets and niggas copped whole bricks… half bricks… quarter bricks. She was a hustler by nature and wouldn't miss out on no money—not a dime. Buyers didn't have to purchase ten bricks or more for her to have business sit-downs and close deals. Semaj was fair and allowed her *people* to get a piece of the pie. Everybody ate, so the streets were happy and her profits quickly proved just how big-time she actually was. Her name may as well been Jack Frost how she was making it snow all across the country. After only two flips Semaj could stop today and still walk away with a pretty penny, but the allure of the game had locked her in immediately and she had fallen in love with the hustle. Just as well as the streets needed her, Semaj needed them to survive like a shark needs water.

The family business gave Semaj something to focus on and her attention was on flipping money and the re-ups. It was a welcome diversion from replaying the murder of her son on a daily basis. She had reverted back into her money hungry self and the cash became her motivation. It was a way for her to cope and she was going hard. The pain of Niran's death had nearly drowned her in a pool of sorrow, but the grind was a pleasurable distraction and

gave her air to breath above water. The sounds of money machine counters were poetic to her ears the same way her seller-buyer meetings were uncannily therapeutic. The dedication that she put into it separated her from her past and she gave the game all of her as she lived in the present and there was no doubt about it that she was the *future*.

Tonight Semaj had canceled everything on her itinerary so that she could surprise Vega for his birthday dinner. *I've been so in tune with this drug shit, I've been neglecting my baby*, she thought as she stepped out of the back of the town car. "Thank you, Arturo," she said as he held the door open for her to exit the vehicle. Semaj walked up the Italian travertine marble walkway and immediately headed to the kitchen. She sat her Prada purse on the centered island.

Semaj set up her indoor glass patio romantically and then arranged their table. She brought out a bottle of Rosé from the wine cellar and sparked up two honeysuckle-scented candles and put on her Keith Sweat CD, setting the perfect mood for the evening. She walked back inside and retrieved the cordless phone and dialed Vega's number as she got ready to prepare his meal.

"Hey, you," she greeted him seductively.

"What up, Maj?" he replied. "I'm on my way home to see you. I miss you."

"Okay, well let me know how much you miss me," she said. "Because I'ma let you know how much I miss you."

"Straight up?" he inquired. She had his complete interest and he wanted to hear more.

"Six o' clock," she confirmed as she closed the oven and made her way up to the master bathroom. She turned on the massage showerhead and began to undress out of the silk jumpsuit.

"How long is it going to take you?" she asked, probing to make sure she had enough time.

"I'm 'bout twenty minutes from the exit. So not that long," he informed.

"Okay, when you get here come out to the patio. I got the

best gift for you to unwrap." She cooed sexily before hanging up and stepped underneath the stream of hot water as she gently washed her body clean. Once she got out, Semaj kneaded massage oil in her silky skin and dressed herself in a red seductive thong set.

Walking over to the vanity mirror, she unpinned her hair that was wrapped from her Dominican blowout and took a seat. After applying mascara onto her lashes, she sprayed perfume on her body and began to brush her hair. Stepping into six-inch stilettos, Semaj was satisfied with her dolled-up look. She glanced at her security cameras noticing the Porsche Panamera 4 pulling through their private gates and rushed to the kitchen to make their plates.

She heard the house alarm go off as she sipped slowly from her wine goblet and waited patiently for her husband to enter.

"Oh, word!" Vega smiled excitedly as he emerged and took in of all Semaj's sexiness. The sunset lighting that came through the shingled blinds highlighted her glazed honey-colored skin. "Damn! That's how you feel?" Vega asked, laughing and nearly tripping down the steps.

"Happy birthday. I miss you," she replied as he walked over to her and pulled her into his chest, cupping one of her butt cheeks. "With business and all, I know that we haven't been able to spend any time together so I had to make up for lost times."

He kissed her on her soft lips and then pulled out her chair as they sat down at the dinner table. Semaj took the lids off of the silver platters where a full-course meal consisting of lamb chops, corn-on-the-cob, mash potatoes, Caesar salad and garlic biscuits awaited them. "You like that I cooked for you?" she asked giggly.

"You made all this?"

"Of course," she replied, telling a bold face lie. She already knew that he knew she was fibbing, but that didn't stop her from trying to get it off.

Vega looked at her with a "yeah a'ight" expression on his face, but found it cute that she was stunting as if she'd temporarily turned chef on him, but albeit her effort to impress him was flattering.

Semaj couldn't remember the last time they had dinner alone and she was going to take advantage of their quality time. She popped the cork off the bottle of champagne and they enjoyed the food and ran through the entire bottle of Rosé.

They laughed and reminisced on the old times, leaving the present in the present and fell out as they mused over their younger lives. No business, no wars, no drugs were discussed and it felt good to reminisce on yesteryears.

"I know you be on your wine and champagne shit," Vega stated, "But you know this shit don't do shit for me. Where the strong liquor at?" he asked with a laugh.

"Should've known. You must want me to bring out some of that white shit you like. I done forgot who in the hell I done married. A damn alcoholic," Semaj laughed. "But because it's your day I'ma hit a bottle of Goose with you."

"Oh, it's gon' be a party fo'real now. Do it like only bosses can, huh?"

"What? You ain't know." She replied arrogantly, her eyes already low and mischievous from the glasses of champagne she had consumed. She stood up clumsily and fell right back into her chair.

"Now how you gonna handle some vodka if you falling and shit off a little champagne?" He asked and scooted his seat back, but Semaj interrupted the gesture.

"Boy, sit down. I got this," she arose, this time slowly. "It's your day. I'ma cater to you and you ain't gotta do shit." She walked goofily over to the liquor cabinet and plucked a bottle of Grey Goose from the top shelf and grabbed two shot glasses. When she returned to her seat she placed a glass in front of both of them.

"You know I'ma bottle type nigga. You can keep the glasses for yourself lil' lady." He playfully grabbed the bottle and filled her shot glass up to the rim. "You talkin' all big and shit. Let's see what you can do with that. What you need some salt and a lemon?" he raised the bottle to his lips and took it straight to the head as if it

was water.

Semaj chuckled as she noticed how he hit a triple shot straight from the bottle waiting on her to indulge. "Babe!" she continued her laughter. "I was just fucking with you. You know I can't handle no liquor."

"I knew your punk ass was bullshitting. This Goose was gon' have your lil' ass loose as a goose too," he laughed. "You got my dick over here all hard and shit. Blood pressure up and shit," he joked. "I thought you was finna be on one, tonight?"

"I am. That's why I can't get too drunk. If so, that mean I wouldn't be able to give you your best gift," she responded. "I *know* you still wanna unwrap your birthday present." She stood and placed her hands on shapely hips as she cocked it to the side, enticing him.

"Quit playing with me," he said as he chased her into the house.

"First you gotta catch her. Once you do… I promise, she's all yours to keep," Semaj stated as she laughed while being chased up to the master bedroom. Semaj stopped running so that she could catch her breath from running through the house. Vega caught up with her at the top of the staircase and picked her off her feet. After entering the room, Vega playfully dropped her on the canopy bed.

"You know, I smoke cush. Got a nigga tired as fuck chasing your half-naked ass around here," he laughed out of breath, as he fell on top of Semaj and she joined in on his laughter. It was at that moment Vega thought about how he missed when everything between them was pure and innocent. He remembered the honest relationship that they used to share, and those beginning stages had been the realest times they spent together. They were so young and immature, but it had been authentic and sincere back then.

There was no doubt that he loved Semaj and he didn't want to bring her no pain, but her grandfather had to go. It had to be done and with Gio's empire within arm's reach, Vega was planning a takeover. He appreciated what he and Semaj had become and loved the family they had created together, but what she didn't

know was he was secretly plotting against her grandfather. *With him out of the way my bitch gon' be able to sit up pretty while I run this business,* he thought deceitfully. Semaj lay on her back, her raven hair spread across the pillow like a large hand fan as Vega stared in her beautiful brown eyes.

"What you thinking about babe. It's like you got lost in my gaze?" she asked.

"I'm just glad you are in my life, bay. I want you to be here forever. I'ma always take care of you and I want you to know that, Semaj," he said as he touched her face. "If I have ever done or ever do anything to hurt you know that it's not in my heart to cause you pain."

Semaj shook her head. "Now, I think you done drunk way too much damn Goose. You getting a little too sensitive for me, gangster." She teased but before he could respond Semaj's tongue was down his throat. She kissed him as both of her hands held his face. Palming her breast, Vega toyed with her nipple and slightly squeezed it. He grabbed Semaj's backside, both of them panting as their lips remained entwined while they undressed each other.

Without reservations, Semaj traveled down low and immediately wrapped her hands around his penis. His lean frame tightened up before she even put her mouth on it. Vega knew her head game was vicious as if she had invented it. The tip of his penis was swollen as pre-cum oozed out of it. Moving her delicate hands up and down his shaft, Semaj made it disappear and reappear. Her handwork was impeccable and that alone had him open. Keeping the momentum going, Semaj licked the tip of his tool while alternating with running her tongue up and down his pole. When her tongue ran down the line on his balls, Vega couldn't hold back his moans and felt like he would explode at any moment, the feeling was sensational.

"Hmm," he moaned.

"Uhh, huh," she whispered softly as she took him into her mouth fully. His hands wrapped around her hair he guided himself

in and out of her wet mouth as she sucked him like a lollipop. She was sure to give him the best birthday sex he ever had, and Semaj felt his body spasm up as he was about to cum. She removed his dick from her mouth, and in one smooth motion she hopped on top of him and rocked her hips as if she was a stripper trying to make a dollar. Her moves were erotic… her rhythm steady… and her thrust amazing. Vega gripped her voluptuous ass and Semaj rode him as her ass cheeks flopped down on his thighs, wetting them up.

"Aghh!" she screamed as creamy liquid gushed from her pussy. The sensation of his penis hitting her G-spot caused her to scream out his name. In a swift movement, Vega flipped her onto her back and filled her back in inch by inch. Flexing her pussy muscles, she held on wanting to feel all of him filling up her insides. Her head fell back in pain and pleasure as he held both of her legs in the air, hitting it from the side. The only sounds that could be heard were their erratic breathing and the familiar sounds of their juices hitting skin. Semaj soaked the sheets beneath her as she rotated her hips until finally they both climaxed.

"Now that's what I call a happy fucking birthday," Vega exclaimed as they burst into laughter. Semaj pulled him up and they walked out onto the balcony wrapped in silk sheets and stared out into the black night. It was the wee hours of the morning and only thing moving were the birds and their chirps filled the quiet atmosphere. Semaj leaned her back against his chest and he kissed her repeatedly on her collarbone while playing with her navel.

"I love you, Vega," she said out of the blue.

"I'ma always love you, Maj." He said and wrapped his arms around her. "Believe that."

"Can you believe that I'm really knee-deep in the game?" she asked as she removed his hands and kissed it lightly. Semaj had robbed and did the whole nine, but never would she have ever imagined her role as a boss in the dope game. She remembered her days of seeking out who the biggest ballers were in town, but now she was at the top

of the food chain and was a part of that community.

"This just the beginning, too," he replied. "This a dirty game and we always gotta stay on top of our shit. Mu'fuckas won't care to clip you just because you a female, Semaj," he put it in her head. "Even when this war is over we gotta be on point."

Semaj turned to face him and stared at him directly in the eyes. "Wars are never over." She reversed it and schooled him. "I locked myself in this lifestyle when I accepted my position," she said calmly. "The game is a battle and I already learned that I can't be too comfortable. Being too lax will get a bitch whacked and you better believe when I go out its gon' be with a bang. I'm all in. There's no turning back. This is all I know now. What I live for, you know?"

"I feel that and you saying it let me know that I'm in this with the right one," Vega stated. "I've been in the game a lil' minute, but I ain't never seen no shit like this. I done seen broads stand on blocks and set up in dope spots, but you on a level that most niggas will never reach," he said. "You realize that this shit is deeper than Fendi bags and red bottoms," he laughed, thinking about what she said and found her motto cute. "Wars are never over, huh? That's how you feel?"

"No doubt," she answered with confidence. "How I look at it, beef is never over because it's a never ending revenge. There's always someone out there plotting rather they execute it or not. Eyes never stop watching and the streets never stop talking. I learned I gotta see it as if we warring with the whole nation and that would keep us ten toes down and several steps ahead."

"Fuck everybody. It's us against the world," he replied.

"Nah. It's our world they're just against us in it," she corrected him, as if she was on some female Scarface shit or something. "But yeah. Fuck 'em all. It's time to get this money." She stood on her tip toes and kissed his lips. "The dope game is ours and I'm finna take this shit to the next level."

Chapter 10

Semaj took to the underworld like she born in it. Within months, she had gotten addicted to the dope game like the fiends addiction for the narcotic, but instead of the drug high, her craving was to see her paper stack high. She had met with top drug dealers all across the country. Semaj was grinding and on her hustle. She had taken office and was attending more business meetings than the president and was having more sit-downs than the secretary of state. She was winning and getting paid in a major way.

The Milano Family's clientele was so large that their buyers were on a specific schedule unless an opportunity to good to pass up came about from a valued customer. Only after Gio gave her the green light did Semaj change the layout like she was a freemason and let the bricks build their empire even greater. She flooded the streets. From New York to California, Semaj was making major weight move endlessly. City to city, region to region, coast to coast, Semaj was the supplier and supplied many dopemen in states all across the nation.

The original order of one thousand kilograms quickly increased to two thousand keys. As Semaj had proposed, she was taking the family business to the next level. With a solid connect money was pouring in like water and Semaj was literally swimming in the money. She fell completely in love with quick flips—easy money and adored the hustle. The power gave her an extreme rush as adrenaline pulsed through her with every brick order she fulfilled;

she was in the driver's seat and hadn't noticed how powerful the Family was until she was actually the one controlling the steering wheel.

"Thank you, Arturo." Semaj said as she slid in the back of the car. The bodyguard closed the door behind her. Semaj had spent half of her day shopping with Sosa, and was ready to wind down. She placed her sunglasses on her head and took a deep breath feeling fatigue. Her phone began to chime. She signaled for Arturo to pull off as she reluctantly answered a call from an unknown number. "Hello?"

"Semaj, this is Valentina. The reason I'm calling is to inform you about a meeting that you are to attend."

"Hey, Ms. Espri—I'm mean Valentina," Semaj chuckled lightly. "I thought another summit wasn't due until the middle of September?"

"This one will be private. Amongst the two of us. You are scheduled to meet with Ortiz in two weeks, correct?"

"Yes." Semaj answered, staring out of the window and couldn't help but wonder what was up.

"Perfect. I'll see you then too. I will have you flown down here from the Dominican Republic and have a helicopter prearranged to pick you up. There is big business in the making for the both of us and I have a surprise that you'd love. Trust me; it's an opportunity of a lifetime. We'll discuss everything then."

"Cool. I'll be there in two weeks," Semaj hung up as she tried to figure out what this one-on-one meeting was concerning.

Vega pulled up to the palatial mansion as he watched Semaj and Sosa climb out of the back of the chauffeur-driven coke-hued

town car with shopping bags in their hands. The car Semaj rode in was the same color of the product that was making her a very rich woman. Vega smirked when he noticed that the bags were all from high-end department stores. *She definitely got a bad shopping problem. Nigga fuck around and be broke fucking 'round with her top-notch ass. Wifey a high society broad and that's all her pretty lil' ass need to be. Not the person to see for some yayo.*

One of his favorite assets on Semaj was her long, luxurious mane and he admired the way his wife's silky, thick curls tossed while she strutted as if walking a runway, making her way inside their home giggling with Sosa. A layer of guilt covered his heart and he felt horrible that he was plotting, but forced himself to believe that he was doing it in order to keep her out of harm's way. Although, it was more so about prominence in the streets and him wanting to become dictator. *She'd eventually get over it*, Vega thought as he contemplated how he was going to warrant Bonjo a death sentence. With Bonjo out of the way too, it'd be even easier for him and his team to assume position. On the day of Bonjo's funeral, Vega planned for Gio to be introduced to the inevitable. He was going to enjoy contributing to Gio Milano's fall from grace.

He noticed the SUV coasting up and saw the family's personal jeweler behind the wheel. Once Vega got inside the house Samisen was already set up and Semaj was seated directly across from him where custom jewels were laid out on the table in front of her. Semaj was so busy trying on the high priced baubles she didn't even see Vega enter the room.

"Baby, I think you'd rather be married to Harry Winston," Vega said smiling while walking towards her.

"Vega, when you get here?" Semaj stood up giving her husband a hug like she hadn't seen him in years. "Babe, you got to see the new hotness he got in. Shits major as fuck," she said excitedly as she returned to her space on the love seat.

Emilia leaned against the patio railing as she stared through the floor-to-ceiling window and watched Semaj interact with her

husband. She could see that Semaj love for him was genuine, but she could also decipher something was off with Vega. Semaj may not have sensed the shade in him, but Emilia could spot a dirty motherfucker a mile away and everything about him spelled grimy. Even the way he had suddenly been on Semaj harder than normal. To Emilia it seemed like the extra closeness Vega was giving, came attached with ulterior motives. Little did Emilia know his motives were worse than anything she had imagined. Vega's focus was to dismantle the Family only to rebuild with his team of thoroughbred street niggas.

"It's something about dude that I really don't like, Sosa. Uncle Gio told me to keep an eye on him because he don't like how he move and I don't either. Something about him ain't right," Emilia stated.

"We're walking down the same line. Jah-Jah was just telling me and LuLu some shit Uncle Gio was saying. You know, I ain't never been the one that was feeling dude and just dealt, because I know what he did for cuz when shit got fucked up for her. I'ma make sure to talk to her though," Sosa assured as she sat back in the chaise longue and split open the blunt and began to fill it with light green cush. Sosa knew that she'd have to watch Vega vigilantly because unlike them, Semaj was just learning how to be a Milano. She was new to how they moved and hadn't completely grasped their notorious tactics and gangster intuition. Although for the most part she caught on pretty quickly, Semaj hadn't come up like them. She wasn't familiar with the duct tape kidnappings and brutal alligator murders, so she wasn't equipped to distinguish certain shit.

Sosa figured she'd have to be extra careful and cautious when it came to Semaj though. She was aware that love could overpower logic, and every pore in Semaj's body wasn't cruel like theirs. She had the wits of a natural born hustler, but Sosa knew that she didn't really have what it took to be a natural born killer. Killing a few people didn't make them cold, they were cold-blooded before they

ever pulled their first trigger. Semaj had a heart, whereas the rest of the Milano's were heartless. They would dead anybody without good reason, including Semaj's husband if need be.

"I think you should try on this piece, Semaj. I received a special order for this necklace for you. I'm not exactly sure who placed it but it was a while back," Samisen said as he pointed to the diamond-filled platinum choker with a half heart chain dangling from the drop. "I think it is perfect for you."

"That is beautiful. How many carats is it?" she asked as she observed each flawless diamond.

"Twenty-two carats."

Semaj shook her head. "Wow! That piece is stupid nice, but I know that cost a lot of zeros. I'm not going to spend that on one item."

"That will not be a problem. It is paid in full and is customized for you only. Look," the personal jeweler said as he grabbed the quarter of a million dollar choker and held it in close eyesight to show her that it had *Maj* engraved on the back of the half heart. "I told you this was custom-made just for you and if I'm not mistaken it was Bonjo who ordered it." Little did either of them know, Bonjo wasn't the one who put in the call to Samisen; it was Quasim and with him having the same personal jeweler as the Milano Family, Quasim knew that it wouldn't bring forth suspicion when the piece was delivered to her front door.

Semaj picked up the necklace from his palm and an eerie feeling passed over her. Her heart began beating erratically and she broke out in sweats. "Okay all of these diamonds are overwhelming and making me dizzy." She said and wiped the sweat from her forehead with the back of her hand. "Thank you Samisen, and as always it was a pleasure having you here. You can add my purchases to my personal account. Thank you."

"My pleasure. I'll be seeing you again in a couple months," he said as he grabbed his chocolate brown briefcase and then extended his hand.

Semaj shook it and replied, "Of course. Again thanks and my housekeeper will see you out." She graciously nodded her head and gathered the small boxes before heading upstairs to her master bedroom.

"Did you tell your granddad about that Labor Day party you trying to throw in a few weeks, babe?" Vega asked as he adjusted his snapback fitted cap and took deep puffs from the purp-filled cigarillo while watching as Semaj moved throughout their bedroom.

"Yeah. He talking about he don't really want me throwing parties. But if I insist, I gotta have it at a club where he's a silent partner. Some shit like that."

"I can feel 'em on that," Vega replied as his mental wheels began to turn.

"Oh, and in a few days I'ma call and let my Uncle Ortiz know that you coming to the Dominican Republic with me on my next business trip. You know he's a greedy muthafucka and ain't too much into the traditional rules and guidelines the rest of the family follows."

"That's what's up. My niggas in Baltimore be moving through them bricks quick too, and I need this shit to fall through. We gon' have to fly back with some of them joints so I can put 'em on my blocks A SAP," he said persuasively.

"You know I hate traveling with that shit Vega, but my people's times never switch up so it is what it is." Semaj said as she pulled her stilettos off and set on the edge of the bed. "But on some real shit, you upping how much work you getting really been fucking my shit up. I am shorting my people on their original order so you have what you need. It's like we losing out on big money. Meeting Uncle Ortiz can definitely mean bigger business for the both of us. If you can prove yourself on this trip your whole operation gonna expand, ya know?"

"No doubt," he said. "But I think your people gon' be tripping on this shit, Maj. You know you the only one 'pose to talk business on a level like this."

"My people ain't gotta know what the trip is about and you know Gio and Ortiz wouldn't dare speak over no overseas phone lines. Besides, I'm the only one who discuss the family drug business with my uncle, so I'll just tell the fam we vacationing there. That you just coming along to spend some time with your wife. We rented a villa on the beach and enjoying our time together, since we haven't had a chance to. Ain't no harm in that. Right?" she asked.

Semaj played right into Vega's hand. When the dust settled, he would emerge unscathed. He didn't want the family knowing that his status was upped until the doing was done. Although Vega knew that they didn't allow anyone to meet with Ortiz, Vega was also aware that once he secured his trust with Ortiz there was no stopping him. Semaj was about to be responsible for his put-on and he could smell the come-up of a lifetime.

"Not at all," Vega finally replied. "Shit, fucking around with what my people pushing, I think we should start me off with five hunnid keys just by myself. I think that'd be cool for now. What you think?" he asked her. He felt that he would keep the amount of bricks in the center. That way once Semaj saw that he could get so many off, when the time came she wouldn't hesitate to give him the spot. Also, he wanted it to seem as if he was including her in on everything he thought, so that way, she wouldn't feel like he was trying to run the show, despite that he was being straight up grimy.

"Everything is on the up and up, bay. When I'm down there he supposed to holler at me about some shit on one of the members at the 16 Tent. Then while you and him touching bases I'ma shoot to Colombia to discuss some undisclosed shit with the Queen," she said, referring to Valentina but wouldn't speak her moniker; at this level in the game it was coded to never mention her name, ever. "We leaving out the day after the party so be ready to leave that morning, Vega."

Chapter 11

It was Labor Day Weekend and the black-tie affair was just right for the rules of the holiday, except members of the Milano family wore all-white everything and everything about them rang long money. Club Mansion was jammed packed as hip-hop blared out of the speakers and Semaj's dominant squad was in attendance. She had invited her valued business acquaintances from all regions of the country to come party with her and the turnout was unbelievable. Real boss niggas and fly ass bitches were in the building to show love.

Rosé and Louis XIII flowed freely in the exclusive VIP section as Semaj, Sosa and Jah-Jah danced by their private tables. As they partied like they were socialites, the rest of the girls played the cut with their hands close to their bangers, never indulging in the theatrics, while armed henchmen were scattered throughout the club. It had been months since they had partied, business had been just that hectic. Then dealing with the war against the Jamaicans, made shit extra crazy, but Semaj thought it would be a good idea to get everyone together in a relaxed environment. She figured the event would allow people to have a nice time while she also reached out to potential buyers.

Six months into the dope game, Semaj was getting paid. She had flipped through millions and was stacking plenty paper. It felt great to be placed on a pedestal so high, and although she played her position low-key, Semaj always shined like a rock star and even

made the most confident look like duds. Her hair was pulled high off her face in a sophisticated bun and the Chanel sheathe block dress and pearl-encrusted stilettos made every girl in the club green with envy, but little did they know she was the connect and pretty much the reason their men were able to eat.

The three women walked over to the balcony and noticed Bonjo chopping it up with a few dudes. Semaj smiled as she watched her uncle interact like a boss. It didn't matter wherever they went, Bonjo received celebrity treatment and he didn't care about being on-scene because his reputation was brutal and everyone had heard of the things that he had done to those who crossed him. *Where is he going?* Jah-Jah thought as an eerie feeling passed over her. She watched as Bonjo and some young cat walked over to a private booth in the corner; the two men were hidden behind black curtains. *Who is that nigga he with?*

"This nigga go so hard. This part reminds me of y'all, Sosa," Semaj yelled over the music as she swayed arrogantly to the beat and femininely chanted along with Yo Gotti. *"Cold-hearted nigga and I run around with lunatics... they be on some shooter shit... I be on some mutual shit... since I got some soldiers I'm on some might as well use 'em shit...,"* she laughed, pumping her fist in the air. She and her girls rocked to the hot track with conceit written across their faces as they continued to have a good time. Semaj had been so focused on the business, that it really felt good to be enjoying herself.

As Vega and his crew sat back, he admired his wife from afar. He watched as a photographer snapped a quick picture of the girls and laughed when Semaj pulled out a wad of money from her clutch and handed it to the man. *Never let an unknown mu'fucka have pictures of how you living life. It could get you nabbed because it might just be the feds or some shit,* he thought as Semaj gave the camera man the money and whispered in the henchmen's ear to dispose the evidence. Semaj turned around sexily and winked at Vega, implying that she'd heeded the rules of the game as she winded her tiny waist while staring him in the eyes. He got mesmerized by

the way she had mastered the art of seduction.

Micah leaned into Vega's ear, and whispered, "Yo', so you know them people ready. You sure you got all the tracks covered with this one, Vega? Your girl people scoping shit out and look very alert, B. They rolling deep, fam," he said skeptically. "If you have the Bonjo nigga hit tonight fuck is y'all gon' fly out and there is a dead family member?" He had thought about it and Vega's plan didn't seem well planned out.

"No matter what happens in this Dominican family, when the connect calls and an emergency meeting is ordered, it must be attended. Trust me on this lil' man. We'd be on that flight no matter what."

"I don't know, Vega, man. I gotta bad feeling now about this shit, fam," Micah confessed.

Vega shot Micah a look. "What you scared, nigga? I'm the one taking the heat. Just let me worry about everything my man," Vega said in a low controlled tone, brushing him off.

The girls finally returned to their table. Semaj picked up her wineglass and sipped on the Moscato as she eye fucked her husband all night. He lifted his bottle of Dom to display him acknowledging her. He was her king and with his knights surrounding him at the round booth, Semaj smiled, respecting their styles. While the dress code was a black tie affair, Vega and his crew donned black V-neck t-shirts and patent leather Jordans with so much jewelry they each could have created an ice rink. Vega nodded to her, summoning her to him and as she arose from her seat, Sosa leaned into her ear to whisper over the music.

"LuLu and I need to rap with you about some shit, ma," she said to Semaj as she grabbed her hand, pulling her through the crowd with LuLu following closely behind them.

"Jah-Jah!" Semaj shouted and nodded her head towards the lower level to tell her to come along. The four women left the other two ladies at their table to watch their handbags and made their way down the wraparound stairs and to the restroom. Emilia and

Marcela knew what the conversation would be pertaining to, so there wasn't any need for all of them. They didn't wanna involve themselves in the heated debate, knowing that's exactly what it would be. It was better for them to stay back because they preferred hollow-tips barking rather than shouting matches.

Vega stopped her just before she reached the bottom step and saw the girls staring at him with screwed expressions. He dismissed it, knowing they were a bunch of evil bitches.

"You ready to shake this shit, ma? The private jet will be at the tarmac in the next hour," he asked pinning her body against the wall. "I figured we should go early so we can spend some time together before you have to shoot straight to Colombia. You ain't gotta worry 'bout getting security ready my people already waiting up there for us."

"We don't 'pose to leave until the morning though, bay. I was trying to kick it with the fam, being we rarely get the chance to hang together all at once, you know?" she whispered, whining. He sealed the deal with a passionate kiss as he wrapped one arm around her small waist and grabbed her aggressively from behind to grip her cheeks, making her panties cream.

"I've got a secret to tell you and we gon' handle it when we get there. Let's bounce." He said with a mischievous smile and automatically she knew he was referring to his sex game.

She removed his hand that caressed her ass and stood on her tippy toes to kiss him on the side of his lips. "Okay. Meet me at the back exit in about five minutes. I need to holla at my cousins and make sure Bonjo don't need me for anything," she said.

He gave her an understanding look, nodded, and said, "Cool. Talk to your people and meet me at the door."

As soon as they entered the restroom they pushed the stall doors open to check and make sure they were discussing business in a private setting. It was an upscale nightclub, so the restroom was on point. From marble tiled floors to the granite marble countertops. Semaj flopped down on the plush Italian white sofa

as Sosa reached the last door. She attempted to shove the door open, but it was locked. She immediately banged on the door with a balled fist. "Hurry the fuck up, bitch. You gotta get the fuck from up outta here."

The stall door opened and a girl frowned as she stared at the girls. "Isn't this a public bathroom?"

"Actually, bitch, it's my people's spot!" Sosa stared down at the girl letting her know it was time for her to bounce.

"Meaning it is still a public place," the girl retorted.

"I don't give a fuck what it is! Get the fuck out!" she shouted harshly as she shoved the girl towards the exit. Semaj looked at her peoples and wondered where did all of the hostility come from and the irritated expressions etched to their faces. Strong arming a chick out of the restroom wasn't uncharacteristic for Sosa, but it was something unpleasant in the air and Semaj wanted to know what it was.

"Fuck is y'all acting so anxious and antsy for?" Semaj asked with an accusing stare. "Something happening that I don't fucking know about or some shit?"

"Yeah," LuLu responded in defense. "Why is your man acting so damn weird?"

"Who you talking about, Vega?"

"Who else, Semaj?" She threw her arms across her small chest while staring down at her. "All of a sudden dude wants to fly out and take business trips with you out of the country. Fuck for?"

Semaj cocked her head back in confusion. She just knew they hadn't pulled her to the restroom to speak with her about her husband. *Fuck's with the extra bullshit anyway!*

Jah-Jah shook her head in aggravation. "Maj, shit does sound mad fishy, mama. He know the rules. No outsiders meet Uncle Ortiz—"

"And how we look at it that nigga is a muthafuckin' outsider," Sosa chimed in, interrupting Jah-Jah.

"So y'all telling me that my husband going over to the

Dominican Republic with me is violating some rules?" Semaj popped up from her seat and waved them off dismissively. "If my memory serves me correctly I make the fucking rules, so if I want the nigga on the plane with me then that's what it is. Fuck!" fumed Semaj.

"So you're willing to risk other people knowing how everything goes, huh? It's bad enough that you probably pillow-talking with the grimy ass nigga. Now you want the nigga to not only know all of the business, but to actually see the shit too, Maj. If I knew you would've been on some gullible shit I would've just took the spot my damn self. Fuck was Gio thinking allowing disloyal niggas in the circle?" Sosa asked no one in particular as she popped her hand on her shapely waist again all the while shaking her head in disbelief.

"This nigga done really got inside this girl head and she really trying to be on some what's mine is yours shit," LuLu said harshly as she leaned against the whitewall. "Am I right, Semaj? That's what it is? You want your boy to be on your level, ain't it?"

"I just don't think it is a problem for me to introduce him to Ortiz and letting him get on with his own dope," she confessed. There was no reason to hide it. Like everything else, they had figured it out. "He already pushing major weight out of the entire DMV area. Why not let him go directly through Uncle Ortiz so I ain't gotta hit him off with the work and let him do his own thang. Fuck is the big fuckin' issue?"

"Then what, he no longer has to cop bricks from you and after he get in good enough with Ortiz he pushes your dumb ass out of the way. How come you don't see this shit, Maj? Huh?"

"That's probably the reason he convinced you to step up and head the family business. Once you were manning the entire operation he knew that he would eventually be promoted and perhaps persuade you to fall behind scenes and let him control the family business." If they hadn't been professional killers, they would have made great detectives. They could sense foul play from anywhere and Vega was

stinking badly. "I can't pinpoint what it is, but the bitch ass nigga on some sheisty shit. I fucking know dude is."

"Y'all can't be serious?" Semaj barked. "Damn, you motherfuckers barely do shit and you mu'fuckas eating lovely but always got the most shit to say. What the fuck? Y'all bitches ain't pushing dope and getting mad bread. What's wrong with Vega wanting to up his bricks and get paid too? I never knew it was disloyal to want to get fucking money. Fuck outta here with that lame ass shit. I'm out," Semaj yelled as she walked towards the door. She knew that she had taken it too far. It was a low blow to down talk their position, and although Semaj knew it wasn't true her anger had spoken for her.

Fuck these bitches on? Think they need a man because they really need a break from Mossberg, Semaj thought in an attempt to make light of the situation as she walked out of the restroom, but the loud sounds of gunshots stopped her in her tracks.

Bang! Bang! Bang! Bang!

What the fuck? Semaj frantically scanned the club as her heart started to beat from the unknown. The entire room was in pandemonium as people ran for cover, afraid of getting hit by a stray bullet. Assuming the shots were for her, she quickly backed her steps up and returned to the same girls she had spazzed on.

"Somebody is out there shooting!" Semaj said with apologetic eyes as she burst through the door. As if she hadn't just given them her ass to kiss, the three of them naturally went inside their white short-length trench jackets to draw their pistols and human shielded the mafia princess. Sosa and LuLu were in front of Semaj wildly pointing handgun Uzis and Jah-Jah was behind her holding two .40s in each hand, as they tried to shoot Semaj out to safety.

Armed Dominican men seemed to emerge from everywhere, all with weapons in their hands ready to pop off. One-half of the Milano Hitters guided the way as Semaj followed behind them and led her to the back entrance where the chauffeur-driven car was parked. As the girls exited, they noticed Bonjo leaned against

the hood of the vehicle and his white three-piece Armani suit was bloodstained. Blood specks decorated his face as if sprayed with a painter's atomizer. "Fuck happened?" Jah-Jah rushed over to her husband.

By this time the entire Milano clan and their henchmen were outside. "This bitch ass nigga tried to pop me but stupid muthafucka didn't even check to see if I was dead. Nigga thought he killed me and as soon as he turned his back I came out with that .357 dumping. Didn't stop until my clip was empty." Bonjo ripped open his riddled button-up and exposed the bulletproof with five bullets lodged in it; the decision to wear it was lifesaving.

"Who was the nigga, fam?" Vega spoke up as everyone's eyes naturally looked over at him. The girls all glared at him as if he was a poisonous snake, because to them, his words were like venom spitting in their faces.

"Fuck you wanna know for?" LuLu scoffed as she gripped the ratchet tightly, but Emilia pulled her away and put her little sister inside the car. She knew LuLu's temper was out of control and she wouldn't hesitate to rock Vega to sleep right where he stood without regret.

"What's up with her, ma?" Vega asked Semaj as he pointed at LuLu in uncertainty.

Semaj dropped her head. "Let's just shake this joint before the cops come," Semaj advised as Vega grabbed her hand and walked her to the car. He opened the door for her as everyone slid inside their own awaiting transportation and the caravan of Lexus LS 600h L's took leave.

Semaj's phone began to buzz in her hand as she boarded the Learjet 60 and quickly answered, realizing it was her grandfather. The lavish private passenger plane had a wet bar, full bathroom, living room longue area, and all of the dash fittings were wood

grain. She sat in the double cushioned seat and sighed in frustration, already knowing why he was calling. "'Sup, Poppa?" she reclined her seat as she placed her pearl-beaded clutch on the console.

"I knew you throwing this party would be a bad idea. No more parties, Semaj. No more," he said calmly, but Semaj knew he was fuming.

"But G-Poppa it didn't have anything to do with me," she explained in her defense. "That was Uncle Bon's people. True story."

"It doesn't matter, sweetheart." He never had to raise his voice with Semaj in order to get his point across.

"I understand," she whispered, feeling bad. "Are you angry with me, Poppa?" she asked.

"You don't get angry with the ones you love, Maj. Remember that. You just correct their errors and mistakes and move on from the situation to prevent it from happening again. Now when you get back I'll have Arturo waiting for you at the landing strip. There is some important things we need to go over." He said before he hung up.

"Looks like you got something on your mind. Wanna talk about it?" Vega asked sweetly as he placed the pillow gently behind her neck, but little did Semaj know he was pissed.

Fuck the nigga didn't give off headshots like I told his clown ass to do. Dumb ass niggas. Everybody knows these Milano's stay vested up, he thought with concealed displeasure. *I'ma have to plan some other shit for Bonjo, but in the meantime I gotta worry about getting Gio to plunge from grace.* He only felt horrible for the pain he was about to cause Semaj. *She'd be a'ight though and she'd never expect anything. Got Micah and 'em dressing in Jamaican wigs when we return home and have 'em rob us to shake her up. They know to hit me and miss her. A nigga can take a gunshot to the leg or something for the position I will assume. Semaj will be so shook and eventually she'd convince her people to let me run everything,* Vega thought deceitfully but had no idea that the real Jamaicans were actually lurking in the shadows, and was gunning for the Milano's head in retaliation for the hit Gio

had put on Ox's family.

"No… not really. I'm just glad you coming here with me. We need this time and I'm going to enjoy it for as long as I can," she whispered as she grabbed his hand and kissed him on the back of his wrist. "I'ma get some sleep because I have a feeling I'ma be up the entire time on this trip." Semaj closed her eyes as the plane ascended into the perfect night skies, having no idea that a storm was brewing.

"I could fuckin' kill Semaj for being so damn blind and naïve!" LuLu yelled as she paced back and forth for the hundredth time enraged, practically burning a hole through the floor.

"Would someone let me know what is going on?" Gio asked as he disconnected the call with Semaj and looked up at his nieces.

"That fucking husband of hers is foul and I can smell the shit surrounding him. He on that flight with Semaj right now," LuLu spilled.

"He's what?" Gio shouted as if he hadn't heard her correctly. "I've made it clear that Semaj was to go on all trips alone. Are you saying that she disobeyed my word?"

"That's exactly what I'm saying," she replied. "Uncle, I promise I've been watching how dude been moving lately and he on some rehearsed shit."

"Let me ask you something and I'll just deal with Semaj concerning that issue once she returns," Gio said. "Security was tight as usual, right?"

"Virgin Mary tight," Emilia answered matter-of-factly. "I still can't get how someone was able to get inside the club strapped and everyone walks through the metal detector besides our crew—"

"And Vega's," LuLu chimed in. "Something is telling me that shit with Bonjo had something to do with his crew or he was involved with it with his crew. Either way, someone has to deal

with the consequences. I don't care who fault it was, but somebody has to be made an example of. I think we should begin with Vega. Sooner or later Semaj will get over it. I'll take care of him ASAP for the Family. Fuck a wait. I've been wanting to sniff nigga's lights out and I'ma make it dark for that dude soon as he get back. He gotta go."

"I feel you on that, LuLu," Emilia agreed. "It was too coincidental that all of this popped off at a club that's wrapped killer tight with ready-to-bust bodyguards. A mu'fucka ain't stupid enough to come gunning for Bonjo, especially knowing that we all up in there. Unless," she paused as if a thought had clicked in her head, and then continued, "Someone tipped someone off and gave specific instructions on how to pan everything out."

"Don't worry about it." Gio said, cool, calm and collected. There was nothing else he needed to know. He picked up his phone scrolling down to Jah-Jah's name and pressed dial. He was determined to find out who this guy was linked to that Bonjo had killed. By any means necessary, he was going to get down to the bottom of it.

Chapter 12

"I can't believe this fucking cockroach is trying to move an operation into the fucking States. Our territory is not appointed to the families by divisions even if our family hasn't tapped into the Miami drug market yet. The fucking prick Julio is stepping out of his boundaries creating a global faux pas amongst our family and the Cubans. Blatant disrespect is what I call it," Ortiz said as they discussed business on Ortiz' estate, sitting poolside underneath the awning umbrella. The pool's nightlights illuminated the massive area. "As long as the International Eight Families has been standing no one has ever tried to pull a grimy move towards each other. We've had a treaty that wasn't to be broken. Greed is a sure enough way to cause conflict and ignite wars."

"So Julio wasn't bullshitting when he said he wanted a piece of that Miami money, huh?" Semaj asked, puzzled, as she slowly sipped on a mimosa. "We're still in war with the Jamaicans, and I can almost guarantee you that mu'fucka Ox still pissed at how Poppa did his family. Now, the Cubans is a whole new beef that I ain't trying to fan the flames to, Ortiz. Who I need to holla at to see about this issue?" Semaj asked casually and knew she needed to nip the problem with the Ordóñez Family in the bud before it escalated. "I'm telling you uncle because if we have to go against Julio and his people I'm sending my goons down to Cuba and stamp our family name on their soils. I'm not finna keep playing with the Jamaicans and most definitely not our own people. Fuck

is this Cuban mu'fucka on?"

"I assure you, Maj that you don't have to worry about Julio or none of his family members for that matter. The 16 Tent takes loyalty very seriously and it is the only thing in this world besides our word that is free. I promise that is being handled as we speak. We don't take kindly to betrayal and Julio is well aware of the consequences for those that display treachery. You don't have anything to worry about and I'm almost sure that the Jamaicans have tapped out this time and is begging for a truce."

"I would like to believe that you're right, Uncle Ortiz, but I don't doubt anyone and as long as Ox is still breathing I'll never let my guards down on him. As far as Julio's goes, I'm for everything that you're saying," she said. "But I'ma allow you two to establish a relationship while I handle business with the Queen. My car is out front waiting. You said my plane leaves out after midnight, right?" Semaj asked.

Colombia, the Cocaine Capital of the World

Semaj was thousands of feet above land as she made her way through the city of Bogotá on a private helicopter that had been arranged to pick her up from the El Dorado International Airport. She wore headphones over her ears to drown out the overwhelming sounds of the aircraft's propeller. The pair barely served its purpose though, and Semaj found herself escaping the annoying noises by consuming herself in her thoughts.

Guilt weighed down heavy on her heart and she thought about her cousins as she watched the beautiful city fly by in a blur. *I swear their asses don't trust nobody. I don't know how I'ma do it, but I'ma have to get them to trust me on this one. Vega is my husband and we all in this shit together. He's my family just as well as they are and Vega would never pull no grimy shit on me. I've known him too long and we've been through too much bullshit for him to double cross me.*

Vega ain't even that type of nigga to betray someone he loves.

Semaj was so engrossed with her thoughts that she hadn't realized that she already flown over the light blue ocean and passed through city limits until the chopper had cleared the water and a beautiful countryside setting was visible. Rocky-like mountains and endless green rolling fields took up most of the land, and twenty-five minutes later Semaj watched as the pilot maneuvered over what appeared as a compound. Her mouth dropped to the floor as the aircraft swayed back and forth as it prepared to land on the estate's landing pad. She hadn't really known what to expect when she got there, but the extravagance before her was beyond anything that she could ever imagine. *This bitch on some super cartel shit,* Semaj thought as she watched through the window as the helicopter descended upon the dirt less field.

To her surprise, Valentina stood leaned against a golf cart awaiting her arrival. *I can't believe she's actually waiting for me.* The gust from the velocity of the helicopters blades created a mini hurricane of whirling wind, causing leaves from the trees to blow wildly. Once the aircraft landed safely and the propellers had stop spinning the ground handler opened the door.

Semaj took a deep breath, instantly greeted by the overwhelming heat as she stepped out off of the helicopter. The thin white Badgley Mischka sundress that she wore even seemed too much fabric for the South American heat. The hot, muggy conditions and Colombia's air was like no other as sweat began to build on the tip of her nose and she was dying to get out of the hell-like climate.

"Semaj, my darling!" Valentina yelled as she waved her over and greeted her with air-kisses. "It's finally good to have you on my home turf. The Milano Family's princess."

"Thank you for having me. It's a pleasure to see how a *Queen* lives," Semaj stated with a friendly smile. "Your estate makes mine look like the slummiest projects back home. I know you couldn't live here all by yourself?"

"Of course not," Valentina answered as they got inside the cart and rode the five hundred feet stretch to the edifice of her complex. "When I purchased this home fifteen years ago I moved my entire family in here. My compound is divided into many sections and everyone has their own private space."

"Wow, now that's what you call living large," Semaj said and looked around in complete awe. The place was unbelievable. Semaj was surrounded by lush mountains, greenery, waterfalls and rock walls. Some of the rock walls even had pure stream cascading down its stones. It was like paradise.

Once they approached the front entrance, Semaj and Valentina got out the motor cart. Surprisingly, the place wasn't guarded. Semaj didn't see one-armed bodyguard on ground. "I find it odd that a woman of your stature doesn't have your home safeguarded. I expected this place to be flooded with security," Semaj said. She walked a few steps behind her and down an extended hall that overlooked a colossal 250-meter indoor lap swimming pool. It was surrounded by stainless-steel ceiling panels and full-length glass walls.

"Just because you don't see any guards doesn't mean that I don't have anyone watching me, darling. As you know we must use enforcers and bodyguards to our advantage, although a fucking prick wouldn't dare step within one hundred feet of me let alone near the vicinity of my home."

They both laughed as they entered a room. There was an extra large sectional sofa with eight roundtables throughout the spacious area. For a minute, Semaj didn't recognize the man that was tied up to one of the chairs. But when she did, it was as if a light bulb flicked on in her head and the conversation she had with her uncle dawned on her. *The 16 Tent takes loyalty very seriously and it is the only thing in this world besides our word that is free. I promise that is being handled as we speak.* Valentina had Julio restrained to a chair with electrical tape sealed across his lips to keep him from speaking.

"See, I finish distractions before they ever get started. If you eliminate the problem before it actually becomes a major one, then there is actually never a problem. I've told Gio this many of times but he's hardheaded. It has caused him to fight many wars that could have been prevented by one simple reaction." Valentina extended her arm and waved her arm dismissively at the problem she had solved for her. "Fuck this Cuban piece of shit. Let's get down to the reason you came here today. We'd discuss everything over brunch."

Valentina escorted Semaj out to the back of her house and they chatted, ate and drank like old friends on the French tête-à-tête outside on the portico. The two of them hadn't spent much time together, but the little time they had, Valentina found herself observing Semaj's laid-back moves and listened to her choose her words carefully. The more they talked, the more she saw the potential in the young woman. Semaj wasn't even twenty-five yet, but if she played her cards right she would be at a place in the game that she'd never even imagine by the time she hit thirty. "You know, I see something in you that I have never seen in a woman besides myself. That's what brings forth this meeting. Since the death of your mother, I've supplied the Milano family with one thousand kilograms of pure cocaine twice a month. Before then it was five hundred kilo's but she changed that. For several years it was stuck at one thousand and it hadn't changed until you came along and doubled that amount in a matter of months. I figured at the rate you're going you will undoubtedly take out your competition back in the States.

"We're going to use a new method to smuggle our cocaine over to your family. Submarines will be the name of the game. I have border protection and coast guards on my payroll from here to Europe. The underwater boat will be about one hundred feet below surface and twenty-five nautical miles offshore so that it goes undetected. This way will give you the opportunity to move business into Miami and expand down south. Can you handle two

and a half tons of cocaine Semaj?"

"Twenty-five hundred bricks!" she shouted as her eyes bugged wide in astonishment. "You mean move through five thousand keys a month?"

"It may sound like a lot, but that's actually nothing compared to the many tons that I'm responsible for. I'm talking over fifty tons every month. Besides, London is an unclaimed market since the Abbott Family was killed off and during the next meeting I was going to consider you as their replacement by default anyway. There's this guy named Nasah out there that has been reaching out to some of my close associates. He's allegedly the new man around the British parts but doesn't have a solid coke connect. He's seeking one though. I was thinking I could set up a meeting between the two of you if you are willing to accept my offer.

"This opportunity would be perfect for you. Not only will you supply the U.S. but have a hand in the U.K. also. This can mean big business for you. I say we can set the increase of product up as soon as possible. What do you say?"

"You know Ortiz is the one who accepts the change in quantities and I haven't spoken with him about—"

"I know a lot of things must be ran by Ortiz, but that's something you don't have to worry about. Between me and you, he's honored to call you his niece and brags to me about how you are changing things and creating bigger business for the Family. Trust me, Ortiz will sign off on this deal. So what do you say?" Valentina asked again.

"That's a huge responsibility, Valentina. I'd need to visit the Abbott's old territory and scope things out before I can accept your proposal."

"There's no need to rush it, darling. You think about it and let me know at your earliest convenience. I suggest you fly out ASAP, though, just to check things out. If you decide on it then it is a go and then I'd set everything into motion. Deal?" she asked as she extended her hand and Semaj shook it with a gracious nod

of the head. "There is something that I will like for you to see." Valentina handed Semaj the binoculars and pointed up at the top of the mountain as a hot-air balloon hovered over the mountain.

Semaj accepted the device and looked through the circled lens to witness Julio badly beaten with a bloody face as he hung upside down in the air by a thick rope attached to it. Abruptly, an amber orange flame erupted and engulfed the helium balloon, sending pieces flying through the air and it looked as if the sky was raining debris. "I've been in this business a long time and I've learned to get rid of the bad seed. You'll last a lot longer in this game, Semaj, if you think likewise. Remember I told you that you have to allow your emotions to be thrown out of the window?" Valentina asked.

"Yes, I remember," she answered.

"I meant every word. Now, I'll be honored to handle them fucking dread heads?" She said sternly and slightly grinned. "I want you to be careful out there Semaj. It is very dangerous and very cutthroat. Never trust anyone because even the closest ones to you will betray you. Over something as valuable as paper with prominent faces on it. I've myself, had to learn that the hard way when I had to murder my husband behind it," she confessed. She had never told anyone that she had committed that murder, but she felt some sort of special bond with Semaj. Sort of like the daughter that she never had. "If you don't believe anything else I say, trust me on that. The closest person to you will turn cold. You see what Julio did for the love of money. People aren't to be trusted, Semaj."

Semaj stood from her seat and walked over to where Valentina was seated. She bent over and hugged her neck and then air-kissed both of her cheeks. "No doubt. I trust you. I really enjoyed our morning together, but I must be going now. I have my uncle and husband waiting for me. I will thoroughly think your offer over and if I need your services in any way I will not hesitate to give you a call." Semaj smiled and patted her on the shoulder gently before she walked away.

Valentina stood and watched her stroll down the unroofed corridor as she strutted through the long passageway. Semaj was one of few that she was willing to take underneath her wing. Valentina knew that if she schooled her right in the game that she'd die at an old age playing it. There were very few players left who understood the rules to being great and Semaj had proved that she was one of those who were in the know and was proving that she, too, could be one of the great ones.

All Valentina could do was nod her head as she watched her soon-to-be protégé disappear down the open-air hallway, and thought, *I'ma make sure that she's the baddest bitch that ever moved dope. From the United States to the United Kingdom, she will flood cities with the purest cocaine in the world.*

Chapter 13

Back to Present Day

The tires from the five Hummers screeched against the pavement as each vehicle came to a fast halt in front of the private hospital. Without waiting for anyone or the truck to make a complete stop, Semaj hopped out and rushed into the ER unaware that there were more sets of eyes on her than before. Uncertainty and apprehension ate away at her as she approached the nurse's station.

"I need to see Nathan Giles!" Semaj said. The nurses looked at her in bewilderment. She was covered in blood and drenched in gore.

"Fuck is y'all just looking at me for? I need to see my husband!" Semaj yelled. One of the nurses recognized her and came from behind the desk. "I understand that but let me take a look at you first to make sure you are okay and get you a change of clothes." The nurse wanted to examine her because all of the blood on her, but actually all of the blood was Vega's.

She attempted to grab Semaj's arm but she swatted her hand away and stepped back. "I'm straight and I don't need to change into shit. I need to see my gotdamn, husband!" She said insistently, so thunderous that her voice echoed through the hospital.

All of a sudden, she felt someone grab her arm and pulled her backward to the waiting area seats as she continued to demand answers. They hadn't told her anything at the previous hospital and the unknown was killing her.

"Calm down, Semaj," Bonjo said sympathetically as he kneeled down in front of her. "I've spoken with a nurse and Vega is on his way out of surgery. He was shot in the arm. That's all I know of his condition right now."

"Where's LuLu?" Semaj asked concernedly.

"Of course she had an on a vest, but a bullet managed to graze her in the neck. She'll pull through though," he explained. "But check, everyone is headed down to the meeting room in the basement. After you get the information you need about your husband come down ASAP."

Just then, a doctor emerged from behind the double doors and Semaj stood up in angst. "Is he okay?" she asked. "Can I see him?"

"He is in stable condition, but the bullet completely severed a main artery in his arm. We were able to remove that bullet but the lost of blood was substantial. Just to be on the safe side we are going to monitor him to make sure there is no hemorrhaging from the artery that we've repaired."

Semaj didn't hear anything past the part where the doctor informed her that Vega was stable. "Can I see him?"

"Yes, he is still sleeping from the pain medication that we injected in him, but he should come to in an hour or so." The doctor said and led Semaj to Vega's room.

As soon as Semaj saw Vega lying in the hospital bed tears built up in the back of her eyelids but she didn't allow a tear to fall. She couldn't, she had to be strong. She pulled a chair up next to his bedside, grabbed his hand, and rested her head next to his head as she waited for him to wake up.

Quasim sat behind the tint of the Mercedes-Benz as he watched man after man emerge from the Hummer trucks. Some stood outside to guard the outdoors while the other half disappeared into the building right behind Semaj. *Fuck going on?* Quasim

thought as he continued to watch the strange activities. He had been in the states for three days and was watching the comings and goings of the private hospital in hopes of coming up with a good plan. He knew that Gio often called meetings in the basement of his establishment, and Quasim's constant surveillance had finally paid off. *Fuck I'ma get by all these mu'fuckas though?* He wondered.

Just as his frustrations consumed him, a young woman with a nurse's smock bypassed his car while texting on her cell phone.

"Ay, ma!" Quasim yelled as he hopped out of the Benz and tried to get the young lady's attention.

The woman didn't seem any older than twenty-years- old and from the nametag on her uniform he knew she was a nurse aide. She was fairly pale but project chick thick, and had small wet and wavy locks on her hair that was micro braids. She stopped texting and looked up at Quasim. She immediately recognized the costly vehicle he was driving and instantly knew he was street prestige. She knew he was associated with money, and thought, *today must be my lucky day because I've been looking for a baller. Think I found him*, she smiled as she ogled him from head to toe. She cocked her wide hip to the side and seductively licked her full lips, obviously vying for his attention. "You talking to me?" she asked as she stared at him with a sexy smile.

"Yeah, ma. I was trying to see if you wanna make some money," Quasim said as he reached into his pocket.

The girl's eye arched as she followed Quasim's hand. Quasim pulled out a roll of money, and the young chick's eye grew as large as golf balls. She hadn't seen that much money in five checks. It had to be several grand perfectly wrapped up. "What I gotta do to make it?" she asked, still smiling.

"I need you to deliver this note and make sure that the granddaughter of Mr. Gio Milano gets it. Many may know her as Semaj Milano. Can you make sure that she gets the message?"

"I know exactly who you are talking about. She the only chick that comes in here always rocking the red bottom stilettos

and draped in crazy diamonds. I'ma make sure that she gets it personally!" Her eyes stayed glued to the big-faced bills that were in his hand. Quasim handed her the knot of money with the note and anxiously watched her go on about her way.

Semaj had spoke healing into Vega's life until finally she drifted off to sleep, but when she felt Vega squeeze her hand an hour later, she woke up instantly. She was all smiles. His blurred vision became slightly clearer as he searched the room, but he couldn't recognize where he was through his unclear sight. The last thing he remembered was Semaj hovering over him crying and a hot internal sting.

After a few moments clarity returned to his eyesight and when it did, he saw Semaj's beautiful face. This time there were no tears and Semaj's beam was refreshing. Like a hot bowl of Campbell's soup on a brisk January night, she was what he needed.

He weakly cleared his sore throat as he attempted to speak. "I'm sorry about what happened, bay," he said, guilt weighing down on his heart.

"There is nothing for you to be sorry about. The Jamaicans did this and they will pay in the worst way. First they shoot you and then they come to the hospital ridiculously deep and try to assassinate all of us. They really tried to kill me. They wanted us all dead, Vega! I can't believe them bastards were able to get that close to us again." Tears started to form in her eyes. "Twice in one night. Fuck type shit?" she continued to shake her head from side to side as the tears rolled down her cheeks.

"What?" he asked in confusion. But before Semaj could respond, Gio emerged from the shadows of the darkened room and walked over towards them in an expensive silk button-up and Armani slacks, his hands tucked inside, and said, "I need you to excuse us for a second, Semaj. This conversation is amongst men

only. One of my men have clothes for you right outside the door. After you get cleaned up head down to the basement," Gio said in a low whisper, but his tone was filled with enough authority Semaj conceded his request.

"You've disrespected me by flying out to speak with my brother. I can't understand your reasoning, but I will deal with that after we discuss my first issue. My concern here is this. A man from your region ends up in a club with my family and now he is no longer here. Either you were aware of this setup or you were oblivious to the fact. One way or another, this guy had inside connections and I'm positive my people are in the clear," he said surely. "Can't say the same for your men though, Vega. Do you vouch for your men?" Gio asked, not even giving him the respect of facing him. Gio pulled at his long pointed nose and then looked at his costly timepiece. Basically, Vega had seconds to respond.

"Hell nah, I don't vouch for no man but myself," he answered quickly.

"You have forty-eight hours to wipe out every man on your squad that was in attendance the night of the party. If this job is unfulfilled there will be consequences," Gio said threateningly. "I don't believe in coincidences. I know someone connected to your low level organization played a role in what happened that night."

"But there was plenty niggas—"

Gio raised his hand to stop him from talking. "There is nothing that needs to be discussed. You carry out the job or else you pay with your life." Gio ordered coldly and turned his back to walk out of the room.

Despite the pain in Vega's arm, he searched his body until he found his bandaged shoulder. He grimaced in pain as his hands continued to probe his body and then aggressively he snatched the IV from his arm. *Fuck is going on? Fuck went wrong? I gotta get out of here so I can find out what the fuck is up. I know these niggas didn't do no dumb ass shit,* he thought as paranoia filled him. All sorts of things raced throughout his mind. *How he find out that I was on*

the trip. Do he know I had something to do with the shooting? Nah, if he knew anything I would've been circled in chalk, fuck conversation. What Semaj mean by two shootings? I know my niggas didn't pull no dumb ass double shooting. They got the work, fuck else they had to do? Fuck is going on? Shit ain't adding up. The setup at the nightclub was botched and now this shit. Don't know why I thought that sloppy ass nigga could pull this shit off or any of them messy ass niggas for that matter, he thought with regret. *I'ma murder all them niggas just for being stupid.*

The setup backfired on him and his situation consequently turned from bad to some shit out of a gangster movie. The real Jamaicans that had beef with the Dominicans had been cooked amidst his meal, but their simmer had caused Vega's shit to burn. They had definitely blown up his spot and he just hoped that fingers wouldn't be pointed at him when the time came. *It would've been so perfect and successful had not them fucking dreads decided to choose today,* he shook his head in pure disbelief.

Semaj took a deep breath as she exited the room and let out a long sigh. *Why couldn't Poppa speak in front of me,* Semaj thought as she made her way down the sterile, narrowed hallway. She was still in a state of shock and confusion plagued her as she thought of how everything had gone down. As Semaj attempted to board the elevator with three bodyguards on her heels, a young nurse's aide stopped her. She turned around noticing the familiar face of one of the hospital CNAs; the Milano family henchmen stopped the girl's approach, but Semaj stepped in front of them and assured that the hospital employee was cool.

"Semaj, I have an urgent message from one of the front desk receptionist," she told a white lie as if she already knew that she was giving Semaj the piece of paper for her eyes only. "She said it's a note to express her gratitude towards you for what your family has

done for her as far as her promotion. She'd love for you to read it once you're calm and relaxed because she said it is from the heart and she wants you to feel it."

"Thank you and I'll make sure to read it later," Semaj promised as she placed the note in her pants pocket. She quickly headed downstairs to the basement to discuss a sure way to put the Jamaicans out of commission once and for all.

Chapter 14

The conference room was in complete silence. Every Milano family member in the room had rage etched across their faces; the rest of the occupants included all of the head of security and they all were afraid to breath, much less speak. It was the first time since the bombing of the family car that they held a meeting with so much tension in the room, and everyone seemed to be consumed by the same homicidal thoughts. Gio stood up from the head of the rectangular table and placed both of his hands on the marble surface as he looked around.

"Family, it has been a long time since we have warred with the enemy in a street gunfight and I'm highly upset at the fact that I, me, Gio Milano was actually shot at today," he said honestly. "We have yet suffered another great loss due to war. Arturo has been with this family for over twenty-five years and like a man who'd died in the service, Arturo has lost his life serving our family. But what I'm unable to understand is how Arturo ended up dead and Vega has only suffered a gunshot wound to the shoulder and Semaj escaped the first attempt against our family unscathed but—"

"Uncle Gio I know you are not saying that Semaj had something to do with this?" Marcela's brow arched in question. She knew Semaj well enough and knew for a fact that she'd never backdoor the family. Never.

"No. What I'm saying Marcela is this doesn't make any sense to me that at the airstrip the Jamaicans just robbed Semaj and shot

Vega. When in fact, they had the perfect opportunity to kill them both. But they didn't kill her or Vega, but made sure to kill Arturo and a few others." He paused, looking around the table, and then continued, "Then on top of everything at the hospital the gunmen were relentless with shooting down Semaj and determined to take her life.

"I picture myself in every situation and it is very hard for me to write this one off as related. I think this was two separate incidents." He was a very clever man and even the most skillful person couldn't get one off on Gio Milano.

"We're definitely reading from the same book, Uncle Gio," Sosa said undoubtedly. "I was thinking the same shit. Ox ain't gon' send no niggas down here to half do some job, especially when his intentions were to erase everything near us. He would have contracted a hit no other way," she scoffed as she clapped her hands together as if she was a black ghetto girl from the projects. "We've been warring with this muthafucka for fucking years and his people has never caught us easily slipping like that and let it ride without taking lives.

"Anytime Ox has brought war to our home front he deaded everything that he could as we have done the same to him. Who wouldn't? It only makes perfect sense when you got the enemy trapped in a corner you kill 'em all. There's no rules to this shit. We know there are no parameters. Ain't no way his people would've just robbed us and let Semaj live like the robbery was a warning for what was next to come. Fuck outta here." Sosa waved her hand dismissively and leaned back in leather chair, pissed.

"I bet my money on it that that bitch ass husband of Semaj's had a hand in this. I wouldn't be surprised if he working for the dreads. Knew I should've been whacked his grimy ass," fumed LuLu. She had never been hit and the bullet-riddled chest vest infuriated her. "I bled today and LuLu don't ever fucking bleed. I don't shed blood for nothing or no one unless I'm on my fucking menstrual." LuLu was very displeased and they all could see it from the dent in

148

her throbbing temple. It was an angry feature that always formed on the side of her head when she was vexed.

"I think everyone just needs to chill and think strategically. Yes, I'm sorry we lost Arturo, but people die every day. This ain't the first time and damn sure won't be the last time we lose someone close to our family. I just hope that none of us seated around this table become one who hearts stop beating anytime soon," Emilia said sternly. "We done lost too many loved ones and we can't afford a huge loss like that ever again, especially from them clowns from Kingston. They're very sloppy, but thanks to their unskilled actions, we survived through the melee. I agree with everything everyone is saying, but being mad ain't going to help anything. If we put our heads together and throw out the BS we can figure out what just happened." Emilia didn't care about the puzzle board pieces. She just wanted to put it together correctly, accurately and swiftly.

Just then, Semaj walked into the room as all eyes shot to her.

LuLu smacked her lips, letting it be known she wasn't feeling Semaj's presence. It was obvious she was still upset with her from the argument they'd had at the nightclub. As Semaj came closer and headed to her seat, LuLu stared her in the eyes with a screwed-face, and said harshly, "Your husband is dead. I'm going to personally handle him myself!" LuLu pulled out her 9mm and slammed it on the table as an indication that she wasn't bullshitting.

Semaj returned the cold stare, not backing down whatsoever, but remained silent as they matched each other's loathing glare. The way LuLu drew her pistol caused Semaj's reflexes to become responsive and she reached in the small of her back and rested the .380 handgun on her lap. Her nose flared with rebuttal. *You ain't the only one that can show a piece. You might be crazy but these bullets shoot the same, my dude,* Semaj thought, really knowing they both understood they were family and it would never escalate beyond harsh words and lashed out thoughts.

Gio cleared his throat and picked up where their discussion and opinions left off. Semaj focused her attention on him and

listened to what was being said in the meeting.

"I've taken in everything you girls are assuming that has happened today and your conclusions are something that I can agree with. There is no way that Ox would send his men up here to rob us. There is no motive with that. Rob us, shoot us and then turn around and get into a gun battle with us does not seem sensible. They could have killed Semaj and got away with it. It is not only very risky, but it is pure stupidity to actually allow Semaj to live when they had the perfect opportunity to kill her. There's no denying that Vega is involved." Gio looked at Semaj hard, his thoughts evident. "He's still alive."

"What? Vega involved? G-Poppa the Jamaicans could have easily set this up like this, knowing that you all would show up at the hospital," Semaj said, her eyes pleading. "That would be the perfect arrangement to hit us all at once don't you think?" Sarcasm laced her voice.

"Semaj! This isn't a ghetto story! This is the mob! One would never do such an act of work just to get us all together. Knowing by that time we would have recruited more soldiers. In this business you'd never get a heads up. Are you really sure that what you saw was the Jamaicans, Semaj?" Gio asked. "One hundred percent positive?"

"G-Poppa, I'm a thousand percent sure. I've went over every single detail that happened and left nothing out. It has to be them and Ox must just be making dumb moves now," Semaj said with certainty.

Gio knew when his granddaughter was serious, and there was no convincing her; like her mother she spoke with assurance and allowed nothing or no one to change her mind. Once she had her mind made up nobody could change it.

"There is no way that you all can point Vega to this. What would be his purpose? I can't believe y'all even doubting my husband," Semaj gasped in disbelief as she tried to figure things out in her head. *Vega would never do this. He loves me and my family.*

LuLu looked at Semaj with contempt. "Semaj, he has a lot of reasons. Fuck you mean? We was just telling you the dude on some trying to up his status bullshit. And now all of a sudden he supposedly gets shot by the Jamaicans that we've been feuding with for years. Ain't nobody at this table green to this shit, but you. We all know if it was Ox's men, trust, we wouldn't be having this meeting right now. We'll be planning your memorial instead."

"No." Semaj denied the accusation vehemently. "It was them and I know it. I was fucking there, LuLu!" she heatedly argued.

"It does not matter if God was there, Semaj! Think like us for a change and get out of the simple mindset. You're acting real naïve. Dude wants to be you. He wants to be in your spot and you allowing him to ease his way all in, Semaj!

"Starting with you allowing him to make decisions for you. And you *really* let him go on that trip with you. Vega is taking advantage of the fact that you have the power to change the rules and he's willing to do whatever necessary to make it benefit him, Semaj. I say he working for them dreads or he got some Jamaicans on his team; you choose one. But whichever it is doesn't really matter to me because he's a dead man walking, either way. I'ma body that man."

Silence filled the room as Semaj debated with herself in her mind. She wanted to take up for Vega. She wanted to cover for him. She wanted to tell them to fucking beat it, but the conversations that she had been having with Vega over the last few months had swarmed her brainwaves and at that moment everything was beginning to come together. He had been more attentive but not in a loving, compassionate way but in an, I have to keep you close to me because I need you. Semaj had tried to reason that he needed her because of the loss they shared and he was mourning like she was, but throwing himself into work kept him sane. But Semaj was slowly admitting to herself that it wasn't that sort of need after all. It was much more sinister. His need came from one of the seven deadly sins…greed. *All of a sudden he convinced me to become the*

leader of one of the deadliest mobs in North America, now I know why, she thought to herself. The Boss Bitch in her started to kick in. Semaj once again went over each detail in her head, and in that instant it was as if a light bulb illuminated in her head. Her body tightened and her breath got caught in her throat as she replayed the gunman's voice at the airfield.

"Don't move, bitch!"
"Don't move, bitch!"
"Don't move, bitch!"
"Don't move, bitch!"

The voice wasn't even laced with a hint of an accent let alone a Jamaican twang. The men were indeed black niggas, but they surely didn't have that rugged Kingston appearance like the hoodlums that was shooting at the hospital. It was two different groups, it had to be. *But how? But why? But for what?* It was all too complex for Semaj to fathom and she instantly became overwhelmed with confusion. Her sadness was written all over her face, but she couldn't reveal what she'd mentally discovered; at least not until she could get the answers she needed to her questions.

"I know this is hard for you, Semaj but your husband has to be accountable for his actions," Bonjo said evenly. "One of my street sources called me before I got down here with some information that the nigga that tried to clip me at the nightclub the other night was some little ratchet nigga close to Vega's camp in Virginia. Come to think about it the nigga was chopping it up with some of Vega's little niggas from D.C., and them cats had to be the ones that slid the nigga the gun," he figured.

Semaj absorbed everything that was spoken, but it was all too much too swallow. Her head spun as she was besieged with her family's allegations. She knew the rules to the game and even if Vega wasn't responsible and his people were he still would die. But as his wife, the woman that vowed to love him for better or worse and the man that saved her life, there was no way Semaj could agree with what they were accusing her husband of. She just couldn't believe

what they were telling her. She didn't want to believe that Vega was on some shady shit. After all, his crew could have set him up, but with all her reasoning, Semaj couldn't shake the voice in her head that was telling her otherwise. Semaj was in a battle with herself and for her it felt worse than any war with the Jamaicans. Semaj got up and rushed out of the meeting room, knowing she had to find her husband. She had to tell him to flee until she could convince her grandfather that he was innocent. She dashed to the door that led to the stairwell.

Her suspicious arose further as she took off up the stairs and thought about everything her people were insinuating. *He said that he think I should start letting him get his own work separate from the bricks I get and he still pay his dues once he get the work off. He said he wanna do his own thing,* she thought as she jogged her memory for clues. She began to go in deep contemplation and pondered on every conversation they'd had months ago, weeks ago, and even the previous day. She was trying to see if she could come up with anything logical that could give her answers. *This is stupid...they just so into the traditional mafia beliefs and shit...they all are wrong.* She pushed the thoughts out of her mind, but she could not shake the skepticism that had taken over her brain. *But what if they aren't wrong?*

"Oh my God, but what if they are wrong? They are going to kill him!" she told herself as she made it up the last flight of stairs. She raced down the hallway and by the time she made it to Vega's room she was out of breath. She stepped into the room and everything was cleared out. She paused in disbelief as she stared down at the crisp, cotton sheets and empty bed. "Please, no!" Semaj screamed and her hand shot over her mouth as she assumed the worst. She rushed to the nurses' station. "Where is my husband? Nathan Giles! He was just here," she shouted, crying.

"I'm afraid he has checked himself out. He signed out right after your grandfather left his room, ma'am," the heavyset nurse informed her.

Semaj just looked at the woman, paralyzed. She didn't know what to think. *Did Poppa order my husband's death? Since they so into the rules of the mafia, they can't do that shit unless I agree. I'm acting boss.* Tears flowed down her cheeks.

Finally, Semaj picked up her feet and bolted down the flights of stairs. *I have to get to him,* she thought as she reached the bottom floor and walked out of the hospital with her heart aching from uncertainty. She froze in fear and her heart shattered when she saw her grandfather directing his goons, automatically assuming he was putting the contract on Vega's head.

She crept back inside the hospital, but almost jumped out of her skin when she bumped into someone from behind. It was Marcela. "Semaj, I understand you might be devastated, but you can't leave by yourself, ma."

"I have to find Vega. I just don't wanna believe that he'd do anything like this. At least my grandfather needs to allow me to get his side of the story. I know I can convince him to tell me the truth about everything. I just have to, Marcela. Even though Niran is gone, Vega is still the father of my child and the only thing I have left that reminds me of my son. Because of the mob I lost my baby I can't lose my husband too. I just can't...I won't." Semaj cried on cousin's shoulder.

"I can respect that. Vega is your husband and you all shared a child together, that can't be taken lightly. I can understand you not wanting to turn your back on him based on unproven assumptions. For your sake I hope Vega is innocent, but if we prove otherwise you know what has to be done. Vega has to go." Marcela was telling her what it was.

"I understand, but that's why I need for you to let me go... alone. I promise to be careful," Semaj said assuredly. Marcela embraced Semaj briefly before she let her go, and didn't protest as she watched her depart in search of her husband's innocence.

Semaj used the parking garage as her escape route. She knew she shouldn't be walking around the city streets alone, but she

needed to get to Vega. She walked three blocks in the light rain before she saw a taxi and immediately flagged the cabbie down.

Once inside, Semaj speed-dialed Vega and asked for his location. He let her know and then she instructed the driver to take her to the unfamiliar destination. When they pulled into the quiet neighborhood, Semaj noticed Vega sitting on the porch as he told her he would. After paying the cab driver, Semaj exited the vehicle and walked slowly up the driveway. He came off the steps as he calmly adjusted his fitted Detroit hat, and approached her until they were standing face-to-face. Semaj looked directly into Vega's eyes. A part of her was relieved to be in his presence, but another part of her was wary that she might be facing the enemy because if he had crossed her then that was what he was. Semaj didn't even want to imagine him committing such an act of disloyalty.

"Come inside, Semaj. I don't want us standing out here in the cold rain, shorty," he gently grabbed her by her hand and led her inside to the leather couch.

"Baby, there is something that I need to ask you. Don't ever think I doubt you or you can't trust me. All I want is your honesty," Semaj stated. It was killing her inside to even attempt to accuse him and Semaj almost broke down completely, but composed herself. Once Vega's eyes met hers, she finally asked, "Did you pull that shit on my family?"

"Hell nah, I'd never do no grimy shit like that. I thought it was them Jamaicans your family has beef with. But after speaking with Gio, nigga think some of my goons had something to do with it. I mean, I told my top lieutenants that I was flying out and them the only niggas besides the Family that knew when we'd touch back down. Never thought they'd do me, but you never can be too sure what a mu'fucka a do. There's no other way around it, so you know I'ma get at them niggas, right? Everyone that knew about it is dead." Semaj searched for the eyes of a liar, but his stare wasn't moving. His gaze was unwavering and still, as if he was telling her the truth. What Semaj didn't know was that she'd been marching

with the devil and Vega was just that deceitful and convincing that his lies seemed genuine.

"I know you will and no matter what they told me, I knew you didn't have anything to do with what happened. You too much of a real nigga to hurt someone that you love. I know it," Semaj arose and threw her arms around her husband as she cried on his chest. She knew it was up to her to clear his name and salvage Vega from the guilty box her family had placed him in. *They can't blame him because mu'fuckas thirsty.* "I'm going to fix this. But while I do so, you have to lay low, Vega. My grandfather is unpredictable and you can't show your face until I'm sure he understands that you had nothing to do with this."

Vega rested his head on top of hers and held onto his wife. He knew that Semaj was unaware that he was responsible for the shooting at the nightclub and the jet robbery, and the secret was eating him up but not to the point he was willing to confess. They had promised to never keep anything from each other and here he was being dishonest. *Fuck this shit go wrong at, B?*

"I got you, Vega. Just be careful and smart 'til this shit is over. I'm your wife and I'ma hold you down. Handle them niggas and I'll handle my Poppa," Semaj said as she kissed him on the lips and reluctantly backpedaled out of the house. *I love you,* he mouthed and she nodded in acceptance. Semaj looked at him one last time with a weak smile and disappeared out of the house. Semaj knew she would have to put in overtime if there was any chance of her saving Vega's life. All dope business was shutting down from this moment on until she cleared her husband's name and he was once again unified with her Dominican mafia family.

Chapter **15**

The morning was unusually still, too still. Everything seemed so calm as Semaj looked out the bedroom window at the clear blue skies, although a dark cloud was forming. She could feel it in her bones. The tick of the antique grandfather clock was a horrible reminder that time waited for no man. She had spoken with her Poppa, called meetings with the Family, but everyone objected her desperate pleas and didn't budge on their decision to dead Vega. Time had come for him to be no longer, and Semaj didn't know how to handle it. Semaj wished that she could stop the black hand from moving, but she couldn't. Her husband's life was on countdown and she knew his end was near.

She shifted her focus and turned toward the bed where Vega lay. His arm in the sling looked uncomfortable, but Semaj knew that the pain in his shoulder was a scratch compared to what was about to happen to him; he had no idea. Vega was about to die at their home. Attempting to overthrow something so powerful had cost him his life. The old adage when a person is near death it is written over them and absolute. A bad omen swept over Semaj. She nervously fidgeted with the material of her short silk robe and slowly walked over to his bedside.

"I'ma love you regardless if you did it or not," she whispered as she bent down and kissed him on the forehead. The morning was so still that even the birds weren't chirping, but the low beeping sounds coming from her security monitor grasped her attention. Her entire house was under surveillance and the noise that erupted from it was indication that someone was on the property. Semaj glanced out the window and

saw a procession of Suburban trucks pulling onto her grounds. She wished her eyes were playing tricks on her, but knew they weren't and rushed closer to the bay window as her heart thumped in fear.

Both her hands flew to her mouth in disbelief as her eyes widened. "Oh my God! No! Why! Vega get up!" she cried in alarm. She didn't really think her grandfather would order his murder at their home. Over twenty Dominican goons swarmed her home in full bulletproof vest gear, all carrying assault rifles or handguns in their hands. Instinctively, the down ass bitch in her came out as her mind pulled toward the artillery that they kept in the rear of their bedroom. They had guns for days and Semaj knew that she wasn't about to just allow them to take Vega away from her. She wished she would have arranged for him to get out of the country. A simple scheduled plane sent to a secret location, and Vega would have been chilling on the island by nightfall. If only she had thought about it all earlier. But he was home, and it looked like there would never be vacationing for him again.

"Vega!" she called out as she sprinted to the corner of the room where the arsenal rack was positioned. He popped up from the bed at her roar. There was no way Semaj was about to let him fight the battle alone. It was until death do them part and Semaj figured if they were going out, it would be with their guns blazing too. She snatched the largest gun off the rack and tossed it to him and grabbed two machine pistols for herself.

BOOM!

She heard the front door's lock get blown off by an obvious 12 gauge shotgun as Dominican goons knocked the door off the hinges and came flooding into her home. Her hands shook violently as she aimed her weapons at the door. She wanted to kill as many of Gio's henchmen as possible, knowing that at least one would take her life in the process. But to her, it was all worth it. Vega had saved her, they had mourned their son's death together and now, Semaj and Vega would elope in death where their baby boy was waiting for them at the crossroad. Just as the bedroom door flew open, paid hit men bombarded into her room, guns pointed their way. Then suddenly, Vega turned and pointed

the gun at her chest, ready to take her life.

The sound of the bedroom door opening snapped Semaj out of her dreadful thoughts, and she looked up to see Marcela. She'd been having the same nightmare for the last couple of nights and in her wake Semaj relived that dream over and over. She couldn't escape it, but couldn't help but wonder what it meant. *It's just a bad dream Maj. Soon this will be over and Vega will be straight,* she told herself.

"The cars are here to carry us to the funeral home," Marcela announced, her voice even toned. She noticed that Semaj eyes were red and swollen as if she hadn't gotten any sleep in days. Marcela knew they more than likely weren't exclusively for Arturo, but for the pending death of her husband. "No matter what happens, I'ma be here to walk through everything with you."

Semaj responded with a nod of the head. It was too hard for her to speak without crying. She perched up from the window chair, put on large sunglasses and descended the steps. Members of the Milano family was already waiting in the foyer for her, and without an exchange of words they all walked out of the house together. Semaj routinely headed to the second to the last vehicle, but Gio grabbed her hand, and said, "Today I'm going to ride with you and I'll let Bonjo ride alone in position of me. You wouldn't mind that would you, Semaj?" he asked. Gio always rode like a boss, by himself, excluding his driver, but today he asked Bonjo to switch places so he and Semaj could speak in private.

"Where is Jah-Jah?" Semaj asked, her eyes moving around in search of her.

"She's handling some important business for the Family. It'd be just the two of us," he said. "Can we talk?"

"We can do that, Poppa," she finally answered, as Gio pulled open the rear door for Semaj and then got into the backseat after her. Nervous energy filled her body and Semaj immediately began to stare out of the tinted window as the driver pulled off. She mentally prepared herself for the deep conversation—one that

needed to be addressed, despite the dire circumstances at hand.

"Poppa, I truly understand but I was just hoping we could come up with a different approach to get at the Jamaicans this time," Semaj said as they pulled onto the block of the funeral home. Flashing red, white and blue lights lit up the gloomy streets and instantly jarred them from their discussion. Over fifty federal agents in full FBI labeled gear and several large trucks filled with agents alike were scattered across the street. Every alphabet affiliate to the police, ATF, DEA, and SWAT were on scene and it was obvious the funeral home was being raided.

"What the fuck!" Semaj hand shot to her mouth as she looked at federal officials bringing out the body-filled coffin as if they were the pallbearers. She watched as they disrespectfully tore the casket up in an attempt to discover drugs. Her eyes misted and Semaj just knew that her family's reign was over. The Feds had come and Semaj felt as if her life was falling apart right before her eyes. She knew all about the front businesses and was aware of the drugs being transported in and out of the caskets, to and from the mortuaries. Every funeral held there and every coffin that entered their funeral parlors had always been filled with bricks with an exception of a Milano family member—and today Semaj wished that Arturo had been their blood, because it looked like tomorrow would never come. She knew that once the feds found the dope, someone…someone close would be held responsible for the drugs and their freedom would be long gone with yesterday.

Semaj looked over at Gio and to see him remaining composed and calm had taken her aback. She was shocked and couldn't understand how he could be so reserved under such circumstances. "Grandfather, aren't you afraid of what they are going to do once they find what they are looking for?" she asked.

"There is nothing for you to worry about. All funerals

that our family attends, every car, and every coffin is clean," he said confidently, referring to there being no drugs around their perimeter whatsoever. He wasn't foolish enough to allow business to operate as usual while his family was present. He smugly smiled as he watched the policemen do their jobs, many who were on his payroll. But Gio got the surprise of his life when he turned around. He saw a federal agent pulling Bonjo from the car as his people recovered kilo after kilo of uncut cocaine out of the vehicle's hidden departments.

"This cannot be happening, Poppa. Those are not bricks, they couldn't be. Could it?" she asked, fearing the worst. Her grandfather ignored the question, but she could see his brow furrow in disbelief. They stepped out of the car and Gio rushed toward the car behind them only to be stopped by a plain-clothed agent.

"Sir, I'm sorry this is a crime scene and you can't come any further," the agent directed.

Gio wasn't into playing big with the police because he knew that with one phone call they would no longer have a job. Besides, he had other things to focus on. So he simply nodded his head and watched the sergeant handcuff Bonjo. As Bonjo's Miranda rights were being read, Gio looked around and noticed none of the other Rolls-Royce vehicles were being searched. At that point, he knew someone had tried to set him up.

Sosa ran up, shocked. "What the hell is going on? Why are they taking Bonjo? *Fuck?*" she fussed. LuLu hurried up beside her sister and shook her head in disgust. "Is all of this unnecessary disrespect really caused for at a fuckin' funeral? Allowing a dead man to damn near tip out of his coffin though!" she cursed as she shot daggers at the other side. She knew Arturo's body hadn't been stuffed with drugs, but from how the cops were handling the casket it appeared as if they wanted to cut him wide open.

"Emilia, get some of our people on line. Call our attorney first and then contact some of our government connections. Tell the lawyer to meet us *immediately*." Before Gio said another word,

Emilia pulled out her cell phone and had already speed-dialed legal counsel. "I need to know exactly what is going on," Gio said, his voice full of irritation. For once, his words were high-pitched but he was trying his best to control his temper. "They've already disrespected Arturo's farewells, so there is no need for us to stay. I can't stand to be surrounded by these pigs a second longer. Marcela, y'all can head back to the house. I don't want Maj anywhere near this chaos," he turned to the rest of his nieces. "Let's go!"

The murky city passed by in a big blur as Semaj stared out of the window blankly, her eyes distant, as she tried to wrap her mind around everything that happened. She had thought the pain from her son's death had numbed her, but with the sequences of events she felt that she would melt to water at any moment. *Who is behind all of this madness,* Semaj thought, knowing that someone was trying to takedown her family. *But who?* she questioned herself, totally oblivious to the fact that her husband was responsible.

When they arrived back at the mansion, Semaj closed her eyes. She shook her head from side to side to clear her mind of the unforeseen pandemonium that had stepped on her family's home front as she exhaled sharply and exited the car. Her iPhone began to buzz the moment her stiletto heel grazed the ground. "Hello," Semaj anxiously answered on the first ring. She listened to what Jah-Jah was telling her on the other end of the line and dropped her head in devastation as she was hit with news that verified it all.

Tears of hurt, anger and regret flooded her mind as the cell phone slipped from her hand, plummeting to the floor and shattering into pieces. Her legs gave out from beneath her and she buried her face in her palms. The confirmation that Vega had been involved all along was the final blow that completely shattered an already broken heart. Semaj felt as if the plug had been pulled and she was no longer on life support.

"Maj, who was that? What happened?" Marcella asked, panicked.

"The setup…" Semaj stopped to clear her throat. "It was him. Vega tried to ruin our family."

"How you know this is a fact, Semaj?"

"Uncle Ortiz puts an invisible stamp on the plastic the coke is wrapped in. You can only read the date that's etched if it is under this special light. Gio had some of his people who have access to the evidence snatch one of the bricks and that date reads when he handed us the work."

"But does that make him guilty? Could it be the people that robbed y'all?" Marcela asked, giving him the benefit of the doubt for the sake of Semaj.

"I was thinking the same thing until Jah-Jah said they pulled the hidden security tapes from the mortuary. Vega knew that Gio would have us ride in our usual funeral transportation, the Rolls-Royces. He planned it all." She cried, doubling over and holding her stomach as regretful pains plagued her. "I just should have listened. Y'all were right. He was behind everything. It had been him this entire time. I've been bedding a man that is intentionally trying to destroy my family. How could I have been so stupid?" she asked herself as her nose began to run and she sniffed loudly. "This is all my fault."

Marcela shook her head, but didn't understand how Vega could be so stupid. So damn dumb. Getting one off on an empire ran so smoothly, so precisely, with no glitches, was unfeasible. Marcela didn't even have to speak his fate, it was inevitable. His actions were unacceptable, he had crossed the line and Vega was definitely a dead man walking.

"There was no way for you to know, Semaj. We never blamed you for not seeing it. We all understand why you were going hard in his defense. That's your husband, a man that you are supposed to love, honor, and cherish. Nobody was mad at you for trying your best to defend him. That's why Gio gave him time. He usually doesn't do that even if he's not sure. He just usually ends lives just to be careful. But he loves you, Maj, and gave you that opportunity to clear your man's name, but Vega the one that's fucked up. Not you.

"He obviously got greedy and now he has to die trying

something that the greatest would never accomplish. We ain't new to this type of disloyalty. It's what we expect, ma and Vega simply proved us right. Believe me, Vega surely wasn't the first that has attempted to end us and I'm sure he won't be the last," Marcela said. "But what he failed to realize is our family's power is endless. Those drugs found in Bonjo's possession won't be able to ride. Believe that."

Marcela took a seat beside her and rubbed Semaj's back soothingly as they sat on the couch for hours. Semaj wanted to take her time because this would be the last pity party that she would ever throw herself. She cried and cried until she was all cried out. She didn't want to leave a slight emotion in her. When she was done she wanted to be a brand new woman an emotionless bitch. She had been warned to leave her emotions out, but hadn't done so all the way. *This nigga really had me going,* she thought. She felt that he had been against her from the very beginning, and if he hadn't, ole well. He had gone against the grain. There was no more understanding in Semaj's heart and no more trying to fathom it all. Vega would pay for the trouble he had caused—with his life.

Finally, Semaj wiped her eyes and dried her face before she walked upstairs to the bedroom for some privacy. She needed to call her grandfather and give him a sincere apology. He deserved it and that was the least she could do. She had doubted him when she knew in all certainty that her grandfather wasn't to be questioned. *I should've believed him,* she thought sorrowfully. As she began to dial him, the small piece of paper on the vanity sat out like a sore thumb. A week had almost passed, and Semaj had forgotten all about the note she had received from the girl at the hospital. For some unexplainable reason a sense of urgency came over her. She dropped the cordless phone on the bed and ran over to the dresser to grab the letter.

Meet me at the Cemetery Thursday night. I'll explain everything then.

PS: Please come alone!!

Oh my God, today is Thursday, Semaj thought as her heartbeat started to speed up and her chest was pounding extra hard. Everything around her seemed to be moving in slow motion and all of a sudden rage passed over her. *I'm going to kill him. I'm going to kill him myself.* Without even realizing it, Semaj grabbed her strap and left out of the side door unaware of who she was actually meeting but thinking it was her snake of a husband.

Chapter 16

Her long silky hair blew to the back as she stood over the large angel monument that was her son's tombstone. Chill bumps covered Semaj's body as the wild airstream kissed her skin. Kneeling down, Semaj hugged the form created out of marble. She desperately tried to pretend that her scars were healing over time, but actually the wounds were as fresh as the day her baby had been removed from her world. She was just able to conceal them well. Tears trickled out of her eyes and stained her cheeks as she laid her head on the gravestone, allowing her soul to release her hidden pain.

"Baby, Mommy misses you so much. You were the most handsome, happiest baby ever and Mommy can't wait to see you again. I love you Niran so much. You was my everything and I loved you more than anything," she said truthfully. "In actuality, you were all I ever had. The one that really loved me back when others faked it," Semaj said in between sobs.

Why would someone I thought loved me betray me like this? Did he really care about our son? Semaj questioned herself. She shivered as she closed her eyes and thought of the picture perfect family that she envisioned only to lose every member in an awful way. She knew the moment her son had died her life would never be the same, but Semaj would have never imagined that Vega... her husband... her son's father would show deceit.

"Semaj." She heard someone call from behind but didn't turn around. "Maj?"

That time the bass of the raspy voice caused Semaj to jump slightly. She was startled and felt as if she was hallucinating. Her heart beat in anxiety and instinctively she turned around only to get the surprise of her life. She wasn't tripping at all. It was Quasim in the flesh and her eyes grew wide as she thought she was seeing a ghost. *This couldn't be,* she thought, because she had seen him in the body bag herself. For all of this time, Semaj thought that he was dead. Now here he was, standing ten feet away from her.

A mixture of disbelief and hatred raced through her veins. It had been nearly two years and it was unfathomable how after all this time had passed, Quasim decided to emerge from the dead. Seeing him had taken her back to a time when she was transforming into a better woman, a time when she wanted to be a better person. But now Semaj was even more ruthless than before, and had completely transitioned into a coldhearted woman.

"Semaj, I'm so sorry that I've waited this long. Shit was just too complicated for me. Still complicated for me because I worry about you all the time," he said. "I know Gio gon' make sure you straight, but that didn't stop me from wondering are you safe."

She closed her eyes. Semaj had dreamed about this day so many nights, but only found it to be a nightmare to wake up without him by her side. She balled her hands as the tears she promised to never shed for another escaped her eyes. She didn't know rather to be happy or sad. So much tension had been in the air the last time they saw each other and that same energy was being felt now. With him in her presence, her stomach began to turn violently, as she doubled over, overwhelmed with confusion and disbelief.

"I saw you dead though, Qua. How could this be?" she managed to ask. "You were in a body bag."

"I was unconscious then and my pulse was so faint they hadn't felt one. By the time they did, I was in the back of the coroner's van being transported to the morgue. But then, I gave the personnel an offer that he couldn't refuse. Money can buy you anything in this

world, ma. Even a fake death."

"But my Poppa went to your funeral. He told me because I wasn't able to make it. I went through a lot that night and was in a medically induced coma, but my Poppa was there. I know he was there." Tears continued to stream down her face.

"It was all staged," he revealed. "I knew once Gio found out who my people was I had to skip town. On top of Block sending some of his people from Queens, I had no choice but to leave and try to start over. I didn't have enough firepower. All the niggas I trusted died that night. My departure was inevitable," he said. What Quasim didn't know was that it hadn't been any of Block's goons from Jamaica Queens that night, but his connects shottas sent from Kingston Jamaica. "Now, you know I ain't afraid of no nigga because we all bleed the same. But I'll never try to be on no superman shit, especially with all my niggas gone," he admitted. "I just want you to know that I'm sorry though, Maj. Real talk, ma."

He's been alive this entire time and all of a sudden he wanna show up and apologize. Fuck! She cursed him silently as she wiped her face and turned to walk off. *All that I've been through and now he wanna show up.* Semaj was flooded with mixed emotions. *I can't believe he'd have me feeling bad all this time because I never got a chance to tell him I was sorry. And now he standing in front of me screaming his sorrow. Fuck outta here.*

"Semaj, hold up." He grabbed her arm and spun her around to face him. He put one hand on the side of her face and swept her hair from in front of her eyes. His heart shattered into pieces when she flinched in fear of his touch. It was a natural reflex from the assault he had put on her. Semaj remembered it like yesterday. "You don't ever have to be afraid of me, Semaj. I'll never hurt you. I promise." He lifted her chin up, forcing her to look him in the eyes.

"I just can't believe that you alive, Qua." She broke down. "You were the one person that I loved and never intentionally crossed, but fate stepped in long ago and created some bullshit before we even met. Why us? Why did our lives have to be so intertwined? If

certain things wouldn't have happened you wouldn't have had to leave. Things would have turned out different for all of us. Turned out different for me. But they didn't. Why though?" He caressed her cheek with the back of his hand.

"Life don't move in ways we want it to sometimes," he whispered and tipped his forehead against hers as he released a deep sigh. He could see the sadness on her face and it was then that he realized that she was hurting. He knew Semaj well and something else was bothering her. "What's wrong, Maj? I know that look in your eyes too well."

She dropped her head full of torment. "I married a man that I thought I knew. A man that I thought I could trust, but he was truly the devil in disguise. He vowed to never betray me, to honor me, but he has caused some unforgivable bullshit to go down. He was willing to sacrifice what we shared so he could satisfy his own selfish needs," she expressed. "I wish I could tell you everything but I can't get into too many details though."

"I feel that. But there is something that I need to tell you. This is a big reason why I am here. There was this nigga name Rude Boy and I—"

"I can't speak about that, Quasim," she said, cutting him off. "You know how it is with the Family. Speak to no one on the outside. You know how strict those rules are when it comes to Gio."

"But, Semaj, this is really important. Just let me explain," he begged.

She shook her head. "We can't talk about this right now. He's dead, he's no longer an issue anyway," she said, remembering how the Milano Hitters said they had murdered him. What she didn't know was that Quasim had really killed him in order to save her life.

"I know he is dead, I—"

"Please. Don't do this, Qua. Don't make this difficult for us. My grandfather would kill you if he knew that I snuck out here alone only to discover that you are alive."

"I want Gio to find out that I am alive, Maj. I want you to

set something up for us to meet soon. I ain't have shit to do with what my Aunt Brina did to Kasey. He can't hold me accountable just like I can't hold you responsible for your pops killing my people," Quasim said. "I know Gio's tradition to murk everybody in the family, but I ain't feeling this for some shit that I had no involvements with. I want us to dead this beef and move on from the situation. Can you set that meeting up for me?"

"I have to be honest with you, Qua. I will definitely speak to him, but it won't be until things calm down. Maybe in the next few weeks we can come holla at you. There is no need to try to settle things when he's angry. It might just fuel the fire. I'm telling you, now is not a good time. He on some pissed shit and everything has to be going good, you know?" Semaj was being somewhat short with Quasim and making his meeting with Gio difficult because part of her was still angry with him.

"I can respect that." He took her into his strong arms. "Gio protects the ones that he love and I can't stunt that nigga was like a godfather to me and I hate what separated us. He always came through rather it was product or protection."

"So now that you got me here this is it? You get the meeting set up with my grandfather and then what?" Semaj gazed down at her feet hating that she was feeling vulnerable to him. Part of her wondered if all he cared about was making things right with Gio instead of fixing things between them.

"When Gio comes, make sure you are there to." Quasim took Semaj by the hand and walked her to where her car was parked. The streetlights up above shined its light directly down on them. "You say you having problems, I wanna come make 'em disappear. I want us to start over."

Semaj wanted to respond, but the huge lump in her throat stopped her from speaking. "You think we can make that happen. I miss you so much. Sometimes I feel like I'm dying without you."

"I miss you so much too, Qua," she managed to say as she nodded unsurely. He kissed her on her forehead. "I really miss your

loyalty and friendship. You was a hunnid and never fell short on being real. That a rare and priceless trait in a man."

"We gon' get all that back, Semaj. Just handle the situation with that nigga and I'ma be waiting for you." He stared deeply into her eyes. "I'll always wait for you, Maj," Semaj smiled when he pulled out the other half of the charm and screwed it on to make it a complete heart. She was speechless. *It was him the entire time.* "With you my heart will forever be complete." He opened her car door, tucked her safely inside and watched as she disappeared down the darkened road.

As Semaj sat in her large dining room with twenty leather high-back chairs seated around her table she causally ate her Cobb salad. She took a few more bites before sitting the fork down. The redundant groans and whimpers caused her to become aggravated and it was pissing her off. Vega sat at the opposite end of the table, and due to his unremitting sobs Semaj was unable to enjoy her meal. "Will you shut the fuck up with all that weeping? You weren't whining and crying when you was plotting and strategizing, nigga. Fuck you bitching up for now?" Something inside of Semaj had snapped.

Vega had been severely beaten but Semaj could care less. Duct tape covered his mouth because she didn't want to hear shit he had to say, although she wanted to see his pleading eyes. She wanted to see the regret and the remorse within them, and like she knew, Vega's eyes were begging her to forgive him. But what he did was unforgivable and his betrayal was unforgettable. His hands were tied behind the chair and his head was pulled up straight by the ceiling's rope. His eyes were semi-swollen shut and blood dripped from his mouth, but he deserved it. For his disloyalty, he warranted his own death.

Since Semaj had found out about his betrayal she knew that

he would die, and after seeing Quasim just the thought of her once being courted by a real nigga to marrying a nigga faker than a Chinatown Louie bag had her vexed. *Fuck was I thinking? Fuck was he thinking? Thought we crossed the lines of lies and deceit before we jumped the broom, but that nigga must've had cruel intentions all along. I hate him for being so damn stupid. Dumb for thinking he'd get away with forcing me out.* She stood and furiously swept her bowl to the other end in one dramatic motion.

"Why would you betray me out of all people? When you could've had it all if we just fucking worked together! You made me look like a damn fool! I thought I could trust you! Here we are in a war with some muthafuckas and all along you secretly at war with us too!" She screamed as she picked up the empty champagne flute and threw it at him in frustration. The glass shattered on contact with his face, reminding her how her heart felt the day she'd learned of his disloyalty. She turned her back on him and took her time as she walked to retrieve her crocodile handbag with her pistol inside.

Gio had ordered his nieces to kill Vega, but like Gabe's murder, this one, too, was personal to Semaj. She had been blinded and allowed Vega to disrespect her family. She knew her grandfather felt some type of way about the fact that she had even considered giving Vega the benefit of the doubt. With his blood on her own hands was the only way to prove that she was sorry for her mistake. The act that she was about to commit would show the family that she was all for them and nothing meant more to her than loyalty.

Emotions have to be thrown out of the window and the number one rule is to get before you be gotten, Semaj reiterated her mentor's motto. She thought it was crazy when Valentina expressed that she had murked her husband, but now Semaj could relate.

As she drew the drapes back from the huge bay window, Semaj sat at the windowsill. Vega's bloody eyes managed to widen in desperation when he noticed the Glock come out, but there was nothing else that needed to be said. He had been dealt a good hand but played his cards all the way wrong. Vega had written his own

death sentence. Semaj raised the gun and fired, piercing his face with three back-to-back slugs. She then called in her henchmen to come dispose of the body. She didn't even bother to watch them carry Vega out. She looked up at the full moon that slightly poked out of the pitch-black night skies.

RING, Ring!

RING, Ring!

The phone chimed and Semaj answered as she continued to peer in the distance. It was Valentina. "Funny thing is I was just about to call you."

"Well, I guess we were both on each other's mind? How is everything coming along with Bonjo?"

"Poppa got some people looking into it," Semaj responded.

"I've hired some powerful people of my own to get on it too. Don't worry, the entire case will disappear. With my people and Gio's connection it will blow over."

"I hope so, because his situation is starting to stress me out. Especially with me knowing that it was a setup."

"Relieve the stress by getting rid of the problem," Valentina suggested. "The sooner the better."

"That's something that I've already taken care of."

"Great!" Valentina caught her underlining meaning and a proud smile crossed her face. "Now what was it that you were calling me for?"

"To ask for a favor. I hope you don't mind, especially since you've already done so by helping out with this Bonjo situation," Semaj said.

"I told you anything you need I'll make happen if I can. What is it, darling?"

"You remember you said if I need your services with a certain situation you wouldn't hesitate to send me some of your people?"

"Of course I remember," Valentina replied.

"I need your assistance helping my people with this one. That man has taken things beyond too far. I'm ready to erase this

problem for good."

"He's throwing this Great Parade this weekend." Valentina was well versed with the affairs of many men and for her, nothing or no one flew under the radar. "I'll have our Russian friends supply us with the needed tools and I'll have everything else set up perfectly. Very soon your problem will be past tense. Trust me."

Chapter 17

Kingston Jamaica

The Milano Hitters rode side-by-side through the paraded streets on saddles. Geared in army costumes and huge hats hid their identities as they neared their intended destination. The extended parade floats in front of them carried Dominican henchmen and shammed National Guard tanks that held Colombian passengers. There was a mixture of both descents on ground in what appeared as a marching military band surrounding all of their moving transportation. Everyone played their positions. There were more than twenty thousand attendees. Flags, instruments, and objects were held by men as they marched the streets. It was the perfect distraction for onlookers because they blended into the activity without causing a hint of suspicion.

The consequences for putting a hit out on the Milano Family would be deadly for everyone near Ox's gazebo. The blue, sunny skies and the scorching conditions should have been every indication that it was about to be a heat wave—one that Jamaica had been more familiar with than any other island—a hotness that drug violence often brought to their streets. Sosa knew she was about to lay motherfuckers down in broad daylight, and she and her sisters were about to show them how you supposed to shut shit down unlike the Rasta boys who had been reckless during their discharge. Sosa promised herself that they wasn't leaving without Ox…dead or alive.

The day has finally come where I get my revenge on this pussy nigga. He's killed my people, setup my Poppa, beat me within inches of my life and this nigga play gangster. We gangsters for real. We breathe this shit. We live this shit. We do this shit. I'ma murder every mu'fucka around that clown ass nigga just fucking because. Her brow arched from a combination of impatience and eagerness. On the outside, one would never know her murderous thoughts, but on the inside, her blood was boiling. This hit was more personal for her and she was about to set it off.

She was jarred from her thoughts as she felt the horse turn the corner with their entourage and made its way through the masses. Sosa went deaf as she looked around the crowded streets, searching for Ox and his hoodlums as she continued to survey her surroundings. She whipped her head eagerly as she tried to spot her mark amongst the sea of faces and then her eyes locked on him. There he was, laughing amongst dozens of young dreadlocked hooligans, carefree, as if he didn't have a worry in the world.

"We got all exit points guarded so your man won't have an escape route. We got this fool," Emilia whispered as she pulled on the saddler-rope and slowed the trained horse down from galloping fast.

Sosa didn't respond. She simply stared down the row at her sisters and nodded her head. She knew they was about to give the Jamaicans a shootout of the century. They each carried either an automatic AK-47 or an AR-15 and each weapon was loaded and ready. The four girls withdrew their assault rifles as they simultaneously aimed at their laughter-filled targets. With bated breaths, adrenaline pumping, rage pulsing through their bodies they opened fire on the *Warfare Clan.*

Rat! Tat! Tat! BOOM! BOOM! POP! POP! POW! POW! BANG! BANG!

The clatter of the different gun sounds was the beginning of the end. One after another, bullets flew in the direction of the perpetrators. The Milano crew had arrived on scene, guns blazing

and relentlessly unloaded their weapons on the Jamaicans. The sound of assault rifles, machine guns and handguns filled the air as the downtown streets became an instant warzone.

The parade suddenly turned into a frenzy as everybody began ducking low and running for cover. Pandemonium reigned. The thunder of feet stampeding and hysterical shouts could be heard all over. They wanted to leave a scene of carnage behind, sending a message that the Milano Family had come to town with no regard for humankind. A blood bath was their only way of retribution for Ox's goons, and the Milano Hitters was making sure they left his entire band of reckless hoodlums drowning to death.

With the unexpected intrusion, the Jamaicans had been completely caught off guard. They had come through on some *Wild Wild West* shit and the scene looked like a clip snatched straight out of an old western movie. Bodies were getting filled with bullets and jerking left to right. Everyone in their camp was on some real natural shooter shit and was laying motherfuckers out.

The Jamaicans was down to only a few members but they needed all of them dead so they could get to Ox. Dead bodies were piled on top of each other and it was a complete horror scene. Even the Milano Hitters were slightly shocked at the sight. It was a gruesome one, but Semaj had given specific instructions and they were following orders. No one from Ox's squad would be left standing.

Hit in the chest, Ox was one of the many men sprawled out on the hot pavement, and since the gunners came there particularly for him no one was willing to leave without his body. A smile of satisfaction flashed across Sosa's face as she noticed the very thin Colombian guy pick Ox up and throw him over his slender shoulder.

I know that broad from somewhere, Emilia thought watching a familiar looking chick run for cover as she continued to let her cannons bark all the while trying to remember where she knew the chick from.

"Don't hit that little girl!" Sosa shouted as she hopped down from the horse and rushed over to the small child. Nearly everyone near Ox had been struck with lead, but the little girl was unscathed. As many bullets that flew, she was blessed. Nothing short of God had spared her.

Shooting kids had never been a concern for Sosa, but there was just something about this little girl. Something had drawn her to the young child, and she instantly grew a soft spot for her. *That must be Ox's daughter,* Sosa thought, immediately noticing the small resemblance. She didn't know if it was because she knew the little girl would have been her child's sister or the fact that she appeared close to the same age that her daughter would have been, but Sosa couldn't bring harm to her. She was innocent and murdering her was not her objective…she only meant to dead Ox's shooters not his seed.

Feeling as if it was her duty, Sosa dodged bullets as she raced toward the little girl while exchanging shots with the remaining dreads. Uncommonly her sisters didn't protest, and continued to shoot cover shots for Sosa as she scooped the small child up in her arms and quickly pulled the lid off the sewer. "Don't come out until the police get here," Sosa said as she placed her in the gutter. "You understand me?"

The little girl didn't respond and looked at her stubbornly. "What's your name?" she asked.

"Nyala," she finally spoke.

Nyala's face reminded Sosa of a child she once knew, a child that she once was. It was as if her past had flashed right before her eyes and Sosa remembered it all. The many murders she witnessed as a little girl, the first murder she committed when she was twelve, and the time she spent with Ox. The pain of premature labor and then all of the blood. The blood! The blood surrounding her baby girl. Sosa had never been able to hold her deceased daughter and now here she was staring at a little girl that brought back all the memories of her own child, the child she lost, but why she began

to wonder before the burning sting of a bullet ripping through her arm took over.

"Aghhh!" Her hand fell over her left shoulder as she realized that she had been shot. In a split second, the situation had gotten out of hand and the blinding pain that shot through her jerked her body forward, but that didn't stop her. It only enraged Sosa, and she snapped back into reality and scrambled to fire her weapon with her uninjured arm. With her right hand, Sosa shot exactly—dropping everything in her view. Her head did a *360* as she searched for a way back to the horse, but noticed a young dread sneaking up on her, gun aimed at her head. BOOM! A loud shot rang throughout the streets, and blood splattered all over Sosa— but not blood of her own. It was the blood of the gunman that shot her. LuLu deaded him instantly and grabbed her sister's arm and they ran for dear life until they reached the horses. Their horses had taken bullets and were laid out with dead humans, so LuLu and Sosa jumped on the back of Emilia's horse and fled from the butchery like some true cowgirls—it was finally the end of Ox's terror...an end of an era of war with the Jamaicans. With Semaj in charge she had accomplished what no other Milano leader had— she had finally got Ox.

Chapter 18

"Bitch, are you even listening to what the fuck we talking about?" Sosa threw a silk pillow at Semaj's head.

"Man, I'm paying y'all asses some attention. I'm not deaf, mu'fucka." Semaj shot the pillow right back, knocking the blunt from her mouth.

"Damn, hoe," Sosa jumped up after the cigarillo landed on her bare thigh. "You didn't have to throw it so fucking hard." She placed the blunt back in her mouth and toked. "You got something real heavy on your mind," Sosa said. "But you need to snap back down to earth. You got an important decision to make. You have a chance to expand our family business internationally. Stepping outside the states to hit niggas off is huge. The global market is big business."

"You only wanna go because of the kid Nasah. Don't act like it's only about family business. I remember you telling me you ran into the nigga at the diner at the hotel that time." Semaj said, her brow arched.

"Girl boo, don't try to reverse some shit on me, because your thoughts blurry up there. Fuck Nasah. Let's get this money," she laughed.

The five girls sat comfortably around Semaj's chocolate brown French sectional while scenes from the movie *Cocaine Cowboys* emitted from the wall-stretched flat screen as they planned the family's next business move. Semaj was trying her hardest to

concentrate, but she failed at it terribly. Every time she blinked, Quasim crept further into her thoughts. Her short time with him had been like a dream that she never wanted to wake up from. All her feelings for Quasim that she had put in a vault and locked away had now opened up and it had Semaj on an emotional high that her heart welcomed.

Semaj nodded her head, folded her legs underneath her and attentively looked at her cousins. They were more than her protectors, her enforcers, but the sisters that she never had. Semaj knew no matter their disagreements or arguments they were there until the casket drop, and knew she couldn't chance another distraction so she refocused. *They all I got*, she thought. *Me and Qua will never be able to go back to what is was or even start over to create something new. I'ma set the meeting up between him and Gio, but after that there will be nothing between us. We are over*, Semaj tried convincing herself.

"You've been real nonchalant lately, distant. You feeling some type a way about that snake-ass-nigga ain't you?" LuLu stared at Semaj accusingly.

"Girl, beat the block. Ain't nobody worried about that. Fuck you constantly bringing the shit up for?" Semaj shot back.

"Whatever. I just hope you ain't regretting shit. That nigga deserved more than a gunshot. Should've put dude in the pond and fed 'em to the alligators."

"The Milano way. Feel me?" Sosa stood up and pulled her .40 from her shoulder harness and pointed the pistol at LuLu. LuLu repeated the same gesture and they tapped guns. It was their way of high fiving each other. It was a silly, playful tradition that they shared since they were young.

"You bitches is so lame for that pistol kissing shit. Who does that?" Semaj asked in annoyance.

"Can you muthafuckas stop bickering for a hot little second? Y'all can get back to the irrelevancy in a minute," Emilia said.

"And irrelevant it is," Semaj told her with a screw face.

"Right," Marcela said. "Emilia, what was that information you received from one of your sources this morning?"

"Oh, yeah, I forgot about this little shit. Too busy trying to convince Maj to take the Queen up on her offer."

Sosa stopped fooling around and returned to her seat, while Emilia pulled the photographs from her purse and spread it across the oak coffee table. Emilia pointed her finger at the pictures and Semaj looked down at them.

"Fuck y'all got a picture of this bitch for?" Semaj asked, irritated at the mere sight of her face as she picked up the photo. It was a picture of Gabe and a girl, the chick looked like Paris. Confusion swept over her. "This must be some joke or something?"

"When we were in Jamaica I could've sworn I seen this bitch. I was staring at the broad so hard 'cause I remember deading her myself. So when I got back I had to go through the flicks of our victims. Then this what I find. You know we had some of our henchmen following her for a minute before we got Paris' ass just to make sure it was the right chick, because I remember Gio saying she had a twin."

"Gio said something about you didn't wanna put nobody else in it so we just got at Paris," Sosa joined in an added. "I wanted to murk both them bitches though."

"I never knew Paris knew Gabe. How do she know him?" Semaj said to no one in particular.

"What you know about the sister?" Marcela asked. "Is she in the streets?"

"From what I know the chick is corny. But what I want to know is what she doing in Jamaica?" Semaj asked, perplexed.

"My point exactly. That's why I looked back at the snapshots we had taken of her. And learned that one of the sister's had been kicking straight bo-bos with Gabe. We don't know which one of them it is because the bitches is really identical," Sosa said. "Now the Paris chick sister all in Jamaica surrounded by hustlers and goons. What got me tripping is how Gabe was with these same

Jamaican mu'fuckas. Did the sister know Gabe too or something?" she probed. "Did they fuck around?"

"Paris never really talked about her sister, so I really can't say. But from what I do know she didn't date street niggas. Vega told me, because he used to date the chick. She refused to get serious with a dopeboy though and left him alone. That's when Paris started doing that crazy shit I was telling y'all about. Faking like she was her twin sister."

"Ain't this some real movie shit?" LuLu chimed in. "I say we just kill the sister too. Just because this shit don't sound right."

"If it don't sound right it ain't right. So what you suggest for us to do, Maj?" Emilia asked.

"You already know. Send someone to take care of the job. Make it clean though and they ain't gotta torture the broad or nothing. They say she wasn't an evil bitch like her sister," she said, venom in her voice. The thought of Paris infuriated Semaj. "I hate even discussing anything to do with that snake ass bitch and I don't want to continue this conversation."

"Now that we got that understood. What's up with expanding to England?" Sosa asked.

"I don't know. That is a huge step to take and y'all know London ain't my favorite place. Nothing good came from that trip last time but my connection, so I'm not really sure." Semaj shook her head. "Something about the town gives me an eerie feeling. The crazy thing is sometimes it could be a good feeling then next bad. Shit is mad weird."

"Well, now that you establishing a working relationship with the Queen ain't shit to worry about. She connected like the interstate and muthafuckas know not to cross her."

"She trusts you enough to have private sit-downs with you and everything. The Queen normally don't do no shit like that unless she's known you for years. Might as well take her up on her offer. We ain't got nothing to lose, but everything to gain in the process." Emilia said. "Dial her up."

Semaj nodded her head in agreement and dialed Valentina's overseas number.

Valentina greeted her as soon as she answered the phone, "Semaj? I thought you'd never call. How's everything? I heard we've finally got our man."

"Yeah, we've finally got 'em. We're just waiting for him to wake from his coma. Because of your help, I can sleep better at night and I wanted to thank you for that. But I also wanted to speak with you regarding that offer you proposed. Is the offer still on the table?" she asked, getting straight to the point.

"It never left. I can set something up for you out there immediately. I already have a few people that you can link up with and you can take it from there. With Pelpa gone I've been losing out on a lot of money."

"No need to worry about that any longer. I'll make it happen for you. I owe you big time. Thank you."

"You don't owe me anything but your loyalty, Semaj. With that I'm paid in full," Valentina stated with sincerity. "Everything will be set up for you upon arrival from housing to transportation."

"Again, thanks for everything and I'll be in touch." She said before hanging up and then turned to her cousins. "Don't just stare mu'fuckas. Get yourselves together we got a plane to catch. It's time to see what some of these British *pounds* be looking like, baby."

London, England

Quasim sat at his office desk that overlooked his nightspot Club America and dragged from a thin cigar. He'd accomplished a lot in the Kingdom, seeing more money than he had ever seen in all of his days of hustling back home. No one other than Quasim had come to town and taken over like he had. His confiscation of territory had been an easy one, especially with his man Nasah

wiping out everyone who resisted partnership, although little to none refused his business proposition. It was too good an offer to turn down and the Londoners were hungry. The British dopeboys dug his hustling strategy, because they had been small time balling until Quasim brought a hustle across the globe that had them eating good.

Quasim arose and walked over to the picturesque glass front window where he could see all of the activity of his upscale club. Quasim had to admit, he was even impressed at how immaculate that place was. The floors were made of white marble, and the walls were made of white porcelain which gave the feel of being on a cloud. But even with Quasim possessing everything in the world a man could want—money, power, respect, it held no value because he wanted the woman. It all meant nothing without Semaj sharing it with him.

She had said that she'd hit him up, but hadn't and for some reason he felt that she wouldn't. It was a blow to his heart. *I thought we was gonna try again, this time slow,* Quasim thought. But Semaj was gone again, and from where he was he felt as if he'd never see her again until she unknowingly walked through his club's door and—

Semaj, Emilia and Sosa led the way as they entered the nightclub, the remaining Milano Hitters behind them. The rest of Semaj's entourage was bodyguards. The girls walked over to the reserved VIP booth solely sectioned off for them.

"This mu'fucka a'ight. Looks like some shit back home for real," Sosa said as she leaned to whisper into Semaj's ear and followed behind the club's escorts that led them to their private booths. The tables were filled with bottles of champagne and the girls sat down at the booth in the corner and waited on the man Semaj was there to see. They had to make sure that they had a clear view of the club, so they were aware of their surroundings.

Semaj sat back watching as most of the women in the club flocked toward the door. She laughed, remembering the days when

she sought ballers, and already had a feeling that the women were waiting on the kid that she was there to discuss business with.

"You looking hard. Thought the trip wasn't about that nigga?" Semaj teased as she sipped on the bottled water. "I see you squinting your eyes and shit."

Sosa smacked her lips, and a beam of guilt spread across her face. Her cheeks flushed and her mocha skin looked as if it had been kissed by roses.

"Bitch trying to play like she ain't checking for the nigga. I know this shit is business but, him being in charge is just an added perk for your 'lil hot ass!" Semaj laughed as she nodded her head to the beat and watched as the man approached them.

Nasah wasn't the flashy type dude and didn't rock any jewels, leaving his boyish features and laid back demeanor mysterious. His under the radar appearance would have the average eye never guessing his role, but gangster recognize gangster and that's what Nasah was.

Nasah formed a slight smirk when he saw Sosa surrounded by her girls. He grabbed a bottle of champagne from the moving waitress before approaching their table. He was actually shocked to see her. "So, you really are the Sosa to see huh?" he said excitedly in a thick Cockney accent.

"Nah, I told you I'm me," she said sassy but sexily. "This is my people. She's the one you'll be dealing with. If you cross her then I'd be the one you'll deal with. Feel me?" Her voice even and serious. "This is my cousin, Semaj Milano," she said as she waved her hand toward her cousin. They often introduced Semaj by the family's surname to avoid any confusion.

Nasah kissed Semaj's hand respectfully and then said bluntly, "My man might wanna wife you. Not cop from you," he acknowledged, taking in her feminine allure with a touch of coldness that would make any true hustler want her on his team. Nasah had known about some of the situations Quasim had back in the States, but without names he barely knew a thing. Quasim

was careful with what he shared with anyone. Although he fully trusted Nasah, he didn't want to chance being discovered, so he kept many things to himself. Nasah was almost certain that his man would be checking for the half-Dominican beauty though. "My people will escort you upstairs to discuss business," Nasah told her.

"I thought I'll be rapping with you. 'Sup with this other shit?" Semaj asked with skepticism.

He laughed lightly, liking how she cut through the bullshit and got straight to the point. "I'm the one who controls pick-ups and our turf. Who you're about to meet handles the connections. Don't worry, you'll get along with him fine. That nigga don't trust a soul either. So I know y'all will get along perfectly." Semaj nodded and he said, "Joell shoot her upstairs to the boss."

What is she doing here, Quasim thought completely surprised, as his eyes followed Semaj to the VIP section in the rear of the club. Disappointment crossed his face as he attempted to keep his sights on her. He could barely see the incomings and outgoings because they were placed in an area so far back. He was straining his vision. *This plug needs to come the fuck on, so I can search for baby girl. Fuck taking this mu'fucka so long,* he thought impatiently as he checked the time every other second.

Quasim's goon lightly knocked on his door but it had gone unheard because he had been so focused on keeping his eyes on the section Semaj was in, but had no idea she had slipped from his view only to be walking into his office. "Your party has arrived," Joell said as he ushered Semaj inside. She took a seat on the opposite side of the executive desk.

Her potential buyer stood behind the plush leather chair

with his back turned toward her as he stared through the glass front. The smoke from his cigar danced in the air, annoying the hell out of Semaj. *Fuck this nigga think I am? Trying to get down to business and he probably eyeing these hoes. The Nasah nigga gotta be mad bugging to think I'ma get with this dude. Never mix business with pleasure,* she thought to herself. It was as if she'd eaten her words and chocked on them when Quasim turned around to face her.

Semaj looked at him and was at a loss for words. She couldn't believe it. Here she had tried to erase all memories and escape every thought of Quasim only to be across the country and run into him. She sucked in air as she prepared an explanation, but stared at him unable to find the right words to say. The chemistry between their gaze was magnetic. She was so struck she had forgotten to exhale, leaving her chest swelled.

Finally she was able to speak and said, "I'm so sorry that I haven't gotten back to you, Quasim. I have every intention of setting up that meeting with you and Gio. Maybe I was taking my time, because I wasn't ready to talk to you about us." Semaj turned away for a second feeling herself getting weak as her eyes got lost in Quasim's stare. "You know as deep as our feelings run for each other, it'll never work between us. Our love is forbidden."

Quasim stood there with a vacant gaze in his eyes. Semaj usually had the ability to read Quasim, but this time she was unsure what he was thinking which made her want to put her guard up, but as ruthless as Semaj had become her soul was still soft for Quasim. "Don't tell me you involved in the family business," he finally said breaking his silence. "Please, tell me this is some sick joke you're playing, right?"

Semaj shook her head no, implying that she was the head of the Milano family business without actually having to say it. He already knew. It was obvious and there was no way to hide it. Both of his hands shot to his head as he shook it from side to side. "This life is not for you, Maj."

"This what I'm on now, Qua. This is all I know. Life has

fucked me over so many times. Every time I tried to do right, fate came through and let me know the joke is on me. Over and over, I lost the people I love most. My mother, my father, my auntie… my…*my son* and then my husband. He backstabbed me for this same shit, Qua. So I understand what you mean, but there is no other way for me to live. This is all I've known for a long time. I've learned to accept the good and the bad as it comes."

"You deserve better than this shit," he said, his eyes filled with sadness.

"There isn't a better life in the cards for me. I don't know if it's crazy, but I love this life. I love the power. I love how it makes me feel. I can't lie to you. That's why I said I learned to take the good with the bad and when my day comes that they put me in the dirt I just hope they bury me a real bitch."

"You think living this life make you a real bitch? You can't be serious," he stated, his head shaking from side to side.

"Yes I am serious. This is who I have become now, Quasim," Semaj replied truthfully.

"You have to get out. Your grandfather will let you walk away. You had so much potential. I can make a few phone calls to Al-B and you can get back into the movie world. You have options. Promise me you're going to walk away. I can't knowingly let you lead a life of self-destruction. This is a man's game. You gotta get out."

"I just can't," Semaj admitted. "In this world you come in on your feet but you leave out in a coffin. Me personally, wouldn't have it no other way. I breathe for the mob. This is my life," she quoted her mother. "This me Qua. I can't change that."

"Baby girl, this ain't a Scarface movie. The director can't yell cut and stop that bullet from putting you six feet under. You ready to die for this shit? Huh? When you in this life, everyday death is knocking on your door, quote that shit."

"I hear everything you saying, Quasim, but I'm good with my decision. I don't want to die, but I ain't scared of it no more.

Burying your child will do that to you. The Semaj you knew doesn't exist anymore…she's dead. She died when she had to bury her son. This mob shit is what breathed life back into me. It gave me a reason to live again. I'm alive because I am the Mafia Princess."

Quasim had to admit to himself that the Semaj he fell in love with no longer existed. She was now simply a memory that he would have to hold on to. The woman standing before him was void of any innocence and not a drop of remorse ran through her blood. It was actually a tragic sight. Semaj was in too deep. There was no doubt in his mind that she would ride-or-die for the family business.

Quasim had wanted better for her. He had never planned on leaving the game, but when Semaj entered his life it made him want to change his ways for the better. He wanted to give her a better life. Seeing how fucked up it had been, Quasim decided to leave his lifestyle behind and marry the woman of his dreams. For her only, Quasim was willing to let it all go. Their future had seemed so bright back then, and visions of her becoming a top actress flooded his brain and him as a legitimate business man crept in his mind. It would have been so perfect, so beautiful and a happy ending. But that all changed when fate had forced them apart and Quasim learned she was partly responsible for the death of his father.

Even with that information Quasim still believed that there was a chance they could start over and make it work. But now he realized that Semaj had fully transitioned into a woman creating her own life. She was the Milano Princess and rocked hard with the Milano Hitters and he could only imagine the deadly combination. With Gio having no sons left, and no longer directly involved in the game, it was inevitable that Semaj would eventually step up. Her mother had, and unlike the golden years of the mafia, the wives and daughters weren't just playing the back. Many had become implicated in the mob business.

Despite what she had become, it didn't make Quasim love her any less. She was no longer the misguided young girl that he

needed to mold. She had become a powerful businesswoman.

"Semaj, I can't judge you on anything that you do. I understand that you're not supposed to speak about it and I'll never question you on your family business. If this is the life you've chosen then so be it. But damn this shit crazy," he said, still taken aback by her presence.

"'What's crazy, me being your new connect?" She joked, but it was obvious that it was the truth.

"So basically you telling me the deal is a go?"

"Don't worry Qua. I'll have a talk with my grandfather soon enough. That problem of yours won't even exist here soon."

"You got it like that now huh, big shot?" he teased as they exchanged pleasant smiles. Quasim still had the ability to melt her heart with just his smile and his intoxicating scent hadn't changed either. When Quasim stepped forward and kissed Semaj gently she couldn't resist him. So she kissed him back.

"Do you think we should try this thing again? I want us to fall in love like we did before," he said in between their lips touching.

"Even when I was married I still loved you. I've never stopped loving you," she confessed. "Since the day we met I've fell in love with you and haven't fallen out. I…I just…I just was too weak to be alone. I thought you were dead and I needed someone to love me, so that eventually our love could fade away someday. That day never came. But now you are here. I'm here. We're here together," she whispered, knowing that there was no way that she could be without him.

"I'ma always be here, Semaj. I'll never leave you and if I do I'll always come back for you," he replied. "I'm here forever. I wanna take care of you forever if you allow me to. You gon' let me take care of you?"

Semaj smiled and said, "Now *Quasim Santana* you knew the answer before you asked. You know I want you to take care of me."

Quasim smiled, laughed and then said, "I don't know what I'm tripping on saying that bullshit. Shit, from how you moving

looks like you gon' be taking care of me."

Semaj jerked her head back ghetto-girl style, and replied, "Ha…ha…ha, real funny, nigga. Don't play, because you know I know you, my nigga. You bossed-up running clubs and probably all kind of other businesses. Plus, you the biggest *street* boss I done seen thus far. So I know ya paper mad long, B." Her strong Brooklyn accent thickened and she laughed. "So don't even act like you ain't caking. Fuck around and have double what I got, my man." Semaj entwined her arms with his and they walked out of the office. Semaj told her bodyguards she was good and instructed them to let her cousins know she was in safe hands. She decided to keep their relationship under wraps until she told her grandfather, knowing the Milano Hitters kept him in the loop about everything.

"You know I really trust you because it ain't too often I'm without my goons." Semaj said as Quasim led her through the rear exit of the club where his Benz awaited. A matching one was parked directly behind his.

"You know your boy don't leave the house without 'em either," Quasim reminded her as he opened her door. "You know ain't shit changed but the country we in." He shut the door and made his way around the car.

Semaj was silent as Quasim held her hand as he navigated his whip through his City. She watched the city streets pass by. Unlike her last visit to London, Semaj didn't feel weird in the foreign setting and immediately recognized why her feelings had been all over the place. Someone she had cared about unconditionally was there and her soul was crying out to her. This was real love. When you could feel it inside without even knowing. The old adage that two who are close in heart and mind the miles that separate them are no more than inches, was more than true, because their love hadn't wavered.

When they pulled onto the grounds of the mini mansion, and the private gate opened, Semaj got out of the car and stared up at the old Tuscan Renaissance styled house. It was beautiful but

small for him; and although she knew he had more than one crib, Semaj just had to shoot jokes. "Yeah, man, you may be right babe. I just might be the one taking care of you with this little ass shack. Shocking, because you used to have the biggest shits on the block my dude," she cracked up.

"Well, you just ought to get used to it because it's your home too," Quasim grabbed her hand and led her inside his home. She couldn't front his crib fit her style perfectly, and at that moment Semaj realized that they were more alike than she knew.

That night Semaj kept Quasim up all night, just talking about everything with an exception of leaving out confidential information about the mob, but Quasim adored her even more because she wasn't loose at the lips. He knew she loved him and Semaj knew he loved her back. Their conversation got intense when they started talking about them, but Semaj needed this. She wanted to make sure this was what he really wanted despite what she had done to him. She refused to have another fake nigga as her partner in any form. Quasim reassured her that he was the realest nigga in it, and that as long as she did her part as his woman, he would rock with her forever.

"I'ma always hold you down," he assured her.

Semaj felt so close to Quasim, and believed every word that he said. She was happy that they were finally at a place that there were no lies between them. He had her mind, her heart, and soul and Semaj knew they were in it for life. He was her best friend. As long as they were together Semaj would be happy.

They had stayed up all night discussing everything, and as the sun rose they lay in bed snuggled together and they both were too excited to sleep. It was 7AM when they finally stopped talking. The purple and orange hues that blended with the morning skies had finally calmed them, and before Semaj knew it Quasim had fallen fast asleep. She kissed his lips and closed her eyes as she thanked God for his blessing of allowing her to find her way back to her lost love.

Chapter 19

Semaj and Quasim had spent an entire week locked up inside in his crib becoming reacquainted. They had seen no one but each other, and were getting that old thing back. Quasim was a true homebody but Semaj didn't mind. Day to day, they were rebuilding their relationship, this time the foundation would be solid and unbreakable. Semaj had actually missed the fact of being out of sight and out of mind, and appreciated it. It reminded her when they used to cuddle up on their spare time and watch movies back-to-back in the home theatre. With Quasim, Semaj didn't need the excitement of the outside world in her life, and realized that if they ever had to be confined to a home as long as they were together she was with it.

Quasim was happy that love was back in his life and found himself even deeper in love with her. She had grown into a different woman and this go around they could learn from each other's mistakes. She was less submissive now though, and not at all intimidated by him, but he found her feistiness and bossy attitude cute. She was no longer a pushover and would argue him down until he waved his white flags; but Quasim liked her strong will. He admired how she stood up to him. He was intrigued by it and never wanted her to hold anything back from him because he respected real shit.

He felt as if their love was unmatched. She would forever be his queen…his leading lady…his homie…his other half…his

confidante…and even his adversary sometimes, but Semaj was his. Unapologetically they loved each other. Their connection was undying. It was one that only they could understand, because only they had been on the rocky journey. London was a city to adventure, and in the seclusion of Quasim's home they had made a passage through each other souls as they became one, night after night. The time flew by so quickly that they didn't want to part ways, but as they sat at the airport's landing strip they both knew that they had to.

"This past week has been great, Qua. Thank you for even being willing to take me back. For taking me as I am," she whispered.

"You ain't gotta keep thanking me. You're the only woman that has been able to teach me how to love."

"And, you've taught me the real meaning of true love. I'll always be thankful for that. I can't imagine my life without you in it now."

"You'll never have to because I'ma always be in the picture, Maj. Even if I'm way in the back and you can only see my shoes I'ma walk through life with you until you all gray and old looking," he laughed.

"Nigga!" she swiveled her neck. "I ain't gon' ever be gray and old looking. I'ma stay dyeing my shit and Botox is something magical in today's world," she chuckled.

"You ain't gone even need that. Your beauty is ageless and even if it wasn't I ain't tripping. I love you more than for your beauty and booty," he said sweetly with a charming smile. "But it is an added perk, though," he gently pinched her cheek. "I'm just bullshitting with you," he sighed, hating to see her go. "Damn, I hate that you leaving so soon."

"I'll be back. I'ma always come back to you," Semaj assured him as she watched the town car pull up at the bottom of the jet's boarding steps. "Ooh, I knew Sosa was feeling Nasah. Her 'ole stunting ass." Semaj cracked up, watching Nasah open up the car door for her and walk to the trunk to remove her luggage.

"Looks like I ain't gon' be the only one spending a lot of my time in London."

"He really feeling *shorty*. Got my man's opening doors and shit. That's uncharacteristic for that nigga. True story." He chuckled and then kissed Semaj on her forehead. "I know you got to be going though. I'ma be waiting on you when you get back. You said seven days, right?"

"Yup, one week. I'ma holla at my grandfather and then we gonna fly back out so y'all can have a heart-to-heart. Gio really had mad love for you and respected you. And my Poppa don't respect niggas," Semaj said straightforwardly.

"You know I already know," he replied, kissing her on the back of her wrist. "I'll see you soon." He leaned over, grabbed the door handle and opened it from the inside, seeing that he was still a secret for right now. "Semaj," he called after her and she turned around before walking away. "I'ma be waiting for you. I'ma always wait for you, Maj." She smiled, nodded, and closed the door. He watched as she climbed the steps and took her seat at the window. Quasim laughed lightheartedly when he saw Semaj *wave* at him, knowing she knew that he'd be looking, and then finally pulled away with his goon following behind him.

Semaj awoke to someone nudging her arm. She squirmed and it took her a minute to adjust her vision so that she could see. "Y'all bitches was all booed up when the rest of us was scoping the town out. Now you wanna be sleep. Get up, playtime is over bitches," Emilia shouted amped, as she lifted the shades up welcoming the sunlight. "The plane lands in another five minutes."

"Girl, I'm sleepy. Gone!" Sosa whispered groggily as she put the pillow over her face.

"Well, I'm up now. That loud ass talking you doing got me all the way up," Semaj said as she stretched her arms wide. "What

'sup?"

"Nah, what's up with you is the question? Rushing us off the phone lines, giving us the "fuck you" button most of the time only to shoot us a text to let us know everything fine. Dude got you hooked like a fish," Marcela said.

"Clasped on tightly and its unleashing baby," she replied excitedly.

"You a fucking retard," Sosa laughed, eyes closed, still half sleep.

"You really feeling this guy huh, Maj?" Marcela asked. "I guess he must be something, getting you whipped doing the first meeting. I heard the dude Nasah run their city so if he's bigger than him he on a level close to you, huh?"

"Yeah, his money long. Thing is he built his shit from the ground up. Started from the cellar now he on the top floor," she bragged, quoting a rapper. A beam stretched across her face. "Y'all a meet him. Y'all a meet him real soon."

"Got you smiling from ear-to-ear dude must be special," LuLu said. "I ain't seen you this happy in forever."

"Only if you bitches knew. He's always going to be special to me and happy would be an understatement." Semaj said as she watched the stewardess gather their belongings as the plane descended on the ground. Semaj stared out of the window and saw her grandfather waiting on her. Her brow rose in question at the sight of him leaning against the last limousine with his hands tucked inside his slacks. *What is he doing here and why is he looking like that? Oh my God? Do he know about Qua? Please don't let him know! Finding out on his own wouldn't be good for us.* She grabbed her bags and stepped off of the jet in a hurry.

"Greetings, Semaj," her driver said as he removed the bags from her hands.

"Hey." She replied quickly and rushed over to her grandfather. "Hello, Poppa. I'm surprised to see you."

"I'm afraid we have a problem. I've just received a call that Ox is no longer at the hospital in a coma."

"That's good news right? Now he can get tortured and we can feed him to the alligators and move on from this finally."

"I'm sorry, but he is not at the hospital, period. A woman posing as the leader of some medical researcher group showed up and by the time anyone noticed it she was gone and so was Ox. The men guarding his room were all dead."

Semaj dropped her head in disbelief. She just knew this problem had been snuffed out but now it appeared as if it had sparked light again. "Who was in charge of security?"

"You don't have to worry about that, I already handled it. All of them are dead," Gio stated, heartlessly. "But there was a note left inside the room."

"What kind of note?" she frowned in concern.

"A note addressed to you."

"To me? What did it say?" She asked but instead of responding, Gio handed her the written message.

I KNOW WHAT YOU DID and IM COMING FOR YOU. YOU WILL PAY SEMAJ RICHARDSON

XOXO

Just then, Emilia walked behind her and read the note as she stood over her shoulders. "Fuck is this?"

"I don't know. Get some people on the phone. Have them run the tapes back at the hospital," she turned to Sosa. "Did you ever handle that shit with ole girl twin sister?"

"We've been searching for the bitch. Can't find the hoe nowhere. Our people still on it as we speak."

"Put more people on it," Semaj ordered aggressively. "I got a bad feeling about this and I wanna make sure all my possible enemies are handled. See who is behind this and when you do bring 'em to me." She walked to the limo with her pencil-thin heels stabbing the dry pavement; she slid in the backseat as she pulled out her cell phone to dial Quasim. He answered on the first ring.

"Babe, we're going to hold off on the meet-and-greet. Shit just got hectic and we have to wait. I don't know when the time will be right but I know it's not now or anytime soon. I love you and I'll call you later."

"Semaj, what is going on? Is everything a'ight?" he asked as he clenched the phone so tightly in anger, it could almost break. He could hear it in her voice that something was wrong. It was as if he could feel the worry from her shaky voice.

"You know there is certain stuff I can't talk about," she explained. "But I have to go. I promise to stay in touch to let you know I'm good at all times." She quickly hung up the phone, because she knew if she hadn't it would only break her down. He was her weak spot. She couldn't think about Quasim right now. She was in another war and anyone outside of their circle would be a distraction. She couldn't afford that, there was no room for it. One day she hoped Gio would welcome Quasim back in like a son and then she'd tell Quasim the whole story, but until then she had to keep him at a distance. *I have to be focus. See who is behind the shit at the hospital. Definitely gotta be someone with Ox. But why single me out from everybody else?* She asked herself as she stared out the window in deep contemplation. She thought of everyone she had ever crossed, but with all the destruction she left in her path, there wasn't any telling who was gunning for her head.

17 Days Later

Ox lay in the hospital bed and hadn't even been awake from his coma for more than forty-eight hours, but that hadn't stopped him from complaining. Paris had pulled some helleva tricks out of the bag on this one. Once word spread through the street grapevine that the Dominican mafia was holding Ox at their private hospital, she set the game plan in motion. Ox had a few good connections

in the States and with the bond they had established over the years, he had hipped Paris on to them. With a simple well executed plan, she had pulled Ox out of the Milano family's deadly clutches and the ball was back in their court.

"Me have ta be outta here as soon as possible. De sooner dem will release me, de sooner me put somet'ing together and hit de Dominicans harder den de could ha've ever imagined. De brought heat ta me parade. Nyala could have been hurt. Me baby girl could have been killed. Me is done playing tit for tat with 'dese slick-haired bumbaclots," Ox said weakly, but his tone was lethal. After rescuing Ox, Paris had arranged for him to be transported to a South Florida hospital. He had a small drug turf out of Little Haiti, so she knew it was all good and made sure they placed him on the top floor under an assumed name.

"Nyala is cool. Since your nanny is British, and she's from England I sent them over there for six months because I know things are about to get out of hand. I know she's your angel so I put them up in a nice safe spot."

"T'ank you, Paris. Me really appreciate what you did for me baby girl. Me will get dem all dis time. Me plan ta murder dem all in one spot, in one night. De perfect night," he said determinedly. "I'm tired. By de time me wake up make sure de physicians have me paperwork ready ta sign fo' me release. Me ha've a lot of t'ings to get in order. Me have ta strike back harder dis time. Me want dem all dead."

"I got you. Rest up, tough guy," Paris said as she bent over and kissed him lightly on the forehead. "Don't worry about it. These mu'fuckas gon' feel us, believe that."

"You have no idea what me ha've in mind ta takedown de Dominican mafia. But it will be like no other. Crazy t'ing, dem bumbaclots won't even see it coming."

The End of the Year
Three Months Later,

New Year's Eve...Times Square

Bachata music played in the background as Semaj stared out the floor length window. Despite the wintry conditions the people took up blocks of the New York City streets to witness the ball drop and enjoy the celebrations of a new year. It was the perfect time to paint the town red and not exclusively, because it was Semaj's birthday, but the charges against Bonjo had been dismissed. Semaj invited all of their organization's Chiefs to come celebrate with them, and the following day she planned to call a meeting at her residence where secrecy and security was assured.

The Chiefs had pledged their allegiance to her out of love and loyalty to the Family and like no other leader of the Milano family, in return, Semaj had silver Caran d'Ache lighters waiting on them. Every prominent rank in the organization would have their own personalized flickers. From silver to the diamond lighters, whoever had one was of great value to the Family. They had help her build something great and Semaj wanted to show her gratitude.

Semaj was running the busiest and most lucrative drug cartel that North America had seen in decades, and it didn't take long for her family to become the biggest importer and distributor in the country. With Semaj in position she took no prisoners as she reigned over the Milano Empire, but with all good comes bad.

It was as if the Jamaicans had fallen from the earth and her people couldn't find Ox anywhere. He hadn't been spotted in months, but the Milano Family was determined to track him down and they had men in Jamaica. *The sooner we get Ox the sooner I can fix this Qua and Gio issue.*

Scanning the front entrance of the hotel, Semaj noticed the Dominican henchman posed as policemen patrolling the area. She was on the third-level of the penthouse suite, which overlooked the second-level. On the opposite side was the main floor. A gargantuan round fish tank was erected in the center. It was filled with miniature sharks swimming through the deep blue sea-like

water, accentuating the midnight marble floors and highlighting the palettes of blues gracing the walls. Single standing, two-sided mirrors decorated the large foyer. The silver fixtures and stainless steel wrought-columns were nothing short of splendor. Diverting her gaze, Semaj turned her back toward the window, and scrutinized armed goons walking in couples on both lower level floors.

Sauntering over to the iron railing, Semaj looked below and noticed Sosa on the sofa by the door with a sad look on her face. She knew it was because it was that time of year for her. But Sosa's solemn mood didn't stop her from being on top of her job. She noticed the light from the sign on the door flashed "open me" and Semaj watched as Sosa grabbed her pistol and tipped her toes to see who was behind the frame.

Semaj heart started to gallop in uncertainty as the concierge carried in about four white boxes and set them beside the door. Five other hotel workers followed behind her and stacked the rest of the boxes on top. Semaj was curious to know what was in the boxes and was already strolling toward a reseated Sosa in the foyer.

"'Sup ma?" What's all this?" she asked as she snatched the taped down envelope on the top box and placed it on the end table. She didn't bother to read it and tore the box open with urgency only to find a white vase with red roses spilling over. Something wasn't right, and she could feel it. She ripped through the next eight boxes, discovering the same thing and finally decided to read over the card that had been attached.

To a very beautiful woman, Happy Birthday and may you have many many more to come. I have another surprise for you at midnight—

Her hardened expression softened and a blushful smile crossed her face as she sighed in relief. *Aww, my Qua is so sweet,* she smiled. "Man, I'm too paranoid. We got way too much security detail for anything to go down. I be buggin'," Semaj chuckled. "I need to chill and enjoy my birthday before it's time to get back to the money."

"Straight up. Your ass thinks everybody is out to get you," Sosa exclaimed, laughing for the first time in over a week. "You be tripping mad hard, Maj. That's something Gio would've done."

"Girl, tell me about it. This shit got my nerves stupid bad." Semaj said and looked at her vintage Rolex watch, "We got thirty minutes until the new year fool. Let's head downstairs and get this shit poppin'. This laid back ass music got me low in my spirits."

"You? Thought I was the only one. 'Bout to have them turn this mu'fucka up with some Jeezy or Yo Gotti. Fuck this Hosea Martino bullshit. That cocaine music and thug motivation series shit go dumb hard. The dumb way."

Semaj burst out in a fit of laughter, near tears. "Sosa, you are a damn fool. I promise you are dumb. You be cracking me up and if I didn't know you I would swear you was from somebody damn 'hood throwing up clique and gang signs." They were rolling.

Once the joking subsided, Semaj and Sosa made their way down the courtyard-styled stairs where everyone was. The party was live and with crystal flute glasses in their hands, their bodies winding and the beat thumping, they were enjoying themselves. Semaj looked around, relishing in all of the power that she and her family had.

"I'm glad you could get Sosa out of her 'lil funk," Emilia yelled over the music. "Seems like every year around this time she be wanting to be by herself. I'm starting to think that she ain't into the whole New Year, party thing."

"She just misses y'all Poppa. That's all it is, Emilia," Semaj said covering for her. "I get down like this at times also, missing the people I lost too. There's nothing for you to worry about. Some of us just deal with shit differently, ya know?"

Semaj felt a hand on her back. It was Bonjo.

"Can I have this dance, beautiful," he asked as the music switched back to Bachata and a laid back number played.

"Sure Uncle Bonjo," she smiled, accepting his hand graciously. They began to dance. Semaj was thankful to have him home. "I'm

sorry for letting that rat into our family. I'm just glad we were able to find out before it was too late. Before he dismantled this entire family."

"With the way you move, Maj, you got everything under control, baby. And if you don't, you know who got yo' back," Bonjo replied. "Gio will forever make sure you straight and protected. You ain't caught on to his new tactic for you, huh? Look." He pointed across the room where a girl chatted with Jah-Jah by the window. She was dressed in a cream one-shoulder chiffon dress with brown rosette corsage detail and brown ankle boots. "He had Jah-Jah on this for a minute and finally she found the perfect match. He said you need this every time you are in a public setting. I agree."

Semaj looked at the woman oddly, noticing something strange. More than half of her face was draped with soft curls and the rest of her hair pulled around into a sophisticated bun. From her head to her toes she was almost identical to Semaj and her role became obvious. Semaj grinned when she noticed her lookalike was missing the one-of-a-kind necklace she wore. It was the one Quasim had got her. "She's a decoy for the enemy. At first glance you'd think she's you."

"Poppa is so over the top sometimes. I thought I could be extra. This nigga just takes the fucking cake though." Semaj chuckled and looked at the clock on the wall. It was 11:55. "Oh, shit, it's almost time for the countdown, Uncle Bon."

As Paris stood on the rooftop of Semaj's hotel, her finger itched to press the red button on the detonator she held. She was the one that had sent flower arrangements to the front desk an hour earlier. But little did anyone know C4 dynamites had been placed in the bottom box. Paris knew what she was up against and it took them months to plan the perfect hit. *This time, this bitch gotta go. I'm tired of playing with her now.*

Quiet, but urgent footsteps resounded in her ear as she watched armored Jamaican snipers run across the pavement and line the edge of the rooftop with assault rifles in their hands. She had an army of shottas on the floor below Semaj's suite waiting on her to give the "green light". From past experiences Paris had learned that coming at the Dominicans with anything less than her A-game was pointless, but tonight she came more on point than ever before. *This bitch gon' die tonight.*

Boom! Boom! Boom!

The explosives from the fireworks show sounded off and laser lights illuminated, flashing the night skies. Balloons floated upward that the people on ground held while confetti danced and swirled around in the air in complete bliss unprepared for the pandemonium that was about to ensue.

"Somebody turn off them lights," Semaj shouted loudly with a bottle of Rosé in her hand. "Everybody grab your people and a glass of champagne and let's count it down." The room fell dim but, the sparklers gave the large space a glow. "To a new day, a new year, a new era."

"Ten, nine, eight, seven, six, five, four, three, two, one— Happy New Year!" the crowd erupted but the sound of bombs exploding rang concurrently and caused everyone to run in a frenzy. The red beams dancing on the walls and then the sounds of glass shattering confirmed that this was a hit on them. Endless bullets came flying through the glass. The girls dropped to the floor and reached for their weapons as the military bullets rained. In that instant the first floor door crashed to the ground as trained shooters knocked it off the hinges and came in, guns blazing. The sound of explosives and machine guns filled the air, and the suite became an instant battleground.

"These muthafuckas shooting from on top of the building

across the street too!" Emilia yelled as she racked the automatic AK in unison with her sisters. "Don't let none of these muthafuckas get through these doors. Kill 'em all!" she commanded. "Sosa, Jah-Jah grab some goons. Y'all get Semaj outta here through the second story door. We right behind y'all." They obliged and ran full speed toward the foyer while Emilia and the rest of them traded shots with the Jamaicans. The Milano crew made a dash for it, all the while never letting up on their targets.

Semaj and Sosa rushed to the second floor and hadn't noticed that was where the explosion had come from. That was until they neared the exit and the overwhelming heat caused them to stumble backwards. Right before their eyes amber-colored flames were in full bloom and there was no way they could get out from this way. "We sure can't walk through fire and there is only one other way outta here. That's on the main floor. Fuck it," Semaj said as she went inside Sosa's shoulder harness and pulled out a machine pistol. *Click! Clack!* She cocked the gun back as Jah-Jah said, "If we gotta die it's going to be in a blaze of glory! Let's get these muthafuckin' faggots."

"These *putas* must thought we don't stay prepared for shit like this. My pussy cums off shit like this you fucking bastards!" screamed LuLu as she continued to fire her weapon endlessly as Ox's men attempted to come upstairs. But before they could reach the bottom step, the Dominicans loaded them up with bullets, dropping them one by one. "Cover me!" LuLu crouched low and hurried to retrieve something that she had hidden behind the couch for occasions like these. It was a shoulder-launched Lau 65-D grenade launcher. She crept over to the glassless window, and then held it over her right shoulder. She fired the missile-like fireball twice and watched as it wiped out every man lining the edge. *Got part of the problem taken care of real fast. Now we gotta kill the rest of these beaded neck fucks,* she thought as she dropped the launcher and ran back to assist her sisters.

"Arghhhh," Marcela shouted as she let her weapon loose.

She was so skilled the second it emptied, she grabbed another gun. She spun back around even quicker, this time with a Mac 10 strategically firing a barrage of bullets as the Jamaicans were still attempting to make their way up the steps. "These sons-of-bitches are fucking endless. They must've sent their whole fucking team to get at us. Fuck?" she was infuriated at their bravery and allowed the sub machine gun to lay them down instantly. *I swear this my last shootout with these unskilled muthafuckas. I'ma make sure I blow Ox's fucking head off personally.* Marcela hadn't noticed the gunman hiding behind the large faux tree below, but wondered where the flying bullets came from as large chunks of the stairway walls collapsed.

Everyone that was coming up was dropping down, but before Marcela could process another thought an unbearable pain shot through her body as she jerked forward. Her mouth fell open in anguish, but no sound came out, only air. Everything around her seemed to be moving in slow motion as she looked over at Bonjo, desperately begging him for help without speaking a word. The gun dropped to her side as her hand fell over her right ear, realizing that she had been shot. She backed out of sight to shield herself from the raining bullets that were whizzing around her head. Enraged Bonjo blazed off, and as he noticed the still tree move, he aimed down at it and immediately filled the hidden gunman up with lead. Not before a bullet had struck Emilia though.

"Aghh!" she screamed dropping the heavy gun as she grabbed her leg in pain. The burning flash of heat terrorized her as the metal ripped through her thigh. That didn't stop her though and she grabbed her piece off her thigh holster and fired, sending bullets sailing. "Now he wanna send some mu'fuckas that really know how to shoot. Fucking maricons!" she grimaced as blood soaked through her trench coat.

Once Bonjo saw that there wasn't a dread head left standing, he rushed over to his two cousins and then looked back at their two remaining henchmen. "Grab them," he ordered. "Get them outta

here. Jah-Jah, Sosa, LuLu, follow them so y'all can keep shooters at bay." The blaze had died out in the foyer due to the sprinkler system, and Sosa noticed it and said, "Y'all let's go out this way," as they ran full speed out of the suite.

"Semaj, come on!" Bonjo grabbed her as he hauled ass, nearly dragging Semaj by her arm. Abruptly, Bonjo's grip slipped and he fell unavoidably through the hole. The explosion had caused the floor to weaken. When the first set crossed over it had depleted the strength even more, and once Bonjo placed the weight of his right leg on the flimsy surface he fell through.

Right before Semaj's eyes he had fell more than twenty feet below. "Oh, my, God! Oh my God, Uncle Bonjo!" she screamed as her hand shot to her mouth in disbelief. She was too afraid to look down and quickly backpedaled out of the space. She damn near jumped out of her skin as she almost tripped over dead bodies. Tears flowed down her cheeks and her limbs trembled as she frantically searched the area. There was no one left alive and she was alone in a room full of lifeless goons. *There is only one way out of here. What if someone is still alive downstairs though*, she thought as her heart was thumping rapidly. It was as if she was having a heart attack. *I have to get out of here. Think! Think!* Semaj spotted a gun in one of the dead men's hand. She grabbed it with one thing on her mind—shoot before getting shot.

The sprinkler system wet Semaj up as she crept down the stairs. Her body shook in chilliness as the fabric of the dress clung to her and her hair stuck to her face. She stepped over dead bodies that sprawled across the stairs and couldn't believe her eyes once she reached the bottom step. It was dark and smoky. The fish tank had been hit and water covered the main floor where dead bodies floated around with the sharks. The putrid smell of death was heavy in the air. Semaj began to cough as the horrible smell robbed her of clean oxygen. Her lungs stung as she shut her eyes and did the only thing she could do; she began to pray.

Flashes of white light snuck through her closed lids causing

her to reopen them in alarm. The front door was gaping now and Semaj noticed a shadow approaching her. She could tell that it was a woman from the hair cascading down her shoulders. "Jah-Jah is that you?" she called out. Her heart jumped with each step the person took. When the face came into clear view, this time Semaj *literally* felt her heart jump out of her chest. She couldn't believe her eyes. *This shit couldn't be real,* she thought as her eyes grew wide in shock and unintentionally she dropped the gun. It was as if she had seen a ghost. It was Paris in the flesh and from the way she glared at her, Semaj realized that the Milano Hitters had failed for the first time on a hit— they had killed the wrong twin and the living sibling was here to settle the score.

The Year of the End

"Well, well, well, if it isn't the golden child all alone," Paris said as she clapped her hands slowly but extremely loud. "Surprise, surprise, surprise, huh?" she asked as she stepped down the three steps, disregarding the things in the water. "Don't look so fucking appalled Semaj."

"What is it that you want, Paris?" Semaj asked.

"Ha!" she scoffed. "I remember all that big girl talk on the phone and I've waited years to see what you were about. Now you all about seeing what I want huh?" She laughed hysterically. "I always knew your bark was much louder than your bite." Paris pulled a .357 Magnum from the small of her back. "You see, I've been here making your life is a living Hell, but I'm coming to grips that I'm bored with it now. I'm sure my brother would say I avenged his death good enough."

Semaj frowned, her brow arched in confusion. "Bitch, you are fucking sick. You went through all that bullshit to make my life a living hell and now you talking 'bout some brother shit. Fuck is you talking about you jealous ass, delusional bitch!"

"Gabe always told me that you were a simple bitch. It was easy to infiltrate your circle and tear that muthafucka up from the inside out." Her words hit Semaj like a ton of bricks. "When I said that you would regret ever trying to shit on me, I meant that shit. Gabe sending me at you was a prelude for a future business move and having Tala shot down had been the perfect setup. But now things are personal and I just had to take everything else you loved—"

This is the sister Gabe was talking about the whole time. He put her on me from the very beginning. This bitch was setting me up that entire time. She befriended me, but was my enemy from the gate.

"Gabe killed my baby he deserved to die!" she argued as the circle-breaker tried to kick in causing eerie squeaking noises and the light to slowly blink on and off. "This was between me and him. Our beef was our beef. That was a baby and he had nothing to do with it."

Paris smiled deviously. "Semaj, you're so fucking pathetic. Does it look like I care about if that raggedy ass baby had anything to do with it? I killed my father and made my mother watch because she allowed him to rape me and my sister and then killed that bitch. Fuck I care about your baby being innocent? You played the tune and I just started to tango to the song. You had my sister killed so I blew your baby up really not giving a fuck. I wished you were in the car, but I found it much more amusing when I watched you grieve."

"You, bitch!" All of the rage that Semaj had bubbled to the surface all at once, "It *was* you at the funeral that day!" she screamed as she completely spazzed out and charged at Paris, her feet flapping through the calf-deep water, but was stopped as Paris pointed the barrel of her gun at Semaj's head.

"Checkmate, bitch! There's no winning with me! Burn in hell with that bastard baby of yours!"

Boom!

Paris sent a bullet sailing at Semaj's head, finally winning the

game of life and death that she had been playing all along. Blood spilled from the side of Semaj's face and into the already rose-colored water. An evil smirk of satisfaction flashed across Paris's face. "Good the bitch is dead!"

Laughing in gratification and smiling in excitement, Paris lowered the gun. She had waited on this day for a long time and finally the day had come. She spit directly in Semaj's face, disrespecting the dead woman. *I spit on your weak ass when you were alive and now when you dead. You just that worthless to me,* she thought.

Paris turned around and looked at the destruction caused on her account. Everything had been destroyed. There were bullet holes throughout the place and blood everywhere, but she wasn't remorseful. That was what the soldiers were for—to get all out of her way just to get that one person. Semaj's death was worth them all. Her glory was short-lived once she heard sirens in the distance.

I gotta get fuck from outta here, but first I'ma fill this bitch up with these bullets.

WHOP!

Before Paris could take a step, Semaj walloped her in the back of her head, sending her flailing in the water.

Semaj had played dead. She had been involved with the mob long enough to know the measures to take in an attempt to survive and outsmart the opposition. She saw the gun, knowing that Paris would shoot her and kept her eye trained on Paris's trigger finger. When Paris's finger repositioned, Semaj slightly moved her head to the side, unnoticed, as the bullet nipped the side of her face and she dropped instantly for good measures.

Paris squealed in pain as she attempted to get on all fours and crawl for a way out. Just as Semaj saw her scoot forward a bit, she forcefully kicked her in her ass. "Bitch, you ain't going nowhere!"

"Fuck!" Paris screamed as her head went flying, banging up against the hard floor.

"Stupid, bitch!" Semaj shouted as she took her leg all the way

back only to kick Paris smack dead in the back of her head. "You just come in my life and fucking ruin everything!" She stomped the back of Paris's head repeatedly.

"You could have fucked with anything else, but my fucking family!" Semaj pressed her foot into Paris's back as she grabbed her long, sodden mane. With everything in Semaj, she banged Paris's face hard and made sure that she met the hardness that was beneath the water. "You should have... stayed... the...fuck ...away...from me!" She shouted.

"You fucking stupid ass bitch come at me, and bring chaos into my life. Bitch everything was 'pose to be about a dollar. You knew that. It was my hustle bitch, a hustle that I turned you on to. Like the rest of the victims, your gullible for pussy ass brother just got caught slipping. It was business, never personal."

"I can accept that y'all hated me for it though and wanted to harm me. But when you killed my son you may as well killed yourself, bitch!" Semaj shouted as she hit Paris over and over again. With every syllable she spoke, she brought Paris's head back and forth like it was a bobble-head and slung Paris's hair every which way, colliding her face with everything hard in sight. For lack of better words—Semaj was fucking Paris up.

"You killed my baby! You set my auntie up! Now I'ma kill you, bitch!"

She delivered her with nothing but head action, and Semaj became so furious she started to pummel Paris's face with her bare hands, hook for hook, right to left and all of her punches were connecting. She hit her so hard that her knuckles had busted open, but she didn't care. Semaj wanted Paris's soul taken.

Semaj loosened Paris from her clutches as she heaved in exhaustion and sweated profusely. Semaj rubbed the side of her face and looked down at her bloody fingertips. Paris had aimed for a headshot that would have sure enough ended Semaj's life, and it left her entire right side ablaze. Tired of bullshitting with the bitch, Semaj picked up a machine pistol by the barrel that had been

floating on surface. It was obvious that Paris wanted to kill her and Semaj definitely wanted the same thing for her. She had done the unthinkable when she blew up the limo her baby had been in, but there was no way that Semaj was about to make the end of her life easy.

Loading her up with these bullets will send that bitch to hell too quick. When she meets the devil I want this bitch bruised and battered the fuck up. This bitch gotta feel me, Semaj thought as she wrapped her hair back into a loose ball. *I'm going to keep beating this bitch's ass until I can't no longer.* Semaj checked to make sure the gun was on safety and walked behind Paris as she weakly dragged herself up the three steps and onto an all concrete floor.

WHACK! WHACK!

Semaj collided the gun with the back of her head with all her might, twice. Paris's head snapped as it jerked forward sharply. Semaj had struck her so hard that Paris felt as if her neck had broken as she chocked and coughed up blood. Stunned and dazed, Paris spit the bloody saliva onto the floor. Seeing all of her blood, Paris was pissed and gathered all of her bearings. Aware that she'd be falling into unconsciousness soon, Paris reached into the pocket of her skin tight jeans to retrieve the bottle of liquid and unscrewed the lid.

SPLASH!

Without warning, Paris had flipped onto her back and threw the sulfuric acid in Semaj's face causing the liquid to come back down on her stomach, burning through her clothes but Paris disregarded the pain because all that mattered was that she got to Semaj's pretty little face.

"Aghh!" Semaj yelled in excruciating pain as she lost all control. She stumbled back, looking at the small container in Paris's hand. "What did you do!" Semaj's hand shot to her face as her skin felt as if it was eating away at her ear and down her neck. "What is this?" she screamed as she brought her fingers to her nose to sniff. There was an odorless smell. Semaj panicked, and her face

felt as if it had been set on fire. She was so focused on the stinging sensation that it gave Paris the chance to gain advantage, and she pulled Semaj down to the ground by her calf. The hard fall gave Paris just enough time to regain her composure and get the upper hand.

"I hope your fucking face burns off," fumed Paris. "See how my brother felt, bitch!"

Paris moaned as she weakly crawled on her knees in search of a loaded weapon. She grabbed an automatic rifle and as she shifted her aim, waving it through the air, Semaj was already on her ass despite the pain.

WHOP!

Semaj had knocked her upside the head in a desperate effort to cause her to release the gun, but Paris wasn't letting up. She had a grip so tight her hands were turning red and hurting from the pressure. Semaj wasn't giving up easily either, and grabbed Paris's wrist and used her on upper position as an advantage as they both struggled for power.

They tussled, flipping each other over, rolling back and forth as they alternated from top to bottom; but all movements came to a slow stop and their eyes darted to the door when black hooded goons came through. Semaj then knew it was over. At that moment, she saw her life flash before her eyes. This was it and her day had come, but what she didn't know was she and Paris shared the same thoughts. *I ain't finna die without a fight,* Paris thought as she wrapped her finger around the trigger and pulled it without hesitation.

Bullets spewed loosely and flew wildly as each shot connected with the single standing mirrors and both their bodies jerked violently with ever slug that discharged. The cracking noises from the frames caused them to look up in fright, but by then the damage had been done. The last thing they saw was mirrors as several came crashing down over them all at once.

Epilogue

The lead homicide detective shook his head as he watched the EMTs load the only breathing body onto the gurney. The crime scene was like none that he had seen in his entire twenty-six years on the job. The bodies found throughout both floors made the crime scene a human slaughterhouse. Familiar with homicide scenes, he knew this was workings of a street war.

"This is a sad, sad way to bring in a new year," he whispered disgusted, as he carefully stepped through all the destruction. The detective knew that the woman was lucky to be living. They had discovered numerous bodies underneath the mirrors and all throughout the suite, but the young lady had been the only fortunate one that came from beneath all the wreckage alive. Everyone else had been D.O.A. Half her body had been trapped underneath the mirror and glass particles had cut into her skin, but she had been a blessed soul. Undoubtedly, her survival was nothing short of a miracle.

Members from the CSI unit had just wrapped up on snapshots and at their access, the coroner's personnel zipped up body bags. Detectives had started to gather the large number of weapons they found and placed them into labeled plastic evidence bags. Homicides were always terrible because most weren't able to accept death at the hands of other, and there was going to be a lot of families hurt, and sadly, a lot of media coverage on the New Year massacre. *The Chief might not even be prepared to explain this to the*

community at the press conference, he thought as he was about to depart, but stopped in his tracks when he heard commotion.

"We have another live one over here!" one of the coroner's personnel announced. He looked back in disbelief and immediately recognized that the man must have fallen through the ceiling. The EMTs raced over and loaded him onto the stretcher preparing to move the victim to the hospital. "He had to have been unconscious from losing so much blood, but there is a pulse. It is a weak one, but nonetheless we have another survivor," the male EMT said pleased to have another one who made it.

The detective nodded at the paramedic as they rushed to transport the other surviving victim to the ambulance and he was quickly on their heels giving orders. As they pushed the gurney down the hallway and stepped onto the empty elevator, the detective said, "Once you get this man to the hospital immediately have the doctors put him under an assumed name and report that name back to the precinct specifically for me. I need to find out what went on tonight."

The man nodded as they exited the elevator and rushed the body out of the automatic doors. Outside was complete pandemonium. Coroner's vans, several medical examiner trucks and patrol cars filled the streets as spectators lined behind the yellow crime scene tape.

As the paramedics prepared to put the body on the back of the ambulance, Jah-Jah broke through the tape again, running full speed in hopes that this time it was Bonjo. Jah-Jah had crippled at the knees when the first gurney came out with a female on there, but was too frantic to recognize the woman. Only face she wanted to see was her husband's. She had been going through it ever since she realized that Bonjo hadn't come out after them. But by the time she noticed, NYPD was already flooding the place and on scene investigators prohibited anyone from going inside.

Please God let this be my husband. He's my everything. He can't die. How would I explain to my daughter that he's dead, Jah-Jah

thought in desperation.

When she saw her husband's bloody head, Jah-Jah felt as if the ground had been taken from beneath her. She fell to her knees, scrapping her kneecaps up. "Oh my God! Please! My husband! Tell me he gon' make it!"

"Get up, Jah," Sosa said as she pulled her onto her feet and turned to the paramedic. "Is he going to live?"

"Hopefully," the EMT replied. "We have to get him over to the hospital, so they can immediately begin surgery. It appears that he had fallen through the ceiling and we need to see if there is any head trauma. Since this is her husband she can ride with us."

Just as she watched Jah-Jah climb onto the back of the ambulance, Sosa spotted Gio racing through the crowd, followed by five bodyguards. *Oh my God! He is about to blow up all of New York if we don't find Semaj alive. Lord Father God, I have never asked you for anything. But I beg that you find some way to allow Semaj to surface.*

"Where is my granddaughter, Sosa?" Gio asked as he approached her with a look that could kill. "They said there were two survivors. Was Semaj one?"

"I don't think so. Jah-Jah saw the girl before they carted her off to the hospital and she didn't say anything about it being Semaj."

At that moment, LuLu ran up with a crazed expression etched to her face. For a minute she didn't speak, but the look Gio possessed reflected hers and LuLu knew he needed an explanation. "All of us are accounted for except for Semaj. I went through all measures and I can't find anything out regarding Semaj." She dropped her head. "Uncle Gio the last place we have to check is the city morgue. I've been told that they have recovered a female body from inside the suite with gunshot wounds to the face and they have already transported the woman to the morgue. Someone needs to come and identify the body."

He clasped his hands together tightly as his cold eyes turned bloodshot red. Gio felt a mixture of indignation and blame pulsating

through him. "What I want to know is how all of you came out of the shooting unscathed and my granddaughter is missing? Missing and better to be found very very soon," Gio said sternly, his strong baritone voice cracking from emotion.

"Marcela and Emilia was shot and Bonjo was inju—"

He cut Sosa off. "Shot, injured and dead is completely different things. If anything has happened to Semaj, all of you are getting a one-way ticket to the Dominican Republic. I never wanna see your fucking faces again!" Gio seethed. "I put her in y'all hands, because I thought it would be the safest, but from how things are looking I've been let down. I made a terrible mistake and I hate that I've trusted you girls with my granddaughter's life," he said cruelly. "If something has happened to Semaj I will never forgive any of you for this." He didn't even bother to stand there and hear their defense. He already knew what had happened but the thought of his grandchild being left to die was too much for him to fathom.

"Gio got me all the way fucked up if he think he gon' send me back to the Dominican Republic. We'll be shooting it out with his goons before I be forced to leave the states. Point-blank, period!" Sosa promised as she felt the nagging tear in her left eye threatening to slip, but she refused to let it fall. "Long as Maj know we did everything in our power to keep her safe that's all that matters," Sosa told herself as she wiped her teary eye.

"You ain't got a muthafuckin reason to shed a tear until they drop that casket in the dirt and then we only mourn for that moment. You know how this shit goes, Sosa," LuLu expressed, her hard nature never wavering. "We've tried our fucking best to protect Semaj and put ourselves on the frontline in order to keep her out of harm's way and this is the thanks we get! Fuck Gio and every muthafuckin' thing he stands for!" She watched Gio get into the back of the limo with hate in her eyes. "If we gotta war with him, too, then so fucking be it. We ain't going nowhere. It is what it is. Fuck Gio!"

Paris slowly opened her heavy eyelids as policemen lifted the weighty mirrors off the lower half of her body. She tried to move her legs but her attempts were futile. The heaviness of it had caused them to spasm up. She felt slightly dizzy from being knocked out as the horrendous smell of death invaded her nose and made her headache worse as they pulled her from the damage.

Please let this bitch be stinking. With all of this damage, she has to be one of the ones, *Paris thought.*

Once she was placed safely on a gurney and the female EMT prepared to push her out, Paris grabbed her by the arms and begged. "Please. My sister was here with me. Could you just hold on a second so I can see if she was able to escape this madness," she managed to say despite the pain in her bottom half.

"I'm not supposed to do that ma'am, so do it as quickly as possible while I strap you in," the female paramedic suggested as she continued her job.

She struggled to lean forward and began searching through the sea of dead bodies with the little strength she still had left in her. Where is she? I hope that bitch wasn't lucky enough to stand it all, *Paris thought. When she got a glimpse of the corpse the men pulled up a slight smile crossed her face. The face appeared as if it had been blown completely off. The face was unrecognizable. Paris knew who it was though. Not from the features but from what Semaj wore. The clothes told it all.* The brown stilettos. I remember them heels. That dress. I remember that rose shit on the dress, *Paris thought as she finally was able to lie back in satisfaction.*

It felt as if the skin on her stomach was frying from the acid burns and her throbbing head was about to explode from the blows she receive, but as long as Semaj hadn't made it through the pain was worth it. Ox must have sent some extra goons through just in case the first set didn't get the job done, *Paris figured them were the henchmen she seen before she blacked out.* Only the workings of Ox, *she grinned as*

she closed her eyes giving in to fatigue.

When Paris came to, she was woozy from the pain medicine nurses had shot through her. Her body was exhausted but Paris felt the feeling back in her legs as she wiggled her toes and then moved her legs up and down. "A bitch felt like she was paralyzed," Paris said and then reality kicked in. Paranoia seeped through her heart as the thought of someone coming to kill her settled in. "I know the Dominicans probably aware that there was a survivor. They'd come looking for me here. That's if they aren't already here. I gotta get the fuck from outta here. I'm on their turf. I ain't scared to die, but I'm not stupid. I ain't built for the torture they'd bestow upon me. Fuck no," Paris crawled out of the hospital bed.

Slipping into the patient paper shoes, Paris tied the hospital-issued gown tight and despite her fragile condition she sprung to the door. All she had to do was get out of the hospital and place a call to the goons she had waiting at the airport for her. *Once I give them a ring they'll be here to get me quick.*

Paris peered cautiously out of the door and saw the nurses manning their daily tasks. She sneakily made her way around the corner and over to the door that led to the stairwell. She didn't want to chance running into any concerned doctors or bumping right into the Dominicans. Just as she pulled the door, Paris spotted two men rounding the corner and then she descended the steps urgently.

As she traveled down the fifth flight she heard a door open, and paused, pressing her back against the wall. She heard a heavy Dominican accent speaking into an apparent earpiece, "Let Gio know that the girl is no longer in her room. Secure all floors and its stairwells." There was a brief pause and then Paris heard, "Tell Gio I'll check one more time but still, you all secure all exits points." The instant the door closed, Paris sprinted down the rest of the

stairs. Finally she reached the bottom floor and peeked her head out. When Paris didn't see anyone, she raced down the hallway, but the sound of heavy and slow footsteps nearing provoked a rare fear and she pulled opened the first door she saw.

An unusual coldness kissed her skin and Paris had no idea that she was walking into the morgue. It didn't take long to realize it though, but she knew that she had to take cover. Gio was coming and he was coming fast, so she hid in the closet.

Gio stepped into the cold room and stared at the bodies lying on the steel tables covered with white sheets. His heart felt as if it would explode in uncertainty. Something inside told him that his granddaughter was lying lifeless beneath the cover. "Just lead me to the table where the female is and leave. I want to be alone." The coroner pointed to the table and departed respectfully.

He walked over as a huge lump formed in his throat. Reluctantly, Gio pulled the cover back, revealing Semaj. Déjà vu smacked him dead in the face. So many years ago he removed the white sheet from his daughter's corpse and now his granddaughter's dead body was lying on the silver table years later. His mind went to another place and he was out of it. Her skin held a blue hue and more than half of her face was blown off. The workings of a shotgun had cleared her of her features. It was Semaj and she was gone.

"I promise baby girl, I will get the bastards that did this to you." He bent down and kissed her bloody cheek. "I will not rest until they're all dead." A solitary tear slipped down his cheek onto hers. It looked as if they were crying together. "I love you, Maj," Gio said before walking out of the room, escorted by his bodyguards who had been waiting just outside the door for him.

To be safe, Paris waited a good ten minutes before she came out of the closet, and fortunately for her she had been in a closet full of white lab coats and medical examiner masks. Dressed as if she was a part of the hospital staff, Paris would be able to leave unnoticed. She would blend in perfectly with the doctors. Just as

she was about to step out of the room, something pulled her to the table Gio had stood at. She just had to see Semaj's dead body. Everything in her tingled and there was no way she would miss an opportunity to see her archenemy dead. She had conquered over Semaj and the body would be confirmation.

All smirks and sneers turned into a look of confusion and disbelief. Paris had noticed something wasn't right. There were no acid burns on her face. *It couldn't just disappear*, Paris thought knowingly. She had put them there. For the first time in a long time, tears came flowing down her cheeks. She knew she had fucked up. *But Ox's goons came and shot her while I was out cold. They had to. Didn't they?*

Little did Paris know the goons that came weren't sent by Ox, but what she did know was evident— the chick on the table wasn't Semaj. The thought caused Paris's heart to pound with fury. Unable to contain her rage she screamed, "Fuuuuucckk!" Paris knew she had fucked up.

As Quasim stood in the spacious room of the air ambulance he removed the black gloves and pulled the hoodie from his head while looming over Semaj. She was cut up badly, bruised and portions of her face were covered with acid burns. Her respiratory system was failing her and she was barely holding onto life. Hardly recognizable, Quasim had only spotted her because of the hallway light that bounced off her iced-out necklace right before the mirrors came crashing down. Undoubtedly if the mirrors hadn't been lifted from her body when they did, she would have died.

Quasim watched as his specialized medical team hooked her up to a ventilator machine and filled her body with IVs as the private jet ascended into the night skies. Every since he had gotten Semaj's frantic call he had been in the States to watch her moves, to make sure she was cool. Her association with the mob put her in

grave danger, and the worry tortured Quasim daily. He had vowed to always protect her, and would chance his own life and freedom to ensure her safety. For the love of his woman, he'd risk everything.

Quasim didn't know who the Milano Family was at war with, but now that Semaj had been severely hurt he intended to find out. Fuck the secrets and codes of the Mafia. Quasim had to find out who was behind the hit. Who had given the "green light" because they definitely had to get it. They had to *go* and Quasim was going through the top man first to make that absolute. He could've easily let Gio's men handle it but with Semaj pulled in the war, Quasim was already putting calls in to get an army of goons together. The Dominicans weren't doing a great job at protecting her, so it was time for him to step up.

Quasim only knew one person where he could get the information he needed, but knew phone calls weren't acceptable and this matter caused for a sit down, however Quasim was unaware that he was headed down to enemy territories. The same man that orchestrated the hit was the same man's guarded residence Quasim was taking Semaj to for refuge.

As he looked at Semaj, the sight of her condition inflicted a fear within him that he didn't even know existed. The skin on half of her face appeared as if it had been sheared off and it was heart wrenching. *I'm going to wipe out an entire zip code behind this one*, he thought as a single tear slipped from its confinement.

All of a sudden the monitor went haywire and began beeping loudly, causing Quasim to rush to get one of the private doctors.

"Sir, you have to let us do our job," one of the nurses instructed. "It appears that we're losing her. Grab the equipment," another said as the doctor placed an oxygen mask over Semaj's face

As Quasim watched them operate on her he grabbed his chest in an attempt to catch some wind. It felt as if he was sharing in the moment with her. His airways were locking up with every breath he took. He prayed and hoped that she would survive. She had to. His sanity depended on it. His life wouldn't be complete without

her. His world would never be the same. Without Semaj, it would be *hell on earth* and Quasim knew that the old adage would become factual for every person ever associated to the people responsible.

Turning to look out the small window, Quasim realized the aircraft was descending upon Ox's landing pad but instead of the overjoyed feeling of having the weight of the world lifted off his shoulders, Quasim now felt the overwhelming weight of two worlds as Semaj's life hung in the balance. He had no clue of the direction God had intended for her, but even if Semaj did pull through her circumstances, the chances of her dying had just heightened as the jumbo jet touched down on the soils of Jamaica Island— the home turf of the malicious devil that started it all…

A KING PRODUCTION

All I See Is The Money...

Female Hustler

A Novel

JOY DEJA KING

Prologue

Nico Carter

"I don't know what you want me to say. I do care about you—"

"But you're still in love with Precious," Lisa said, cutting me off. "I can't deal with this anymore. You're still holding a torch for a woman that has moved on with her life."

"Of course I have love for Precious. We have history and we share a daughter together, but I want to try and make things work with you."

"Oh really, is it because you know Precious

has no intentions of leaving her husband or is it because of the baby?"

"Why are you doing this?" I shrugged.

"Doing what... having a real conversation with you? I don't want to be your second choice, or for you to settle for me because of a baby. Nobody even knows about me. I'm a secret. You keep our relationship hidden like you're ashamed of me or something."

"I'm not ashamed of you. With the business I'm in and the lifestyle I'm in, I try to keep my personal life private. I don't want to make you a target."

"Whatever. I used to believe your excuses, but my eyes have been opened. I'm a lot wiser now. I've played my position for so long, believing that my loyalty would prove I was worthy of your love, but I'm done."

"Lisa stop. Why are you crying," I said, reaching for her hand, but she pulled away. "I was always upfront with you. I never sold you a dream."

"You're right. I sold myself a dream. More like a fairytale. But when I heard you on the phone with Precious that fairytale died and reality kicked in."

"What phone conversation?" I asked, hoping Lisa was bluffing.

"The one where you told Precious she and Aaliyah were the loves of your life and nothing would change that, not even the baby you were having with me. It was obvious that was the first time you had ever even mentioned my name to her."

"Lisa, it wasn't like that," I said, stroking my hand over my face. "You didn't hear or understand the context of the entire conversation." I shook my head; hating Lisa ever heard any of that. "That conversation was over a week ago, why are you just now saying something?"

"Because there was nothing to say. I needed to hear you say those words. I knew what I had to do and I did it."

"So what, you're deciding you don't want to deal with me anymore? It's too late for that. We're having a baby together. You gonna have to deal with me whether you want to or not."

"That's not true."

"Listen, Lisa. I'm sorry you heard what I said to Precious. I know that had to hurt, but again I think you read too much into that. I do care about you."

"Just save it, Nico. You care about me like a puppy," Lisa said sarcastically.

"I get it. Your feelings are hurt and you don't want to have an intimate relationship with me

any longer, I have to respect that. But that doesn't change the fact you're carrying my child and I will be playing an active role in their life so I don't want us to be on bad terms. I want to be here for you and our baby."

"You don't have to worry about that anymore. You're free to pursue Precious and not feel obligated to me."

"It's not an obligation. We made the baby together and we'll take care of our child together."

"Don't you get it, there is no baby."

"Excuse me? Are you saying you lied about being pregnant?"

"No, I was pregnant, but..."

"But what, you had a miscarriage?"

"No I had an abortion."

"You killed my child?"

"No, I aborted mine!"

"That was my child, too."

"Fuck you! Fuck you, Nico! You want to stand there and act like you gave a damn about our baby and me. You're such a hypocrite and a liar."

"You had no right to make a decision like that without discussing it with me."

"I had every right. I heard you on the phone confessing your love to another woman and the child you all share together. Making it seem like our baby and me was some unwanted burden.

Well now you no longer have that burden. Any child I bring into this world deserves better than that."

"You killed my child because of a phone conversation you overheard. You make me sick. I think I actually hate you."

"Now you know how I feel because I hate you too," Lisa spit back with venom in her voice.

"You need to go before you meet the same demise as the baby you murdered."

"No worries, I have no intentions of staying. As a matter of fact, I came to say goodbye. I have no reason to stay in New York."

"You're leaving town?"

"Yes, for good. Like I said, there is nothing here for me. I don't want to be in the same city as you. It would be a constant reminder of all the time I wasted waiting for you," Lisa said, as a single tear trickled down her cheek. "Goodbye, Nico."

I watched with contempt and pain as Lisa walked out the door. I couldn't lie to myself. I almost understood why she chose not to keep our baby. I wasn't in love with Lisa and couldn't see me spending the rest of my life with her. The fucked up part was it had nothing to do with her. Lisa was a good girl, but she was right, my heart still belonged to Precious. But I still hated her for aborting our baby. I guess that made me a selfish

man. I wanted Lisa to bless me with another child that I could be a father to, but have her accept that she would never have my heart.

At this moment, it was all insignificant. That chapter was now closed. Lisa was out of my life. In the process, she took our child with her and for that I would never forgive her.

Seven Months Later...

"Look at her, mommy, she is so beautiful," Lisa said, holding her newborn daughter in the hospital.

"She is beautiful," her mother said, nodding her head. "What are you going to name her?"

"Angel. She's my little Angel." Lisa smiled.

"That's a beautiful name and she is an angel," Lisa's mother said, admiring her granddaughter. "Lisa, are you okay?" she asked, noticing her daughter becoming pale with a pain stricken expression on her face.

"I'm getting a headache, but I'll be fine," Lisa said, trying to shake off the discomfort. "Can you hold Angel for a minute. I need to sit up and catch my breath," Lisa said, handing her baby to her mother.

"I would love to." Her mother smiled, gently

rocking Angel.

"I feel a little nauseated," Lisa said, feeling hot.

"Do you want me to get the nurse?"

"No, just get me some water," Lisa said. Before Lisa's mother even had a chance to reach for a bottle of water, her daughter began to vomit. In a matter of seconds Lisa's arms and legs began jerking. Her entire body seemed to be having convulsions."

"Lisa... Lisa... what's the matter baby!" Lisa's mother said, her voice shaking, filled with fear. "Somebody get a doctor!" she screamed out, running to the door and holding her grandbaby close to her chest. "My daughter needs a doctor. She's sick! Somebody help her please!" she pleaded, yelling out as she held the door wide open.

"Ma'am, please step outside," a nurse said, rushing into Lisa's room with a couple of other nurses behind her and the doctor close behind.

Lisa's mother paced back and forth in front of her daughter's room for what seemed like an eternity. "It's gonna be okay, Angel. Your mother will be fine," she kept saying over and over again to her grandbaby. "You know they say babies are healing, and you healing your grandmother's soul right now," she said softly in Angel's ear.

"Ma'am."

"Yes... is my daughter okay?" she asked rushing towards the doctor.

"Ma'am, your daughter was unconscious then her heart stopped."

"What are you saying?" she questioned as her bottom lip began trembling.

"We did everything we could do, but your daughter didn't make it. I'm sorry."

"No! No! She's so young. She's just a baby herself. How did this happen?"

"I'm not sure, but we're going to do an autopsy. It will take a couple of weeks for the results to get back. It could be a placental abruption and amniotic fluid embolism, or a brain aneurysm, we don't know. Again, I'm sorry. Do you want us to contact the father of your granddaughter?" the doctor asked.

Lisa's mother gazed down at Angel, whose eyes were closed as she slept peacefully in her arms. "I don't know who Angel's father is. That information died with my daughter."

"I understand. Again, I'm sorry about your daughter. Let us know if there is anything we can do for you," the doctor said before walking off.

"I just want to see my daughter and tell her goodbye," she said walking into Lisa's room. "My sweet baby girl. You look so peaceful." Lisa's

mother rubbed her hand across the side of her face. "Don't you worry. I promise I will take care of Angel. I will give her all the love I know you would have. Rest in peace baby girl."

Get Caught Up
On The Entire Bitch Series...

A King Production

ORDER FORM

Name:

Address:

City/State:

Zip:

QUANTITY	TITLES	PRICE	TOTAL
	Bitch	$15.00	
	Bitch Reloaded	$15.00	
	The Bitch Is Back	$15.00	
	Queen Bitch	$15.00	
	Last Bitch Standing	$15.00	
	Superstar	$15.00	
	Ride Wit' Me	$12.00	
	Ride Wit' Me Part 2	$15.00	
	Stackin' Paper	$15.00	
	Trife Life To Lavish	$15.00	
	Trife Life To Lavish II	$15.00	
	Stackin' Paper II	$15.00	
	Rich or Famous	$15.00	
	Rich or Famous Part 2	$15.00	
	Rich or Famous Part 3	$15.00	
	Bitch A New Beginning	$15.00	
	Mafia Princess Part 1	$15.00	
	Mafia Princess Part 2	$15.00	
	Mafia Princess Part 3	$15.00	
	Mafia Princess Part 4	$15.00	
	Mafia Princess Part 5	$15.00	
	Boss Bitch	$15.00	
	Baller Bitches Vol. 1	$15.00	
	Baller Bitches Vol. 2	$15.00	
	Baller Bitches Vol. 3	$15.00	
	Bad Bitch	$15.00	
	Still The Baddest Bitch	$15.00	
	Power	$15.00	
	Power Part 2	$15.00	
	Drake	$15.00	
	Drake Part 2	$15.00	
	Female Hustler	$15.00	
	Female Hustler Part 2	$15.00	
	Princess Fever "Birthday Bash"	$9.99	
	Nico Carter The Men Of The Bitch Series	$15.00	
	Bitch The Beginning Of The End	$15.00	
	Supreme...Men Of The Bitch Series (Coming February 29th, 2016)	Pre Order $15.00	

Shipping/Handling (Via Priority Mail) $6.50 1-2 Books, $8.95 3-4 Books add $1.95 for ea. Additional book.

Total: $_____ FORMS OF ACCEPTED PAYMENTS: Certified or government issued checks and money Orders, all ma
in orders take 5-7 Business days to be delivered

Imagine That!

Fuzz and the Glass Eye
Which Way, Jack?
The Wish Fish
Famous Animals

Pie, Pie, Beautiful Pie
My Word! How Absurd
You Can Canoe!
A World of Imagination

Written by **Elizabeth Pulford**
Illustrated by **John Bennett**

05 04 03 02 01 00 99
10 9 8 7 6 5 4 3 2 1

Published in the United States by

a division of Reed Elsevier Inc.
500 Coventry Lane
Crystal Lake, IL 60014

Printed in Hong Kong
ISBN: 0-7901-1866-1

FROM ELIZABETH PULFORD

Is there a real Fuzz? Absolutely! Just like Fuzz in the story, the real Fuzz was a scrawny kitten that had been abandoned. Eleven years later, Fuzz is still with us. And the man with the glass eye? Well, I was ten years old when I met a man with a glass eye – it squeaked when he rubbed it! I nearly fainted when he took it out and I saw it staring at me from the palm of his hand...

FROM JOHN BENNETT

Fuzz was modeled from my own cat Silj (pronounced Seal-ee), who shared much of Fuzz's feisty nature. I think that my fond memories of Silj surface in these drawings and help to make the book *Fuzz and the Glass Eye* special.

Now, after all the excitement, I'm lying in bed, grinning – you'll never guess about what. I'll give you a clue. It has something to do with Mr. Pedosky and what he gave me for helping him find his eye. I'll give you three guesses what it is. Nope. It's not a cookie or a piece of cake. It doesn't have anything to do with food. Money? Dream on. Mr. Pedosky hardly has enough for himself. And now, with keeping Fuzz, he's going to have even less.

Do you give up? OK, here it is. Mr. Pedosky gave me his very first glass eye. How's that for coolness?

The End